(CONTINUED FROM FRONT FLAP)

well, which is notorious for the number of accidental drownings it has caused.

The final parable, *The Angel*, is written from heaven by a candidate in a training school for angels, addressed to the girl on earth with whom he had a lyrical, sensuous love affair that ended unhappily before he died.

Whether Vassilikos is suggesting, as in the first novella, that to love only from the heart is unrealistic, or that to love only from the mind, as in *The Well*, is to love unsuccessfully, or, finally, that we are not completed until we are loved in return, he has found original approaches to this universal theme.

REX WARNER comments that the translation by Edmund and Mary Keeley "has been done with admirable tact and skill," and adds: "I've admired and enjoyed all the stories. This seems to me a very moving and poignant kind of fantasy; and there is a pure Greek element in it.... It is fresh, vivid, really human."

THE PLANT,
THE WELL,
THE ANGEL

THE PLANT,
THE WELL,
THE ANGEL

by Vassilis Vassilikos

A TRILOGY
TRANSLATED FROM
THE GREEK BY
EDMUND & MARY KEELEY

New York : ALFRED · A · KNOPF

1 9 6 4

L. C. catalog card number: 64-13446

THIS IS A BORZOI BOOK,
PUBLISHED BY ALFRED A. KNOPF, INC.

Manufactured in the United States of America,
and distributed by Random House, Inc.
Published simultaneously in Toronto, Canada,
by Random House of Canada, Limited.

FIRST AMERICAN EDITION

Originally published in Greek as *To Phyllo* (The
Plant), *To Pēgadi* (The Well), and *T'Angeliasma*
(The Angel) in three separate volumes in 1961.
A condensation of *The Plant* has appeared in *Greek
Heritage*.

TO DEMETRA

CONTENTS

THE PLANT

THE PLANT

IN THE BEGINNING was chaos. Mist, fog, rain, snow, and hail. A void, and darkness was upon the face of the deep. Wind systems and the meeting of waters inhabited it, and birds flew within it: crows and swallows. Until one day a somber Landlord appeared, with sunglasses and brief case in hand. He took the papers out of his brief case; with a tape measure he plotted the space. And the Landlord said: let the digger come first. And there came a metal monster with the mouth of a beast, all teeth, and it started to dig the earth. It worked for days with passion. It ate up the earth, then spat it forth into a dump truck. And the Landlord said: let the digger go and let the workers come for the foundations. A crowd of workers came then, workers who mixed the thick cement, and workers who bent the steel bars, and mold makers who prepared the molds with wooden planks and clamps. A concrete mixing machine, taking strength from a generator, worked on the side, churning the sand, gravel, and cement. And the Landlord saw that the base had been set and that the supports of the house were steady, so he said: let the first-floor slab be poured. And when that had cooled and solidified, they moved on top of it and started pouring the next. They worked an eight-hour day, with a small break for lunch in a nearby taverna. They worked hard, and as the scaffolding rose higher, their work became more dangerous. With satisfaction, the Landlord saw the building take on proper dimensions and said: let the walls rise. And the square slabs were gradually enveloped by bricks, and so the house, which until then had been a simple skeleton, started taking on flesh and separating from the chaos around it. Only a few rectangular holes for the doors and windows remained open, communicating with the darkness of the chasm. And the Landlord saw that the cement mixer below stopped grinding, the hoists too stopped lifting and lowering, the scaffolding was dismantled and most of the masons were leaving, so he said: let the carpenters, painters, plumbers, and electricians come in. And through the main entrance, crowds of new workers pushed their way in, each with his own tools, to thread the nerves, infuse the blood and paint the soulless face of the house. The carpenters put in the frames for the doors and windows, fitted the closets and the shelves, dressed the floors with hardwood parquet. With planetree brushes, the painters coated the walls with oil paints, the door and window panels with water colors. The plumbers brought in water, fixed the faucets, the bathtubs, the pipes, the water mains. And the electricians completed the elevator installations, placed the meters down by the entrance, passed wires and cables everywhere, installed the switches, the plugs, the fuses. And other workers polished the marble staircase with sanding machines. And when the Landlord saw that everything in the apartment building was ready—five months had elapsed since he started building it—he said: now let the tenants come too.

Lazaros, before going in, stood by the entrance and read the names of his fellow tenants, listed in two columns on the doorbell panel. He read from the bottom up:

4

TOULA and MARY
Dressmakers

GERASIMOS ANAGNOSTARAS
Neurologist-Psychiatrist

EMMANOUIL LADOPOULOS
Textile Merchant

KONSTANTINOS A. PLYTAS
Civil Servant

KEVORK POPOLIAN
Lumber Merchant

RAILWAY WORKERS' CLUB

SYMEON EXADACTYLOS
Brigadier General, Ret.

He jumped to the next column and started down:

JEAN-JACQUES LEBELLE

RAILWAY WORKERS' CLUB

PERICLES L. KARMIRIADIS
High School Principal

ANTONIOS ANTONAKAKIS
Former Member of Parliament

MALVINA PERIVOLARI
Midwife

IOANNIS SOUSAMIDIS
General Agent

CHARALAMBOS I. KALFOGLOU
Cattle Dealer

PORTER

5

The names of the tenants danced in front of his eyes. He saw them changing places in a thick, diaphanous liquid, each leaving its narrow, circumscribed world. He saw that he could not distinguish one from the other any more, as in the unending parade of supporting actors and production assistants on a movie screen, as between the thickly planted vertical crosses of a graveyard. He rubbed his eyes to get rid of the dizziness. Then he went in.

He and his parents took the right-hand apartment on the seventh floor of the new apartment house. His room was somewhat apart from the rest, one of its walls adjoining the retired brigadier general's apartment. His parents took the room to the left of the living room. There was also another room, which stayed empty for the time being. The toilet, the bathroom, and the kitchen were at the back. The house had too many doors and too few windows.

It was winter when they first moved in. The Vardar wind was blowing in from the cold northern plains. On the very first night, when everything around him still seemed foreign, he got up to secure the shutters, which were banging freely, but a hinge broke loose and so he had to seal them shut to prevent their clatter from disturbing his sleep.

He didn't tell anyone about this mishap. He was so pleased to have acquired a room of his own that he couldn't bring himself to complain. In a few days, though, there were more small mishaps of this kind. The door handles quickly became disjointed. The enamel paint on them began scaling from the heat of the stove. And the light switches started coming loose. In the kitchen the sink would clog up every now and then. And when the rains started, large water stains appeared on the walls.

6

—This is some house, his father said, annoyed, as he carefully sipped his burning soup. They used the cheapest materials they could find. And hurried work. What can one say? It isn't even worth half the rent, But there's nothing we can do.

The other occupants, he said, were saying the same thing. Nobody was satisfied. At the meeting they had held the day before, when they voted the principal, Mr. Karmiriadis, head of the apartment house committee, they had hardly agreed on the operating expenses before all the occupants started airing their complaints. The materials were worthless. The elevator had already started breaking down regularly. "And who knows if the whole building might not collapse on our heads the first time we have an earthquake." Yet nobody could leave, because they were all bound by leases. Mr. Papadopoulos, the landlord, had fooled them. They all proclaimed it. But in vain.

—Why in vain? asked his mother. Why don't they sue him for fraud?

—How can they sue when the landlord's disappeared from the face of the earth? her husband answered. He had finished his soup and was now boning the boiled fish. He usually ate them together, but today's conversation had distracted him and he lost the necessary co-ordination.—Try and get your rights when you're mixed up with scoundrels . . .

They spoke about other things, too. The gossip and oddities of the apartment house. The principal was taking steps to get rid of the two whores, Toula and Mary—who had the gall to put up a sign outside the entrance—because living as they did in the basement, they contaminated the very foundations of the house. Lazaros was not listening to what his parents were saying. He was watching the snapper slowly disappear from his father's shallow plate,

7

and deep down inside him he was pleased, very pleased, that he finally had a room of his own.

It may have been narrow, the ceiling lower than usual, the whole constructed with cheap materials and often asphyxiating from the pressure of furniture crowded in its corners—a table, a small bookcase, a bed, two chairs, an armchair, a sideboard full of his mother's china and silver—it may have looked like all the other rooms in the world, but what attracted him from the very first minute was finding himself in a room that was virgin, untouched, unsullied, where no one had lived before him, where no one else's memory would lie heavy in the corners. Its whitewash still smelled new, and its four walls were unpierced by foreign nails. So there would be no basis for comparison. The room was given to him like a young girl whom he could decide either to sully or to make beautiful, to fill with his story, which would be the first that she would come to know in her life. That is why he loved it and put his hopes in it—and, besides, the view from the balcony door was such that he wouldn't exchange it for any panoramic screen in the world.

"From this balcony door," he wrote his friend Kosta, who was studying film directing in Munich, "I can see the whole Upper City of Salonica, the width and breadth of it, the battlements, the prison of Yiadi-Koulé (remember the song?), the Rotunda and the minaret, the Vlatadon Monastery, which seems so close I could stretch out my hand and catch the roaming peacocks by their tails. You don't know what a joy this is for eyes turning dry among the pages of my agriculture books, what a relief it is for my imprisoned

8

soul to look upon this sea of roof tiles, shivering, unsettled, with the church domes surfacing between them like the backs of whales, to see this unfolding upward in waves that end in the seven towered walls which seem to be biting into the sky with a toothless mouth. And the Turkish houses with their courtyards, the red windows at twilight, the wooden corner stones, and the twisting staircases, all these things, Kosta . . . Only when there's a fog and I can see nothing, I imagine myself in a void, and I'm lost. In the afternoons I go out and walk through the narrow streets of the Upper City, and there I can savor at close quarters what I see only at a distance from my hermitage; I feel it with my hands, I live its every detail.

"Unfortunately, I also see the university from my window, the lecture halls—those crematoriums—and sadly this reminds me every now and then that I have to study. And you, how are you getting along with your studies? Have you finished the twelve-minute documentary that you wrote me about?

"But what can I say to you! It's strange, very strange, to live on the razor's edge, on the border between two worlds. Because the way our new house is situated, on this side of Egnatia Street, opposite the Arch of Galerius and the row of low houses with their cracked and worn masks, I have the feeling that I am indeed living on a border, in the no man's land between the new town, with its square monsters, and the old, with its poor and humble houses. In the world I belong to there is ease but no joy. In the world opposite there may be poverty, misery, unhappiness, but there is also a certain disposition toward gaiety which spreads out with the coming of night, and the singing there is more carefree, one breathes more easily, because there is less heaped-up stone and there are still trees and flowers in the courtyards. The streetcar tracks are the borderline. The kiosks are the guardhouses. That's why I tell you that it's difficult to live on the border. Every now and then you feel the need to escape, to go live for a while in the world to which you do not belong, leaving behind the world to which you do belong but where you do not in fact live at all. Until finally the only thing you gain is not knowing where you are, while losing sometimes whatever security you may have found within whatever boundaries.

"This is more or less the way I feel in our new home. It's still too early to make predictions. The only thing I know that I want for the time being is to build within my own room a world of my own. Forgive my babbling. I expect a letter from you with all your news.

Lazos

P.S. Wait a minute. I can't resist describing to you what I saw as I lifted up my head just now: the sun is setting behind Mt. Olympus, and its rays are lighting fires on the windowpanes and tin roofs of the Upper City. The hour is full of sweetness, and the sounds grow dimmer in the purple of sunset. The windows of the houses have turned red like eyes at the moment of parting. The sun has shattered into a thousand fragments against them. Only after this last reflected light, God, how quickly night falls. . . ."

II

IT WAS THROUGH neither luck nor coincidence that one afternoon, in the narrow streets of the Upper City, he met her. He was ripe for her now, because for some time in his lonely walks it seemed he was looking for her. The weather too had softened, as it was April. He had gone out for a short afternoon walk to clear his mind of his reading, when . . .

He suddenly saw her coming out of a side street off St.

Demetrios. And she immediately turned the corner, without his having had a chance to see her face. He didn't know her, he was sure; her bearing didn't remind him of anyone. Unwillingly, almost magnetized, he followed her. He shortened his step so he wouldn't overtake her. He noticed first her delicate white legs with the short red socks, her calves beautifully molded. She wore no heels, and this made her walk even lighter. Then he noticed her brown raincoat, belted at the waist. But what really captured him was her blond pony tail, caught up high with a bone pin so that her hair fell straight down and apart from the shoulders it covered, dancing there, swinging like a bell, bouncing free and unleashed like the mane of a horse, silent like a distant waterfall whose roar never reaches the ears. The hour was deep and calm. The sky resounded with the ringing of vesper church bells scattered among the houses. And the sun, near its setting, gilded her straw-colored hair, deepened the dark earth-brown of her raincoat.

She walked on, and she was so light-struck among the already darkening houses, so rich amid all that poverty, so much of the future in the heavy past around her, that he asked himself: Who on earth would be he who wouldn't follow her? I'm not doing anything wrong, was his next thought. Her rhythm is drawing me on like a poem.

She walked on, and she seemed to know where she was going, because she didn't hesitate at all among the complicated, twisting little streets. Now she was going up Ioulianou Street. At Kassandrou she took a right turn. And then left again, uphill. She ran on like a partridge—red socks like partridge claws—feeling the threat of a hunter behind her and continually raising the angle of her flight. He noticed that her feet did not stumble on the stones as his did and that she chose the paths that were most feasible. Therefore, he concluded, she must live somewhere near here.

This must be her neighborhood, and from one minute to the next I may lose her. He was now filled with curiosity to see her face. He had no fears that he might be disillusioned, that the cobblestone path might suddenly cease to be the wake left by dreams. His instinct told him that her face would be as alive as the pony tail, and just as golden. But how could he possibly see it? If he passed her, she would know that he was following her and so would only run faster. Somewhere we will meet, we have to, he told himself again and again. At some corner, some crossroad.

Then he noticed that her hands were not free. She was holding something. What could it be? he wondered. A dress? A star? Or bread from the baker's? What's she holding in her hands that would tire her so?

Absorbed as he was in his thoughts, he must have slackened his pace, because suddenly he saw that he had lost her. He ran to the corner. He looked: a small square opened out in front of him, with an old plane tree in the middle, and a fountain. Three roads led out of it. Which of the three had she taken? He noticed two old crones sitting on their doorsteps bent over their knitting. They wouldn't be able to tell him. Some little urchins were playing wildly with a rag ball. He started over to ask them, but a priest, upright and proud, chose to cross the square that very moment, and the children, abandoning their game, ran over to kiss his hand.

He had no time to lose. Every second that went by increased the distance. And night wasn't far away. Throwing it to chance, he took the middle road. He was running now, searching despairingly for the lost pony tail that swung so free and insubordinate. The vesper bells had stopped ringing, and silence had spread across the sky.

As he ran on, the cobblestone paths, instead of unwinding, became all the more entangled. A labyrinth, he thought. And if he lost the thread of sun which sustained him, surely he would find no exit from here. And he was unfamiliar with this part of the Upper City. It was the first time he had come so far east. A labyrinth . . . A real labyrinth. And the unknown girl who had entangled him here he baptized Ariadne. Ariadne . . . Ariadne. He murmured her name in the rhythm of his running.

He now suspected every door. He looked into every courtyard. She could have vanished into any one of a hundred openings. In his distraction he nearly ran down a yoghurt peddler, would have scattered his yoghurt containers all over the ground if the peddler hadn't twisted his wooden tray out of danger at the last instant. But where did she go? How could she disappear so abruptly? She was cut off like a song, erased like the color of the sea at sunset. That priest: a bad omen. And what if she'd taken one of the other two roads? Where, then, am I running like a madman? Where am I going? What do I want? I want . . . I want to see the face of Ariadne. A dog started following him. Then, in the midst of his turmoil—the barking of the dog, the curses of the yoghurt peddler, the people looking at him suspiciously —he suddenly recalled the surfacing fish, the fish that emerge for a moment on the face of the water, beat the waves with their wings, scatter snowdrops and particles of silver, and are then sucked in again by the sea to go down deep, deep, deep, where no diver can reach them, where even the arms of the sun terminate.

Now he found himself on a wide dirt road which had no houses on its one side. He recognized it immediately. Somewhere around here was the rabies clinic, where he used to come, when he was a freshman in the school of agriculture, to get injections in his stomach (he had been bitten by a rabid cat he was trying to save from attacking dogs). Yes, that was it. The clinic was deserted at this hour;

only one light on at the front, under the roof. Next to it was an old Venetian wall overgrown with weeds. He leaned against it. Further down, the Jewish tombs and the great cemetery of Our Lady of the Annunciation, fenced in. Yet he could see the full plot, sown with crosses, and the death beds with their lighted lampions. The tops of the cypress trees kept their calm. A young couple was slowly climbing the wide dirt road that ran alongside the cemetery wall. Each was so much a part of the other's embrace that he couldn't distinguish their separate forms. Further down, like a cypress tree that had escaped its proper limits, rose the tall minaret, unperturbed in the twilight. He remained where he was, leaning against the old Venetian fortress, watching the road anxiously in case he had overtaken the young girl by mistake, in case she were to appear from somewhere, when his eye was caught by the new wall of recently built apartment houses on the far side of Egnatia Street, hiding the view to the sea where the sun had disappeared. He was suddenly afraid, as this ashen fortress, this long battlement with symmetrical ramparts and dark loopholes, seemed to him nightmarish. But he became even more afraid with the thought that he too lived inside it, that one part of it was his house, one of its loopholes his window. He counted, he calculated, he discovered the green sign that was right under his balcony, RAILWAY WORKERS' CLUB, and there was his window. It was looking at him like a dark eye, reproachfully. What was he searching for out there? What was he doing in the meadows of the poor? His place wasn't there. His place was inside the castle. Come on back, quickly, it seemed to say, come on back now, you delinquent sentry, leaving your post like that, traitor, back into the fold, you lost sheep . . . No, let me stay here a while longer, he begged. I'll come in a little while. I'll come . . . He turned away in disgust. And

14

then he saw her. She was coming down the hill. She was coming straight toward him. And she was holding a flower pot in her arms.

At first he was stunned. He couldn't believe his own eyes. How could she be coming downhill now when she was going uphill before? Somehow he himself must have turned downhill without knowing it. In the middle of the flower pot, like a trembling green flame, a single-leafed plant rose. He couldn't make out her face clearly from that distance. He saw only that it was pale like the moon at the beginning of night. And it rested on a long neck like the stem of the plant. Under her half-opened raincoat, he could see a full blouse that had the same brick color as the flower pot she was holding so tightly against her.

He pulled his arm abruptly away from the ruined wall. He now wanted to become a wall himself in order to stop her.

There was a light breeze. In the distance, from the various alleyways, one could hear the cries of children, the call of the yoghurt vendor advertising his sheep's-milk yoghurt, a dog barking at shadows. And the young girl was coming closer. But as she did so, the opposite of what he expected happened: the plant's leaf slowly fastened to her face, covering it completely with its green flame, so that he could see nothing of her lips, her eyes, her forehead. Only when the road was very uneven and one of her feet sank deeper than the other would the leaf and the face separate, but for such a short interval that he still couldn't manage to grasp anything, as though a door had opened and shut quickly in his face; and then, the moment her step evened out, the two would become one again, as the idol joins its shadow. It got on his nerves. He didn't like this game at all. But it annoyed him even more to see that not only did her neck gradually become one with the stem of the plant, as she came closer, her full blouse was slowly absorbed by the brick-colored flower pot. So transformed, she passed close beside him, passed beyond him, because he stood motionless as though turned to stone, unable to comprehend the mystery of her change. The only thing he saw was the stem of the plant bending lightly toward him as she passed him by.

He came to his senses only after the critical moment —the moment when he could have seen her—had passed. He followed her with some hesitation. He could again see the gold of her pony tail, dulled by nightfall. Her legs shimmered in the deep darkness. She now knew that he was behind her, and she quickened her pace. It was too late now. He knew it. Too late. So late that the city lights had come on.

He saw a woman, leaning halfway out her window, saying good evening to her. Something now prevented him from following her further. He knew that this was her world, her neighborhood, her friends. Slowly he slackened his pace until he had stopped altogether. A moment later he saw her pause to open a heavy iron gate and then disappear behind it. Passing by there, following the scent of her footsteps, he saw a courtyard behind the iron gate, and at the back of the courtyard, a small two-story house with orange windows. He noted the number: 17. On the faded street sign at the corner: IERISSOS STREET.

Leaving, he turned downhill on Apostle Paul Street. It was only then that he noticed the pain of a nail in his shoe. He eased into a small taverna and downed three glasses of ouzo straight. It made him tight, but he calmed down a little. He rolled along as far as the Arch of Galerius. Opposite, on the other bank, the illuminated towers rose. Crossing the "boundary line," the streetcar tracks, he tripped on the rails. Back to jail, he thought as he hopped up the stone trunk of the apartment house like a sparrow.

But that night—he was listening wide awake to the train whistles from the Old Station—his room betrayed him for the first time since he had come into the apartment, and he was left unprotected. Chaos returned to his room, the chaos that was there before the building rose: a void, and darkness was upon the face of the deep. Mist, fog, rain, snow, and hail. Wind systems. The meeting of waters. And the crows flew low, searching in the night for their secret selves.

III

IT WAS ON WEDNESDAY, April 11, the feast of St. Yclasios, the martyr, and at exactly ten minutes to ten that suddenly the first noise was heard.

The elevator door banged shut. And this noise detonated like a grenade in his room, utterly destroying any further attempt on his part to concentrate on his reading. They've found me out, he thought, sighing, and his first impulse was to go out to the staircase and curse the maids of the apartment house, who were screeching hysterically as though they were being drowned. But he held himself back: if he went out there and made a fuss, what good would it do? He would only succeed in getting them to bang the doors harder and to shout even louder now that they knew it annoyed him. No, he shouldn't reveal himself so soon; it wasn't smart to let them celebrate their victory. His blood was boiling. The battle had begun, yet he had to pretend indifference.

17

It wasn't the first time he had heard them. Every morning at the same time, after being notified by the porter, the maids brought the garbage cans down to the entrance. And every morning he heard the same shouting, the ones up above yelling at the ones below to shut the elevator doors, and banging with their fists and laughing, and the ones below yelling back at them to stop screaming and . . . Every morning. And yet only today, on the eleventh of April, the feast of the martyr St. Yelasios, had he ascertained for the first time that the noises were falling in his room like shells and smashing everything in there, knocking down anything standing and shattering his tranquillity. That does it, he said to himself, they'll annihilate me now.

There was a moment of relaxation, a few minutes went by when nothing at all could be heard; he breathed deeply, succeeded in gathering his forces and saying, with the joy of one who has escaped from danger, "I'm still alive," when suddenly loud machine-gun fire resounded in his ears. Bullets were sown everywhere, on the floor, on his table, on the walls, with the speed of a sewing-machine needle. It was the garbage collector's bell ringing down in the street, like reveille. He forgot his decision not to show himself, and, totally distraught now, went out on the balcony as he was, in his underwear. He leaned over the railing, to find the city garbage truck below, the garbage collectors emptying the cans one by one onto the truck with gloved hands. Further off, the servant girls, like a chorus, were gurgling laughter. He felt an impulse to jump from the seventh floor—he counted on hitting soft ground so as not to break a leg—and snatch that bedeviled bell out of the driver's hand and pummel the whole bunch of them over the head with it. He realized, however, that he couldn't jump, because he would get caught up in the electric wires below him. So he went back in. There was a suspicious calm. But, as the garbage truck moved off, the same machine-gun fire echoed again, like a parting volley, sowing its bullets this time in his own body.

He dropped into his chair out of breath, his elbows on the desk in front of him, his head buried in his hands. That does it, he said to himself again. They found me out. Now they'll never leave me alone again. They'll always keep coming. He touched his forehead; it was on fire. They'll keep coming.

He stretched the whole upper part of his body across the desk. He tried to calculate how many they would be. I must defend myself. He opened his drawer: there was no gun. Then he picked up the metal letter opener and nailed it violently into the desk top. I must defend myself. I must dig trenches, set up flank guards . . . But how could he manage to protect himself? The invisible enemy could strike at him from anywhere. The walls of his room proved to be made of cardboard, since they had crumbled under the first surprise attack like a house of cards. The important thing is that they not find me. Now . . . The battle would be uneven: he expected help from nowhere, and his defeat was already assured.

There was only one hope left: leaving his room and going to study in the public library. But he remembered hearing from a classmate that it was full up every day and that no more pass cards were available. There was an excess of new applicants every morning. So he wrote off this last hope.

He gave himself over to gloom. Wherever he might go, even to the farthest corner of the world, wouldn't they discover him, since he carried with him the magnet that gathered them in? Everywhere the noises will find me and fall upon me like starving dogs. Everywhere and always. Day and night. Then he took on strength again. But I won't let them get me so easily. They'll realize themselves that I have a tough skin.

Fortified behind his desk, he waited. The mimeographed book on tree culture had been lying open for a long time at the chapter on buds. It had to happen, there was no avoiding it: in a moment now they would hit him again. Feelers ready, like an ant poised in front of danger, he waited.

Outside there was sunshine. An April sun was warming the world. But too much light in the room was dangerous, it might betray him. So he closed the shutters.

The agony of waiting tormented him. The delay was cracking his nerves. Why don't they strike? Having nothing to do with his hands, he started picking his nose, removing the snot with his finger and gluing it to the underside of the desk. Every time he added a bit, he would run his finger along the length of the underside, which was covered with hardened scabs, like the hulls of ships covered with barnacles. Why are they delaying? What are they waiting for? He had used up his snot, so he now turned to another job: he started uprooting his pubic hairs one by one, burning each with a match, squeezing the speck of ash between his fingers and inhaling it lustfully. It smelled like chestnut, boiled chestnut.

He must have fallen asleep at his desk, because he suddenly found himself startled awake by a strange new rustling. He jumped up like a guard caught napping by a patrol.—Halt! Who goes there? No answer. He gave his serial number: 11. He advanced on the password: martyr St. Yelasios. No answer. His mind cleared, and he realized that the strange sound was caused by human footsteps in the dining room. They've come, he thought. But he didn't hear merely the familiar footsteps of his parents. There were foreign footsteps as well. They're having lunch here, he said. My God! He had no desire to see anybody, to speak to anybody.

His floor was squeaking. The boards were sighing in answer to those outside. Wood is a good conductor of noise, he mused. While stone, cement, and iron are bad conductors. The feet were gabbing non-stop. He divided them into three categories according to the shoes they were wearing: rubber, squeaky, and high-heeled. Then the footsteps ceased and the voices came. They pierced the walls of his room unhindered, riddled them thoroughly. They reached his ears with their full intensity as though they had originated next to him. He plugged his ears, but he could still hear them. The enemy was besieging him, smothering him, waging a war of nerves against him. They want to force me out alone, he thought, to give myself up.

—The meal is ready. Please sit down.

—What a lovely view you have from here! Wonderful . . .

—And where is Lazaros?

—Studying for his exams.

—Good for him. Bravo.

—The food will get cold. Do sit down.

—Yes, she left the Council . . .

—Look how clearly you can see the Vlatadon Monastery and the AHEPANS building!

—The food is frozen. Will you please sit down.

—And Lazaros?

—I'm going to call him.

—Good. Bravo . . .

He heard footsteps approaching his door. He assumed a defensive stance.

—Good Lord! What darkness! Why, for God's sake, did you close the shutters? You'll ruin your eyes.

He gave up and went out.

At the table he found two dried-out old ladies, friends of his mother from the Council of the School for the Blind. She had run across them by chance in the street and had brought them home to try out one of her new culinary concoctions. One was a widow and the other an old maid. His father, who showed clearly that he was bored by them, devoted himself to the food, carefully alternating mouthfuls of fish and soup. And then he himself said, quite irrelevantly, that all the maids in the apartment house were registered whores. Yes, whores, simple whores. His father gave him a fierce look. His mother sat gaping, her fork in mid-air. The old maid choked, and the other lady had trouble swallowing. He said the word again, loudly, with passion. And where was the special Felizol insulation promised by the contractor? The house had the acoustics of an ancient amphitheater. He just couldn't live there any longer. He said it all, let himself go completely, then ran to hide in his room.

Fortified behind his desk, he waited, no longer remembering how many hours, how many days, how many weeks. Easter had gone by, snuffed out like the candle he had held stupidly in his hand on the night of the Resurrection in the courtyard of the Church of the Immaculate Virgin. With a little more effort he remembered the noises made by the firecrackers, the Bengal lights, the gunshots, the noises of the fireworks, the bells, the noise of the priests chanting "Christ is risen," the noises, other noises, the cherubim . . . He could remember nothing else.

Fortified behind his desk, he saw the days lengthen on the windowpane of the balcony door, the hills turn green, the swallows drown in the light, whose glare gathered like pus in the wound of his room. Spring. Spring. Yet he . . .

In the meantime, the noises had manifested themselves from all sides. The children of Mme Lebelle— Jacques, Marilaine, and Pepo—would play above, and their games collected the plethora of apartment-house children. They ran, they fell, they quarreled. They played cowboys, trains, rolled steel bearings along the floor until they grooved veins into his temples. He called the noises stalactites because they dropped from above. And when these stopped, other noises, stalagmites, emerged from below like thorns: the applause of the railway employees who were meeting in their club, so stimulated by the speech of a potbellied labor leader that they thrashed their chairs around. And from the side, through the wall of the retired general's apartment, came the bayonets: Miss Exadactylos, arriving home from school every afternoon, would turn on her victrola at its loudest. Elvis Presley, Bellafonte, Bill Haley, Pat Boone—all shattered his eardrums. And the elevator went up and down. The doors banged open and shut. The cat meowed. The phone rang. The doorbell rang. The radio whined. These were the interior noises. But did he suffer less from the exterior ones? Every time a big truck went by, the whole house trembled as though it were a tree with its roots in the street. Then there were the official funerals with all the fanfares, on their way to the cemetery of Our

23

Lady of the Annunciation. And the crowds on Wednesdays and Sundays going wild in the football stadiums of PAOK and HERACLES. The demonstrations. The tinsmith established across the street. The parades. And the church bells which rang every afternoon.

So his room changed its substance. From the private refuge which it was in the beginning, it now turned into a Center for Transient Noises, a House of Alien Noises. He even started a record of Noises Received and noted every new one that appeared, with consecutive numbers.

He then sat down and wrote his only friend, Kosta in Munich; he wrote him that he could no longer create his own world, because his world, even before he was born, had become a prey in the claws of noises. He asked him for immediate advice on what to do. And Kosta replied: "In the trees. Only there, for all of us, is the tranquillity we long for."

But he reacted against this too. "In the trees? What trees are you talking about? Have you asked the sparrow perched in the fork of a big tree whether it is ever quiet at night? Have you asked it what noises it hears? Because it is not only the birds of prey that return from their hunting and fight over who is to land first on the highest branch; nor the restless lovemaking of the doves among the leaves; nor the ornamented hens trying to settle down in the branches, bringing to the tree a ceaseless turmoil; nor even the little birds chirping at one another. But it is also the wind tearing itself apart in the branches as it strives to uproot the tree whole; it is the leaves which rustle as they fall, the sap which hums as it climbs. And even when every-

24

thing calms down some night and you think the tree is relaxing, a strange cry comes from the earth demanding more fertilizer from the leaves, the fruit, the birds. Who said, then, that trees could ever be peaceful, and especially during an April night?"

He signed: "The sparrow who lives in the stone tree."

And yet one day, when he had come to feel that all was finished and his sentence had been pronounced by God, creator of all visible and invisible noises, he remembered the blond pony tail, the red socks, the brown raincoat, he remembered even more sharply her blouse, so much like the brick-colored flower pot that she held in her arms—her face, covered by a green leaf that gave her its shape and freshness.

IV

IT WAS EVENING. An unmarred evening in May. He had crossed the "frontier" and was now climbing Apostle Paul Street in a great hurry. The scent of mimosa from the court-yard of the Rotunda touched his nostrils sharply. He stopped for a moment and breathed deeply, greedily, as though he wanted to hold within himself all the coolness of the eve-ning, all the sweetness of spring. For the first time, after so many weeks of asphyxiation, he felt his senses alive. He raised his head high and looked up at the minaret, whose tip was tickling the stars.

At that hour the Upper City was just coming to life. Girls strolled along arm in arm, singing. Boys kidded them from behind. The café was full of people. Children were chasing each other in gangs. They jumped over walls, stole apricots and plums. The shoe shops and grocery stores of daytime were transformed into small taverns where neighbors sipped drinks together.

He swerved right, where Apostle Paul Street meets St. Demetrios, and headed straight for her house: 17 Ierissos Street. A bus on the regular route, all lit up, sprayed him with gas fumes. It was moving so tightly against the line of houses that they brushed it with the flower pots in their windows. He turned up another cobblestone road. It wasn't easy to find her house in darkness so sparcely sown with street lights. There were no signs on the back streets. And those elsewhere that had not been torn down were washed out. He again found himself doubly lost in this labyrinth. Ariadne. He recalled the name he had given her the last time.

He had set the wrong course. This he discovered when he found himself in front of the Turkish Consulate, and the city policemen who guarded it looked at him suspiciously. He turned down quickly on St. Demetrios Street, the road dividing the Upper City in two. He paused in front of one of its movie theaters to decide which way to go on. He gave the posters a quick look; two features were showing, as was usual at the end of the season. They were announcing the opening of the outdoor theater on the terrace a few days hence. Summer was coming. And spring has gone by without my knowing it, he thought bitterly.

This brief lingering in front of the neighborhood theater was the last memory of light that he held, because immediately thereafter, turning left, he lost himself in the side streets. He turned right and left, sniffing his way like a lost dog. He was in fact fooled a number of times, thinking he'd found her house, but he quickly recovered from the traps of night.

He was moving in circles like a fisherman trying to

find the cave where he once saw a wriggling fish hide. But the rocks of the sea bottom look so much alike!

Then, a moment later, as suddenly as she herself had once appeared in front of him, the heavy iron gate of the courtyard loomed ahead. He looked at the number to make sure: 17. And his heart beat with a flurry, as though it had hooked a big fish.

He hadn't come all the way here out of curiosity or nostalgia. On the contrary, he had started out with a specific purpose. He had conceived a daring plan, an act of piracy. And he had been waiting for the cover of night: he would then go into her garden and steal the flower pot with the plant.

He looked down the street, which was closed off at the end by a house. No exit that way. Deserted. He moved in closer. Through the gate railings he could see her house, with the orange light in the window. A shadow moved behind the curtain. He imagined it was her shadow. Then, at the last minute, he lost his nerve. What would happen if someone came in or out of the house while he was in the courtyard? Her brother, her father. They would humiliate him. They would call him a chicken thief, a bum. She would come out, would recognize him, would say he had once followed her. But I must, he said inside himself to build up his courage. What he was doing was cheap. But I must, I must . . . he kept saying inside himself. He heard some footsteps in the street. They faded away. We have to live, he said finally. And the longer he put it off, the worse it would be. The neighborhood was full of eyes.

He put his hand through the railing and lifted the latch inside, then pushed. The heavy iron gate gave way without squeaking. Two cats bolted in the darkness and jumped nimbly onto the wall. They gazed at him with glass-bead eyes.

He moved ahead on tiptoe, his shoulders hunched. The courtyard had a little flower bed, two trees, a fountain, some metal objects, a hose curled on the ground. He continued further, arriving almost under the window with the orange light. From inside came muffled talk. He started searching with his hands among the flower pots. There were many. A whole collection. They probably sold them. In one corner, isolated, he finally found the plant he was looking for. It now seemed bigger to him. He remembered the leaf as having the shape of an egg. It was now rounded like the moon. Carefully, so as not to make noise, he lifted the flower pot from the earth and nestled it in his arms. It was heavy and damp. With his lips he touched the pale skin of the leaf. This momentary contact filled him with delight. He was no longer empty. He had a sweet weight on his chest which calmed his heart.

He left on tiptoe. Luckily nobody noticed him. He turned and glanced for the last time, gratefully, at the window with the orange light. The cats were watching him from the wall with their glass-bead eyes; he couldn't manage to close the iron gate behind him.

He didn't return home immediately. His parents would find it very strange if they saw him actually come in with the flower pot, but they might react differently if he confronted them with an accomplished fact. So he would wait until it was midnight and they were asleep before he entered the house with his trophy.

He hid the plant in a dark corner of the little Byzantine church half buried in the ground opposite the entrance to the apartment house. There was no danger that anyone would find it there. It was as safe as it would be under a trap door. Then, finally liberated, with a feeling of triumph, he gave himself up to the central streets of the city.

He walked high-spirited, carefree, light as air, winged. He moved down the right-hand side of Egnatia Street, where only an all-night pharmacy and two tavernas were still open. The kiosks were closing one by one. The glare of two advertising signs from the opposite side of the street knifed through him. And the white funeral home, also still awake. He crossed St. Sophia Square. The Achilles pastry shop tempted him for a moment, but he didn't want the stench of people. Alone, he was more completely given to his joy. His thoughts returned every now and then to that dark corner where he had hid the flower pot, and this filled him with warmth as though he were spreading his hands above hot coals. He passed between the Symplegades of the Floka and Astoria pastry shops; then, turning left into Metropolis Street and finally right, he reached the quay.

It was deserted, just what he was looking for. The sea stretched before him enigmatic, faceless, dumb, jelled in darkness. The roots of night dipped into her, milked her silently. He walked slowly along the edge of the pier to pass the time until midnight. Without realizing it, he reached the White Tower. He passed the theater on the lower side, the Electric Power Company still working, got lost among the cement pilings. He was now far from the roar and glare of the city, alone, facing the double abyss of sea and night. Then, certain that nobody could see him or hear him, he bent over a rock and confided to the rim of the sea the most precious secret of his heart. He was full of joy, he told her, because tonight he had stolen from Ariadne's courtyard the flower pot with the plant that she was holding in her arms one afternoon. The small wave that heard it turned back and spread its circle to infinity.

He whistled with a lighter heart now that he had made

the night and the sea the accomplices of his theft. He was
walking by the Society of Macedonian Studies when he ran
across two of his classmates. He cursed his luck for finding
them. They started talking. He told them he was in a hurry.
They asked him if he was studying for his exams. He said
he was, but not very hard. They asked him if he'd registered
for the exams. He said he hadn't yet. Then what kind of a
world was he living in? Tomorrow was the last day. They
told him that right then, during their walk, they were asking each other questions to test their knowledge. They
differed, however, concerning the surface roots of trees and
wanted his opinion. He told them he was in a hurry and
left. This encounter deflated his easy mood. People, he
thought, only succeed in terrifying you. He looked at his
watch. It was quarter to twelve. He headed for home.

The plant was waiting for him in the dark corner of
the church where he'd left it. He saw it from a distance,
luminous like a large green glow worm.

Even the door of the apartment house resisted him,
as though it wanted to prevent his bringing inside something foreign, odd, hostile. He battled with the key in vain
to get it open. His hands trembled nervously. What would
happen if one of the tenants came back and saw him? The
tenant would comment on it. There would be gossip about
it. "You see," he told his plant, which was standing immobile by his knee, "you see what trouble I go to because I
want you near me." Finally, the edges of the key coincided
with those of the keyhole and the glass door gave way. He
went in with his prize. He choose the stairway rather than
the elevator to get to the sixth floor so that the noise wouldn't

betray him. And without turning on the light—he knew the stairs well enough—he started up the winding staircase.

On the first floor he could hear the sound of Mr. Kalfoglou snoring. " 'Cattle dealer' is what it says on the door of his apartment," he explained in a whisper to his plant, "but in actual fact he's a butcher. He has three daughters to marry off, you see . . ." He was about halfway up to the second floor when he heard a door open and close in the basement, and then a man's footsteps. "A customer," he whispered into the plant's ear. "Toula and Mary work at night and make fifty drachmas a visit, while Dr. Anagnostaras, who works in the daytime, makes two hundred and fifty drachmas a visit. He's a psychiatrist. Very popular." He was now on the second floor. Darkness and silence. Doors blind. With the reflection of light from outside, he could see two empty milk bottles in front of Ladopoulos' door. "He's also sleeping," he told his plant. "He sells fabrics. A *nouveau riche* type. And his wife is expecting her second child." He found the same silence, the same darkness, on the third floor. "Mrs. Malvina, the midwife, lives here, and opposite her, the Sousamidises. The husband's a Mason, of high rank. Man gets reborn from his ashes." On the fourth floor there was a light behind the door of Mr. Antonakakis, the politician. "They're playing cards. Coumcan or canasta. They've turned their house into a casino. Until the next elections . . . We're now halfway there. Mr. Plytas sleeps here, a high public official. He wears a mourning band on his sleeve because he lost his wife after her thirteenth abortion. He also keeps a dog on the roof terrace because he has a mania for hunting." He was talking to his plant; he wanted to enlighten it about the apartment house and the people it would be living with. But he was starting to get tired. The higher he went, the heavier the flower pot became, so that he could hardly lift it. He re-

membered a movie he had seen when he was young, during
the Occupation; it was called *The Iron Treasure* or something like that, and the treasure was a precious stone which
the hero had stolen and which became constantly heavier
as he carried it off; it didn't grow larger, only exhausted
him little by little until at last he knelt under the weight
of it and the stone covered him and became his tombstone
in the desert. "Courage, we're almost there," he said to his
plant. "We've come two thirds of the way." On the fifth
floor, darkness reigned absolute. He set the flower pot down
to rest. "Some Armenians live here, the Popolians," he explained. "They're the only ones who've put a glass peephole
in their door. They've suffered so much that they're suspicious of everything; but they're wonderful people, the
only ones I like in this place. Maybe that's because they,
too, are exiles like me . . . And next to them, over there
at No. 12, lives Mr. Karmiriadis. He's a theologian, school
principal by profession, and a fanatical catechizer. Cerberus
of the high school and head of the apartment house . . ."
And then, as he was resting there, he heard the elevator
coming up. He froze. They'd catch him. It might even stop
at the fifth floor, it might be the principal himself. He followed the ascent with agony. As it continued to pass the
floors below without stopping, his heart tightened, was about
to crack. He was lucky again: it cast its light for a second
through the wire netting of the window on his floor, then
moved on up. He heard a door open and close on the penthouse landing, followed by the grinding of a key. And then
all was quiet again in the dark pharynx of the stone monster. He picked up his plant, his knees trembling. On the
sixth floor, the Railway Workers' Club was deserted as
usual at this time of night. "We've arrived," he whispered
to his plant. "Our neighbor's a retired general. Symeon
Exadactylos. He fixed himself up with a job on one of the

International Fair committees, and now he makes out all right. He never stays out late and he always gets up early to do his exercises . . ." His own door showed no light. They must be asleep, he thought, satisfied. He unlocked the door quietly, entered like a thief, closed it carefully. Crossing the dining room in the dark to get to his room, he tripped over a chair. Luckily no one woke up. Except the cat, Daï, who was sleeping on it, but he just stretched, yawned, and curled up again voluptuously.

V

—AND NOW where will I put the sideboard? his mother complained at the table while they were eating two days later. There's no room for it anywhere. All the other rooms are full. Where? In the kitchen or the hallway? Whereas if you would put your flower pot out on the balcony . . .

—But the purpose of my experiment is to study the influence of a closed space on vegetation, he said, awkwardly swallowing a mouthful of rice and spinach. So how can I put it out on the balcony?

His father believed him. An honest and unsuspecting man, he was convinced once again that his son had what he liked to call "a passion for his science." That was why he was now on his side in the argument at the table. His mother, though, was not so gullible.

Besides, he had seen it in her eyes from the first moment that she saw the plant in his room. It was yesterday morning, Tuesday. Monday night he had stolen it from Ariadne's courtyard, at midnight he had brought it home, and when his mother came to his room the next morning to wake him up, she stood in the doorway astounded. "Who brought it in here?" she asked, and her voice sounded cold.

33

"I did," he answered, pretending to stifle a yawn. He could see, though, that there was something more than surprise in her eyes; a certain hatred had already started smoldering deep inside them, in the very pupils, a certain hostility, as though she were facing not just a simple plant but another woman that her son had brought in from the street. And she didn't then ask, as he might have expected, why he had brought this flower pot, or where he had taken it from, but with the flame of jealousy already growing in her eyes, she said: "And for how long?" "That will depend on the results of the experiment I'm working on," he answered. And he then told her for the first time the story he'd invented. He saw her look at him suspiciously, then leave his room, banging the door behind her. Yet today, Wednesday noon, at the table and in front of her husband, she said nothing about the plant. She complained only about the banished sideboard and all the problems this created for her.

—In any case, just put it in the attic, in the store-room, her husband said. Burn it, sell it. Are we going to waste our time arguing about a prewar sideboard?

—It isn't just the piece of furniture, she answered back. It's all the household things I have inside it. The silver. The china. Where am I supposed to put all that? You think it's so easy to keep a house running?

—We don't use the best silver and we don't eat off china plates everyday, her husband said, with some irritation. Hide them in the trunk, and if we have a guest, you can bring them out. It isn't the end of the world, for God's sake. Here our son is trying to better his grade in the exams and you want us to hinder him?

· · ·

34

This is what had happened exactly: yesterday morning, Tuesday, when his mother left the room banging the door behind her, he had to face the problem of finding a permanent place for the flower pot, since it couldn't stay forever where he had set it down the night before, not only because it blocked traffic in his room, so that he had to go under the table to get out, but because he knew from his studies that a plant such as that one needs light and air to develop, to grow naturally, and where he had it for the moment there was only darkness and asphyxiation. On the other hand, he didn't want to put it out on the balcony, because he was afraid that those who saw it might give it the evil eye, even if he put a blue bead around its neck. The important thing for him was that they live together and breathe the same air, that whenever he might want to, he could stretch out his hand and touch it. He wouldn't allow any separation between them, even if this separation were just a clear glass window. So the only space left in which to settle the newly arrived flower pot was that of his own room. It was in there that he had to find the right place. By any means he could he had to arrange some place that would serve as its nest. But where? If the room were big and spacious, there would be no problem. But crowded as it was with all kinds of furniture, things looked very difficult. This problem, which he had started thinking about in the morning, became more and more complex as the day went on. He could find no solution. He moved the furniture around here and there, made diagrams on a piece of paper; but in practice he found that the furniture was too varied, that each piece had its own personality and couldn't easily tolerate another beside it, that each needed a margin of space to display itself. So they clashed, scratched each other, groaned. He despaired. He had tried all possible variations without result, when finally, toward the end of the afternoon, he decided that the source of the evil, the root of the incompatibility, was that long, narrow red sideboard with his mother's silver and china in it. So, without asking anyone, one—two—three, pushing away by himself, he got it out into the hallway. Along with the room, he now breathed more easily. At last! The space had thinned out. The other pieces of furniture relaxed. Now that the heavy sideboard was gone—that massive prewar monstrosity, that dried codfish—everything found its right place. He arranged it all beautifully, then spread a mat on the floor so the boards wouldn't get wet during watering, and placed the flower pot with his plant where he had wanted it from the beginning: near the window and next to his bed.

—All right, I'll put it up in the storeroom, his mother said, finally giving in. What bothers me, though, is that the plant will use up all the oxygen in his room. We even take out flowers at night, let alone such a . . .

She was addressing his father, but he himself answered her:

—I'll open the balcony door every night.

—So you can catch pneumonia again.

—It's May, for God's sake. How can he catch pneumonia! her husband answered, picking cherries out of the fruit dish.

—All right, his mother said, getting up from the table nervously. Father and son are in league. From now on I accept no responsibility for whatever happens. . . .

Yet his mother had been right when she said it would use up all the oxygen. And this is why: last night, Tuesday night, when he lay down to sleep, all tired out from the joys and agonies of his first day of living with the plant, he couldn't manage to get his eyes closed for a long time. Lying awake on his bed, he followed the slow retreat of moonlight along the surface of the plant, which had taken on a bronze-green color. As the light of the moon slipped off it, the plant became assimilated with the darkness until it was lost completely and only its shadow could be distinguished like an imprint on the night. Satisfied that his plant was sleeping, he turned over on his other side. At three in the morning he woke up with a bad dream: in his sleep he had seen his mother steal secretly into the room and tear the flesh of the plant with her painted fingernails. It uttered no cry of pain and patiently suffered its coming death. He jumped up. He couldn't see it right away. He moved blindly until he stumbled against the flower pot. Then he relaxed. Luckily it was still there, sleeping with its wing spread. He caressed it, and a sweet numbness moved through his fingers like mist. It was there, thank God, unhurt, untouched. Then, this morning, Wednesday morning, as he woke, he saw it glued flat against the glass pane of the balcony door. It frightened him. The sunlight pierced its damp flesh unhindered and, tinged with green, entered the room, highlighting with silver its delicate nerves, its tender veins, its outline sketched like lace on the glass in the shape of a large heart. Taking care not to tear the leaf, he separated it from the glass pane, which was coated with beads of perspiration like drops of rain. He realized what had happened during the night and opened the balcony door immediately. Then he saw the plant open out as though calling "air, air," breathing in hungrily the fresh morning breeze. Think what might have happened! he said to himself. It could have died of asphyxiation. His mother was right when she'd said that it would use up all the oxygen. So in order to save his plant, not himself, he decided to open the balcony door every night before going to sleep.

—What do they call it, that is, scientifically? asked his father as he got up from the table and went to sit in his armchair to smoke a cigarette.

—I still don't know what category to put it in, he answered as calmly as he could. In a few days it will become apparent, that is, it will manifest itself, as we say in botany.

His father seemed satisfied with this answer. It was enough for him to know that his son in fact possessed "a passion for his science." So he unfolded his newspaper.

But he himself was very worried. From the first moment that he had seen the plant settled in his room, he was tormented by the question of what it would turn out to be. It could go either of two ways: become a monstera deliciosa or a philodendron. And his father's question about its scientific name again aroused his anxiety. For the moment all its characteristics indicated that it would become a monstera deliciosa. But this didn't preclude its turning into a philodendron later, since its struggle to survive inside the room would be difficult and harsh. Because it wasn't only the confinement that it had to fight, with so little light and air; even the furniture had now assumed a hostile attitude toward it. He noticed how the various pieces surrounded it on all sides with sharp corners turned toward it like bayonets. An he couldn't throw them all out as he had done with the sideboard. The plant, with its liveliness and warmth, helped him to see them for what they were:

38

soulless like cenotaphs and lusterless like varnished coffins and completely superfluous like formalities. And he began wondering why they hadn't bothered him at all until then. Only when you start acquiring something of your own, it seems, do you realize what really doesn't belong to you, he said. That's why he was so anxious about the evolution his plant might undergo. If it remained a monstera deliciosa, it would have a delicate and transparent skin, soft, downy, sensitive to light and changes in the atmosphere. And it could generate new leaves on its sides, grow offshoots, because, being female, it would give birth; yet the plant would always remain unprotected within the circle of the furniture's enmity, like a girl whose beauty creates death. On the other hand, if it became a philodendron, its skin would harden, its nerves would swell, its flesh would become firm like cactus flesh, and it would sprout thorns if coerced. It would be a male. And it would be better able to fight the wardrobe, the book shelf, the table, the chairs . . . He himself didn't know what to wish for. Sometimes he would hope for a monstera deliciosa because their sensitivities would match; other times he would hope for a philodendron so that it could endure the battle. And for the time being, during this murky period of adolescence, anything was possible. That's why, deep down, he was very worried. And as he watched his father put out his cigarette in the ash tray, he thought: Time will tell. The days, the weeks ahead will show me the real sex of my plant.

The following Wednesday, a week later, as they were by chance eating rice with spinach again, his father asked him:
—How's the experiment coming along?
—All right, he answered indifferently.

—I see you . . . I see you've got your head buried in your books all the time. Is your work about finished?
—Unfortunately it's hardly begun, he said.

It was true, as his father suggested, that he'd buried himself in books. He didn't go out at all. He read and read, everything that had to do with the monstera deliciosa and the philodendron; he wanted to know all there was to know about the subject. But his plant daily contradicted his reading. Every morning he found it different from what it had been the night before. It ripened in the darkness and the silence like fruit, so that he had to rub his eyes to recognize it. He was pleased that it grew by such leaps and bounds, rendering useless all the scientific books. During the first week its stem had become a branch, a trunk, a flag pole, and its sheath the halter that a flag-bearer wears around his waist. And its blade had broadened: a mere plate when he first brought it home, it had soon become an oblong platter and now looked like an elliptical tray. Its under surface had formed a belly and was covered with down like the leaf of an olive tree, and its upper surface glittered like the sea in sunlight. Its middle nerve, its backbone, ended in a small spiral, as he knew happened with the Indian Flagellaria. And there was no holding back its growth. So he abandoned the books, which could tell him nothing now that his plant eluded definition under the usual types and forms. It was still without a name, like the girl who had owned it, and without a face, since it changed its face every so often.

—Now do you know what it's called? Scientifically, of course, his father asked him while smoking a cigarette.

40

—It's called a philomonstera, he said, combining the names of its two possibilities. And to cover up his deeper ignorance: —It also belongs to the category of the glutinous. Two pitchers of water a day hardly satisfy it. And of the lofty genus, since it grows taller all the time. Its species is rightist, except that the day before yesterday, finding the wardrobe an obstacle, it turned and became a leftist, so I'm not sure. . . .

Every day the plant changed the perspective of the room and made the massive furniture look smaller. It would turn this way and that, sometimes straighten out so that it was parallel with the ceiling, other times dip to the balcony door and ask to be let out (but he was determined to protect it from the eyes of the world), or fall against the pane like a curtain. Only as the leaf grew heavier and the stem appeared too weak to support it, he was forced to tie the plant, with a girlish blue bow, to its first prop.

It had a stomach that changed the starch of the fertilizer into chlorophyll, and a lung that breathed through all its cells, filling the room with vapors. And when the vapors cleared, he could see its naked rib cage as he would a human rib cage exposed by an X-ray photograph: in both instances the ribs were symmetrical bows rooted in a vertebral backbone. In both instances there was night between them. He nowhere saw a spot, a shadow, that should have him worried. The green X-ray plate, against the sun, showed him that his plant throbbed with life and health. And by reflection he received some of this vitality from it. He moved back so that his eye could take it in whole; he admired its looks just as it admired itself in the wardrobe mirror: proud, broad-chested, firm-bodied like a philodendron and, at the same time, sensitive like a monstera deliciosa. With a feather duster he had bought especially for the plant, he dusted the cobwebs off it, standing on a chair. Only at night

41

did it frighten him a little, when the electric light turned it into something outside reality, something implausible, like certain plants that move sluggishly and silently on the floor of the sea.

Then, at the end of the second week, he sat down and wrote his friend Kosta in Munich that he no longer heard any noises "because my plant absorbs them all like blotting paper." So with what hands, tortured by loneliness and privation, could he caress it, thank it? With what words uncorrupted by daily use could he express his gratefulness? "And it has spread around me," he wrote, "a great green shade—and luckily its chest is clear, with no spots—it has enveloped me in its green silence—and it's greedy, two pitchers of water a day are not enough to satisfy it—and it has opened before me a green valley with meadows of untrodden grass and rivers of joy, where the feet of noise fade away and drown."

This letter hadn't yet reached its destination before he woke one morning to discover with surprise and fright that his plant had torn itself, had divided into smaller leaves which had also torn themselves, had formed clefts and fingers. And his room was now full of palms, palms in a bouquet on a single arm, like that of a monster, palms spasmodically open and striving, grooved with wrinkles, striving to hang on to something because otherwise they would collapse, breathing and moving with difficulty, like the hands of shipwrecked swimmers, palms, fingers, palms . . .

VI

—WHAT KIND of tree is this?

The voice of the electrician startled him. He hadn't

heard the knock on the door or the "excuse me for bothering you," but his ear clearly caught the question concerning his plant and he jumped as though hit by an electric charge. He looked up, trying to decide what this young man with the checked shirt and blue jeans wanted. And why was he standing there in the doorway looking at his plant with such a persistent stare, one eyebrow raised, as the neighborhood boys might in trying to catch the eye of a girl, his hands playing with a screwdriver.

—It looks like a palm tree, said the electrician without lowering the arc of his eyebrow.

—No, it's a monstera deliciosa, he said nervously, without raising his look from the small and treacherous screwdriver.

The young man told him he'd come to have a look at the plugs and wiring. In a few days the City Power Company would be installing the new current; he was an employee of that company and they had to check the electrical installations in all the houses because the new current was dangerous. Nobody ought to touch a switch with wet fingers unless he was standing on wood.

From behind his desk he listened, a little calmer now, though his ear couldn't readily get used to the intrusive voice, and with a vigilant eye he followed the man's every movement.

The electrician took a pair of nippers out of his back pocket and looked first at the switch that was at the left of the door. He tightened a loose screw with his screwdriver, tried the switch once or twice, the light went on and off, then he stepped on a chair, examined the wire that went up the wall, then got off the chair, bent down, looked at the plug below, went up to the table where Lazaros was sitting, took his desk lamp in his hands, turned it upside down and

43

told him to bring it in to the shop one of these days, right across the street, so he could change the wire for him because it was worn in one spot.

—Where's its plug? he then asked.

They were very close to each other now, almost face to face.

—There, he said, pointing out the place behind the flower pot. But it's very difficult to get to.

—Don't worry, I won't touch a thing, said the young man. I have to look at that one too. Some of these plugs need changing.

—Just be careful how you make your way through the supports, he warned him, and got up to see that there wouldn't be any damage.

When the plant divided itself, its palms weighed down dangerously. To prevent their breaking, he went to a carpenter and ordered a dozen narrow plywood slats with which to support the hanging segments of the plant until they grew strong enough to stand on their own. And through the railing that these supports formed in front of the flower pot, the young man with the checked shirt and the blue jeans now passed lithely like an eel, while Lazaros watched in agony, as though it were a heart operation. He saw him bend, balance himself on one foot only, look for something, then straighten up, then stand on both feet and skillfully glide through the forest of wood slats.

—O.K., he said at the door, returning the screwdriver to his back pocket. Only don't forget to bring in the lamp so I can change the wire. Good-by.

And he left, with a last glance at the plant and an undefinable smile.

—Good-by, so long, Lazaros said, relieved to see the

44

door slowly close. He breathed again. The foreign presence
in his room, the screwdriver, the lifted eyebrow, the detailed
examination of his world, as though to verify that his world
was all right, had upset him. He had to wait some time
before his nerves relaxed again, before he could forget that
undefinable smile—was it jealousy? admiration?—that he
had seen on the man's face as he left.

Outside, the sun was burning. Summer. The days had
expanded with the heat and the sky was red. On the day
he attended his last class at the university he also settled
his accounts with the outside world. He passed his exams
successfully, even better than he had expected, so his family
would have no reason to complain. He had silenced them.
Now he could live as he wanted to.

And he lived shut up hermit-like in his room, locking
it the few times he happened to go out under the pretext
that the cat, Daï, might go in and relieve itself in the fertilizer of the flower pot. He even forbade the cleaning
woman—Kyra-Katina, who came twice a week—to go in
there. And he had given specific instructions to his mother
to tell whoever might happen to ask for him that he was
away, that he had gone on a trip.

Some time after the electrician left—he was calm now,
he had found his equilibrium again, He and the Plant were
once more alone—he still remembered that question from
the doorway: "What kind of tree is this?" He remembered
it now independent of the man's face and the sound of his
voice, and in turn he asked it himself: what kind of tree
was it indeed? He looked at it from below, protectively covered by the green planes of its ceiling, and for the first
time the truth unveiled itself to his dazzled, ecstatic eyes:
the plant was no longer the single-leafed plant he had

known, the plant he had stolen one night in May from the humble courtyard of the young girl, but had become something else, something heavier with experience and sap and strength; it now really did look like a tree. And the fact that a third person's observation had been necessary to make him see its proper dimensions didn't bother him. He knew this often happened with people very close to us: exactly because they are so close, we're the last to become conscious of their changes. It was an infant when I took it out of her hands, and look at what a giant it's become! he thought with pride. Would the same thing have happened in her courtyard? he then wondered. Or maybe the difficulties it encountered in here made it grow ahead of time, made it mature, so that it wisely tore itself to provide new fronts on all sides. He looked at it, admired it, took pride in it as he would in a son. The only thing was that the terms had changed: it was no longer the plant that needed his protection; it was he who needed its protection. He laughed. What joy!

He had no doubt any longer that it was a full tree. It had outgrown all the furniture, which cowered in the corners panic-stricken; it dominated the whole room with ease, untamed, imposing, a little inaccessible, like an elephant in its cage, and also prophetic, without he himself knowing the reason. The only trouble was that he couldn't determine exactly what kind of tree it might be.

He would have called it a philodendron without hesitation, because it had acquired all the same characteristics —a hard and firm flesh, thick ribs like branches, a stem like a mast, and the central nerve like the backbone of a gigantic fish, terminating in a propeller tail, as in the case of the Indian Flagellaria—he would have called it a philodendron without hesitation had it not generated two new stems out of its sheath, each with a leaf about as small as

46

the original leaf at the time he'd stolen the plant; and he knew for certain that this kind of reproduction was a basic characteristic of the monstera deliciosa. And the question was even more vexing now that the plant was no longer in its adolescence—when its sex, still unformed, remained justifiably undetermined—but had filled out fully and entered its mature period, as he could see so clearly. What was it, then? Monstera deliciosa or philodendron or palm tree or none of these but something totally different, which, growing in a strange world, could nowhere find its mate? In the end it doesn't really matter, he thought. It's enough that it always remain strong and vigorous, graceful and beautiful. He got up and measured himself against it. It was even taller than he was. Each of its rib cages was wider than his chest. They gazed at each other in the mirror, cheek against cheek. And then he saw for the first time that his eyes, normally brown, had now turned green, olive green, like two small leaves.

"What kind of tree is this?" He recalled the electrician's question some days later when, on waking, he saw the flower pot—the broad, brick-colored flower pot—in pieces on the floor. The earth in it, black and lumpy, had spilled out over the mat, reaching the floor boards. It frightened him. The roots shot out this way and that, twisted like ground antennas, coiled like snakes frozen stiff in the dead of winter. And hairs protruded at the ends, compounding the horror. At first he thought he was seeing a nightmare. The plant, near death, was asking for his help. It was held up by its supports alone and these were bending under the weight. He imagined that people had come in and deliberately broken the flower pot. But how could they have come in since the door was locked and the bed blocked the

47

open balcony door? Now the flower pot was in fragments on the floor, the pieces concave, tinged orange on the inner surface. He picked up two or three of these, tried to fit them together, studied the brick coloring of their outer surface, recalling the brick-colored blouse she had been wearing. The last thing that still reminded me of her is broken too, he thought bitterly. The room was full of vapors. And outside, the steam of summer.

For hours afterwards he was tortured by remorse. Why hadn't he thought of it ahead of time? Why hadn't he forseen what would happen and bought a bigger flower pot? He had sat there admiring the growth of his plant, forgetting completely that the roots would be growing also, suffering from asphyxiation in the hell of their prison. Its body had the whole room in which to expand. A room 12′ by 12′ by 12′. But what about its feet, its toes? How would he himself feel if he were wearing his childhood shoes? Yes, he saw it all clearly now: the roots had become twisted, had turned back on their axes, had formed themselves into a ball, had become so entangled among themselves that they couldn't stand it any longer and had kicked through their clay prison. Now they were breathing freely, were stretching numbly. The plant moved, was about to fall . . .

He got dressed and rushed out into the street like a madman. He was in a hurry to find a bigger flower pot. He tried all the flower shops, went to the various places that sold jugs, searched, asked, could nowhere find what he was looking for. They told him he would have to place a special order. "And when will it be ready?" "In two or three days." Two or three days? Even two or three hours would be too

late. "Then why don't you get a barrel? That ought to do
the job for you." He liked the idea. Without wasting any
more time, he went and bought a small barrel with hoops
around it, took its lid off, bought some brick-color paint with
which to coat it and enough fertilizer to fill it up to the ears.

He returned home, covered with sweat, carrying this
strange-looking barrel. Inside the entrance of the apartment
house he ran into several electricians working on the meters,
fiddling with some capricious wires. These he saw as entrails
torn out of some stomach, frigid snakes, and recalling the
roots he had faced on waking up that morning, he was
compelled to move with even greater speed—when, suddenly, someone addressed him. He came out of his preoccupation, looked, saw a young man with a checked shirt and
blue jeans. The face seemed familiar, but he couldn't remember where he had seen it before. "How's the monstera?"
he was asked loudly. "Fine," he answered dryly, and to
cover up his agitation while waiting for the elevator, he said:
"When are we going to get the new current?" "Soon, very
soon," said an electrician on top of a ladder. "Soon," added
another, "people in here will die like flies." "And that barrel,
did you buy it for her?" asked the boy with the screwdriver.
"No," he answered nervously. This discussion of his plant
out in the open bothered him. And to change the subject:
"I'll bring the lamp over to the shop tomorrow." In the
meantime the retired general's daughter had arrived and
was standing beside him with a victrola in her arms. The
elevator, named TITAN, finally came down, and the two
of them got in: first the girl with the victrola, then he with
the barrel.

—Is it new? he asked her in order to say something.
—Yes, she answered, all affectation. The old one no

longer worked with the new three-phase current, so I bought this one.

As they went up, he began worrying about whether or not anybody had heard about his monstera deliciosa. If it were just the porter, he wouldn't care. Nor would he care about the electricians, strangers who were leaving tomorrow, anyway. It was the tenants he feared. Had the sensitive ear of the butcher's wife picked up anything? Had this young girl, who pretended indifference, caught on, so that she would now spill it all to her family? How long had she been standing next to him? He was now ready to go down again and find an excuse for picking a quarrel with the electrician who had almost betrayed him. No, that wouldn't do any good. It would be better to take him aside and tell him: "How much do you want to keep your mouth shut from now on?" That way he would buy his silence and keep the plant secret. He would pay the man anything, just so long as he didn't . . .

—Why did you press the STOP button? asked the general's daughter. Aren't you going to the seventh floor too?

Why had he pressed it? What good would it do to go down? It would only make him look more suspicious.

—I just made a mistake, he said, turning red with embarrassment.

They got out on the seventh floor. Nobody knows the name "monstera deliciosa," he thought, to console himself. Even if they had heard it, they wouldn't know what it meant.

—Good appetite.

—Same to you.

And each rang a separate bell.

He plunged into his room, thirsty for coolness and quiet, thoroughly shaken by the world he had seen, a world whose existence he had nearly forgotten—plunged with a passion, as he used to into the sea when he was a small boy, wanting to drink it up totally, immersing himself fully in its wet bosom despite the shouts and threats of his mother from the shore.

From his mother's point of view, the barrel touched on the verge of sheer madness. She now had serious doubts about her son's sanity and wanted to go consult the neurologist on the first floor, Mr. Anagnostaras, without letting her husband know. But she would always put it off at the last minute with the hope that this mania would eventually pass.

Every day she would complain about the stuffy smell that came out of his room and spread through the whole house. She said it might not bother him, he might even think it natural, but the others were not obliged to put up with it, and he shouldn't be so selfish and always think only of himself. It was his right to isolate himself if he wanted to, but he was very nearly isolating her as well. She didn't dare ask a friend to come over and have an iced fruit juice as she used to. The house smelled. And she had no desire to be ridiculed in society because of him.

Today, the barrel brought on one of her crises. She saw him come in rolling it along the floor, steering it into his room. She recalled him rolling his hoop along as a small boy and then falling into her arms out of breath; now he was rolling a whole barrel, with four hoops, and all for this damned plant. That was all he thought about, her darling boy, never about her.

She had asked him to bring her a glass of water because she wasn't feeling too well today. She was sitting in the dining room in her nightgown, copying a pattern for embroidery out of a foreign magazine that the French woman living in the penthouse, Mme Lebelle, had lent to her. He

51

answered that he was in a hurry. A little while later she
saw him carrying a jug full of water for his plant. Everything, everything for the plant. Nothing for her.

She couldn't hold back any longer. She had smothered
the pain inside her for so long. Now the tears welled up
in her eyes of their own accord. She cried quietly, without
sobbing. She was telling him how very much alone she had
felt lately, how useless. And, yes, she didn't hide the fact
that she was jealous of the plant that had stolen him away
from her forever in her own home, in her own territory.
She had no other children to console her, to devote herself
to. She had him alone, her only cherished one, her pride
and joy. And now! She reminded him of what she had suffered to bring him up. During the privations and hardships
of the Occupation she had always arranged to give him the
cream of everything. And what was her reward in the end?
Her son had fallen in love with this freak of nature, this
abortion, this monster, and she'd lost him forever. If it
were at least something beautiful that had drawn him away
from her! The tender arms of a woman who would take care
of him as she did. She would still be jealous, but in a different way. She would become reconciled to it and would console herself with the thought that her son, her child, lived
happily near her. But as it was now, she knew that he suffered with the monster, that the monster dominated him,
tortured him sadistically . . . Her tears became more profuse.
She could hardly speak. And why wouldn't he let her go into
his room? Why did he lock it up when he went out? He
said it was because of the cat, Daï. But Daï was just an
excuse, she knew that. What harm would it do? She wanted
to smell his sheets, put his room in order, pick his dirty
socks off the floor, mend them. He had deprived her abruptly
of every motherly joy. And what about her desserts? He
used to be so crazy about the sweet things she prepared for

him . . . Why did he scorn them now? Why did he eat nothing? Couldn't he see for himself how thin he'd got? He was just skin and bones. It frightened her to look at him. And his friends, boys and girls alike, were looking for him. Everybody was asking about him. Where had Lazaros gone, where had he disappeared? Couldn't he realize himself that the way he was going he'd become tubercular one of these days? . . . Her whole body now shook from the sobbing.

He watched her, stood in front of her, listening at first with indifference and cynicism. Gradually, though, the jug he was holding tipped, and a little water spilled on the floor. Gradually, watching her tired face—which seemed older now without make-up—and her dyed hair showing white at the roots, and her tears falling on the embroidery pattern and soaking the paper, he began to unbend, his knees lost their rigidity, his heart, which he'd walled up with stone, softened, and he felt something pushing him toward her, urging him to fall at her feet and ask her forgiveness for everything—as he used to do, when small, before going to communion on Good Friday—urging him to tell her—as he used to in childhood to give her courage when he was sick and she would sit up by his bedside all night—: "Mama, I'll be all right tomorrow, I'll go to school . . ." But how could he give her courage now? He couldn't tell her that anything would go away, that he was sick but would be well someday soon; he didn't believe that he would ever be well the way she meant it, because the decay had reached the nerve, the tooth was rotten, it stank; yes, she was right about the smell that came from his room, she was right about everything, and he was clearly an ungrateful son. "Mother," he said inside himself, "Mother, don't cry . . ." But in the end he didn't go near her.

· · ·

53

The memory of the burning sun all morning long while he was looking for a new flower pot, the sweating people, the melting asphalt on the road, the flies, made him muse —now that he had transferred the plant and had finished painting the barrel—on how happy he himself was in comparison to all that, especially as the plant was now pouring a green coolness around him, like a plane tree by a stream, in the heat of high noon, laying traps with its smaller leaves for the troublesome flies that stuck there and died, thus turning his room into a true oasis in the desert of the summer, an oasis that many would envy if they knew about it. What of theirs, then, could he possibly envy? What was he losing by not going out at all? Even the sea was less cool than the shade of his plant, not to mention the discomfort of coming and going in the excursion boats.

Then he remembered what his friend Kosta in Munich had said: "In the trees, only there, for all of us, is the tranquillity we long for." Only now did he understand what Kosta had meant, now that he had acquired his own tree. And he wrote him to say so, adding that he didn't know exactly what kind of tree it was. But this didn't bother him as much as it used to. The nature of a relationship, he believed, mattered less than its intensity. The nature is for others, the intensity for ourselves. And this simple fact, impossible for him to understand while living with people, he now understood once and for all through his plant.

But the intensity that existed between them dropped at times. The plant's silence tired him, its immobility numbed him, the thought of their inability to communicate turned nightmarish sometimes. Because he had the courage to admit that in essence he didn't know the plant. And if he lost it this very moment, he would be left with endless regret that despite their living so long together, the essence had escaped him in the end, since they hadn't known each other. At first the plant might have had some distant connection with Ariadne. But now that it was so transformed, that it had grown monstrously, that it had changed fundamentally in the barrel, now that it had become a whole tree, what was it, what did it represent? He didn't know. And since it couldn't become human, in order for him to get close to it, he was gradually taking on the manner and way of life of a vegetable. Hadn't he tried so many times to break off their relationship? He would go out, pretending that he had work to do or that he longed to talk with human beings, but all that ever came of it was his wanting passionately to return to its side, so that they would find themselves alone again in this exquisite silence, in the coolness of its corner, where everything became peaceful and closed up like a wound covered by green oil. What tortured him had nothing to do with their life together. It was something deeper, something unfathomed, something enigmatic. The plant is me, he had said once, but quickly discovered that such an easy answer couldn't satisfy him because it simply wasn't the truth. And when he went outside to think about it, beyond the influence of the plant's presence, he lived with nothing but the yearning to return.

In the end he found the answer and settled down. It was his error, a big error, to try and explain their relationship in terms of human logic. The plant far outstripped his very humble logic, and their relationship was located elsewhere. Exactly where, it would do him no good at all to discover. In any case, surely not on this earth, so dirty and garrulous and worried about its own skin, but somewhere higher, where cloud mingles with cloud in the net of the stars.

The only trouble was, it started to expand beyond the limits of the room. Day by day the room became narrower, like the flower pot. Having already been through the exper-

55

ience of one breakage, he wondered what it would now do
to the room. Would it knock it down? Would it then have
the strength to break up the roof terrace? And where would
it go from there? To the sky, clearly, he said, to the sky. Its
propeller would start turning and it would rise into the sky
like a helicopter. The wind would lift it like a zeppelin. I'll
get into the barrel too, I'll have enough ballast to jettison,
and we'll go high together, higher and higher, and together
we'll rise to the limits of the sky.

For three days now the sky had been covered with
clouds. The sun had hidden behind their quilt. An oppressive
sultriness. And there was no light. He watered his plant,
but the water wouldn't go down to the roots. Without the
slightest sun, with no light, the plant was gradually losing
its sap, was gradually wilting. Its ends turned in, it shrunk,
and on its deep ocean-colored surface, yellow stigmata began
to appear, round like islands, with a black core in the
middle. For three nights now he hadn't been able to sleep.
His worry about his sick friend tyrannized him. What did
these yellow spots mean? He was afraid of carcinomas.
He could see the plant stirring restlessly, suffering. For
three days, as long as the sultriness lasted, he was sick.
And when sudden heavy rain finally came, he too cried with
joy. And then, with the light, the plant recovered its health.
The yellow islands sank in their deep ocean, where he was
sailing again on *lobed, serrate, lanceolate* dreams.

VII

SUMMER WAS BOILING. July with its apricots was dying
and August had begun to hang its black grapes in the sky.

The days, big as bulls, let warm breath out of their nostrils, breath like a sirocco wind. And people lounged motionless like sheep, offering their shadows to each other.

His parents went off to the country. They were going to spend their vacation on Ammouliani, a quiet and unknown little island at the foot of Mt. Athos. They implored him, uselessly, to go with them. "The experiment I'm working on," he explained "is just reaching its critical point and I can't abandon it in the middle." "But the sea, the sun, will be good for you . . ." It was impossible to make him change his mind. Before leaving, his mother left him the key to the cupboard where she hid her preserves, and his father gave him some money so that he could eat out.

For some time now he had been waiting for the day when his parents would finally leave. Other years he had been afraid to stay home alone because he would disintegrate in the sudden solitude, stretch himself through the empty rooms, thinned-out like air. He craved others in order to crawl deeper into his isolation. But this year was not like other years. This year he craved isolation in order to give himself more fully to his plant.

That's why he opened all the doors and windows the moment they left, as though he were preparing the house for a reception, then closed the shutters except for the one that gave light to the plant. He had got undressed and started walking around in the nude when—less than an hour later—he heard the phone cackling in the hall. He hesitated. He didn't know whether to pick it up or let it ring itself dumb. The phone was insistent. He finally went over and said "Hello" in a changed voice. They were asking for his mother. "She just left for Ammouliani." "Is that you, Lazaros?"

57

said the voice at the other end. "Yes. Who is this?" "Your
godfather. So they've left already. And I thought they were
leaving tomorrow . . . All right, all right. It doesn't matter
. . . How was your trip? . . . Good. Now that you'll be alone
you must come to the house often for lunch. It'll make your
godmother very happy. All right? You hear? You come
often . . . Where did you say they were going?" "To Ammouliani."

He saw his godfather twice a year: on his nameday
and on New Year's Eve. On both occasions his godfather
would give him some spending money. The rest of the year
he didn't even know whether he had a godfather. Yet the
whole time he was speaking to the man, he could see his
naked body in the big mirror behind the table stand where
the phone was, and it filled him with a sense of shame. He
imagined that his godfather could see him from the other
end of the line, naked, as he was when the man had im-
mersed him in the baptismal font. With the difference that
at that time he was pink and round, whereas now you could
count the ribs in his chest, like the ribs of the plant. I've
gotten thinner, he thought, looking at this white and hairless
flesh. I'm half what I was. But how would my plant grow if
it didn't feast on my flesh? He had put down the receiver
and its click spread through the empty house to infinity,
like the circles created by a stone thrown in water. Then
he unplugged the phone. Now you rest too, he told it. I give
you a month's leave. And with his little finger he cleaned
the ear where his godfather's voice still buzzed its "All right?
Hear? You come often. It'll make your godmother very
happy . . ."

He was worried. What would his plant do now? The
whole house was at their disposal. He went near it and

58

caressed it. "I want you to spread," he told it. "We'll never have an opportunity like this again. And the sooner we take advantage of it, the better. I want you to fill the other rooms, rub out the memory of others, just as you filled my own room and rubbed out the noises of others . . ."

For two days, however, the plant didn't make a move. It stood thoughtful, undecided, as though it were playing with his impatience, with his longing to see it spread. This immobility got on his nerves. And because he thought the two side leaves which had emerged from the sheath were responsible for the situation, and because he had a deep fear that these might expand instead of the whole plant, that they might fill his room and exile him from it forever —what could happen to him worse than this: not to be able to sleep with his plant any more?—he took the bread knife from the kitchen and cut them off. He saw his plant go into painful spasms. "But it had to be done, it had to be done," he kept saying like a man lost, as he threw the knife aside. And with his two hands he struggled to stop the hemorrhage. Where he had cut off the two side leaves the stalk wrinkled like the stump of an amputated leg.

He waited a while without seeing any result. Then, for relief, he went out, on the excuse that he had some shopping to do. Down at the entrance he was stopped by the kindly porter. "All alone now, huh? A bachelor." "Can't be helped," he said, and opened the letter box. He found an invitation from the Council of High School Graduates for a nighttime boat excursion under the full moon. He had until Wednesday, August 6, to sign up. Price: 30 drachmas. As he was going up in the elevator loaded with fruit, eggs, tomatoes, and bread, he tore up the invitation in disgust.

On the night of the full moon—which he saw coming up behind Mt. Hortiatis like a red zero—trying to force sleep through his agitation over the strange immobility of

59

the plant, he heard a mysterious creaking in the dining room outside, as though thieves had come in and were walking on tiptoe. A few days earlier he had read about a theft in a neighboring house, and, relating the circumstances, he felt his blood run cold. It's better not to move, he thought. Let them take whatever they want. As long as they don't come in here. The creaking, fading slowly, lasted until dawn. Then, with the first light of day, feeling certain that the thieves had left, he got up to see what remained. He searched the house thoroughly and found that everything was in its place. They had touched nothing. Strange, he thought. But if they weren't thieves, what were they?

The following night he moved the couch against the front door for security, and balanced the garbage shovel on the edge of it so that whoever came in would reveal himself. He then lay down and, with ears taut, waited in the darkness. A section of moonlight progressed slowly along the floor. Shortly after midnight he heard the same creaking again. This time it seemed to him the grunting of small children in their sleep, and it was accompanied by the strange sounds of furniture moving. Afraid that he was having hallucinations, he got up, turned on the light in the dining room, and prepared to receive a blow from an invisible arm. At first he couldn't see clearly. Possibly from too much light, or possibly because his eyes were closed out of fear. When he opened them, he found that the couch was still thrust up against the front door and the shovel resting as he had left it. A big cockroach, scared by the light, scurried to hide behind the armchair. "You won't escape!" he shouted at it fiercely, and went after it. He moved the massive old armchair and then, as he was ready to crunch the black cockroach with his foot, hovering there with his right leg poised in the air as though he were doing gymnastics, he saw it: a small leaf lifting up its tender body fearfully, alone and unprotected, held tightly in the clutch of the floor boards.

He stepped back, knelt down, blew it gently, kissed it. It was round like a mushroom and hollow in the middle like a coffee-cup saucer. "A leaf! A leaf!" he whispered, amazed, full of a strange joy. How did it sprout here all by itself? he wondered. Through the opening of his bedroom door he saw the huge plant shyly extend one of its heads, like a turtle coming out of its shell. "What's been going on? Won't you tell me what's happening?" he asked the mother plant, which was gazing at him from the opening, enigmatic as a sphinx, voiceless. "Did this green tear fall from you?" After more careful scrutiny, however, he discovered that the little leaf hadn't fallen there; it was rooted in the floor, and its roots, like underground wires, had split the floor boards. To trace their source, he followed the split on all fours until his head struck the barrel.

He relaxed. All the black thoughts that had kept him agitated for so long scattered. His plant was progressing underground, while he had expected it to spread aerially. That was it. No hallucinations, or thieves, or exhaustion from illness . . . Tears of joy came into his eyes. And to celebrate, he filled a glass with brandy, got some ice from the kitchen, downed the brandy in one swallow. That was it, he said again. The spreading has started. Now there will be no stopping it. I think I hear new creaking already. The fullness of time has come. The fullness of space. The fullness. This small moment of eternity that we pursue all our lives. And afterwards I don't care. Afterwards I'll be able to die more easily.

He picked up the shovel, almost staggering, pushed the couch back to its place, saw the black cockroach scurrying again, and said "Tomorrow I'll put out some poison," then turned out the light and went back to sleep in his bed, which was now floating in a sea of moonlight.

The days that followed were days of glory for him. His happiness multiplied every time he saw new leaves sprouting through the floor boards, so green, emerging always where there was a touch of light to warm them as they started out. A lot of them, though, happened to be born at night, and he would find them in the morning hidden under shadowy traps in the furniture. That's why, without hesitating, like a man of experience, he moved the tables, the chairs, the couches, and the armchairs. He piled them on top of each other, freeing more and more floor space for the leaves to walk on. He didn't even hesitate to dismantle the wide matrimonial bed in his parents' bedroom, leaving only the springs, since these didn't stop the light and actually formed a wire latticework where the leaves could later find support. And now the mother plant, immobile by the open door, gazed pensively at the flourishing of the new generation.

Every morning he woke with joy. His first thought, the minute he opened his eyes, was: how many came up last night? And he purposely delayed getting up so as to postpone the rare pleasure of seeing them multiply. The floor became for him a military map, with mountain ranges of furniture and thick forests of wood, where he daily marked the advance of his leafy army with tiny green flags. And their variety was unending: *oblong, orbiculate, gymnogamous, cryptogamous, palmate, cordate, dentate, lobed, serrate,* and *lanceolate*. He never tired of looking at them. Then he would sprinkle them with a watering can, cautious in his movements, since the slightest misplaced step could be fatal to a leaf.

And the roots of the mother plant spread everywhere. She was like an octopus that remains in its lair—the barrel —and spreads its tentacles one by one, watching them unwind ceaselessly under the rocks. The roots too, like octopus tentacles, had spaced projections and pith. They were like wires that hold up electric lanterns. And the small leaves were phosphorescent in the darkness, a full meadow of lights, like the Upper City after dark, and the plant itself shining in the shadowy corner of the church where he had left it that first night. Everything is going along fine, he told himself. Someone else in my shoes might have gone crazy. It's very lucky that I'm an agriculturist rather than an engineer. Thank God . . . And he made up a prayer which he repeated every night before going to bed: "You, God, who live up high and see everything, do not deny me your sun again tomorrow, and give my young leaves health and happiness so that they may grow tall and strong to glorify Your name now and forever more. Amen."

And the roots later progressed into the tiled hallway that led into the kitchen, disturbing the symmetry of the black and white tiles. These didn't creak like the floor boards. They came loose noiselessly and easily, like a row of medals hiding the flower in a buttonhole. Some of the roots went askew into the toilet, became caught up in its basin, climbed up the pipes, dipped into the NIAGARA flush tank, plugged up its orifice, and drank water greedily. They stormed the bathroom in a frenzy, crawled into the openings of the faucets, covered up the bidet, twisted the water pipes in their thirst, and knit a whole network in the marble bathtub, where they swam gleefully like water snakes.

One day, toward noon, his doorbell rang. It couldn't be the ice delivery at this time, he thought. It must be some-

63

one else waiting for me to open up. He was lying down, in the nude, among his newly born leaves, studying them. The bell rang more insistently this time. And then again, with a different rhythm, staccato, and again. Through the frosted glass panel in the door he could see the moving shadows of two men. Who can they be? he wondered. Maybe the bill for electricity or water. But why two people? He dragged himself to the entrance hallway on his belly and waited with his ears taut. Then he heard the voices.

—There's no question. He's in there. I know it. He never goes out, said a voice that he recognized immediately as that of the porter.

—Maybe he's asleep, said the other voice, which he didn't recognize.

—Let's see, said the first voice. I'll ring again for the last time.

And the bell rang again stubbornly. Then the porter banged on the door with his fist. He shouted:

—Mr. Lazaros, a telegram . . .

What sort of telegram? he thought. Who could it be from? Maybe from my parents saying they're coming back. Father was suddenly taken ill and . . .

—Why don't you sign for it? he heard the voice of the mailman say.

He saw some movements behind the opaque panel: the porter probably putting on his glasses.

—Where should I sign?

—Here.

And lying as he was on his stomach, the telegram, shoved under the door, nearly came into his mouth. He waited for the shadows to go away, then crawled back and tore open the transparent envelope with trembling hands. He stood stunned. It was from Ammouliani, from his parents. He couldn't read any further. Exactly what I was afraid would happen at the high point of my happiness, he said to himself and unfolded it, ready to receive the disagreeable message.

ON ANNIVERSARY YOUR BIRTHDAY WISHING YOU EVERY POSSIBLE HAPPINESS AND LIFE FULL OF LAURELS. FATHER, MOTHER.

His heart slipped back in place. Feeling the relief spread spread through his whole body, he looked to see what time they had sent it: 9:30 a.m. It came very quickly, he thought. Then he looked at the signatures, at the seals. He counted the words: sixteen for the text and five for the address, twenty-one. He put it back in its transparent envelope. Then, hands behind his head, he stretched out on the floor, which was still damp from the watering. So today is August 17. On a day exactly like this, twenty-one years ago, I too came into life, into the light, like these small leaves, twisted, unprotected . . . Twenty-one years! he thought with a shiver. And I'm still playing with the leaves, just as I used to play in the garden of our prewar house when I was a small boy. It was the same then as now. So what has changed? Twenty-one years old. I've turned Twenty-one. I've entered the twenty-second year of my life . . . It was hard to realize. And he started singing old songs: "Where are you going, little ship, in this weather?: the sea is rough, so aren't you afraid? . . . And the lot falls to the bravest, who hasn't jour-jour-journeyed before, who hasn't jour-jour-jour . . . Riri, Riri, Ririka, you're some creature, my child; you're better than Marika Kotopouli . . . Bring me another glass of red wine, just one more and don't you worry . . . In our time the girls knitted stockings, now they go down to the beach with men . . . Eany, meany, miny, moe . . ." He stopped. The prewar years were good, he said to himself. But now I'm

65

twenty-one years old. I have responsibilities in life. I can't be carefree like I was then.

But he soon lost count of the days again. He mused: Yesterday was the seventeenth. It was my birthday. I received the telegram. Today must be the eighteenth. Time closed over him again like a wave. He ascertained that it passed by the thinning of the moon and the growing of his garden.

In the dinning room, to which the shadows of the leaves gave another perspective, another depth, the *dentate* now dominated together with the *alternately* and the *spirally arranged*. In the living room he found more *entire* and *lyrate* leaves, while the *oppositely arranged* had their own corner, like a minority, and were neighboring the *pinnately lobed*.

In the room reserved for visiting relatives, something else had happened. Here the roots had emerged to the surface—they called them "surface roots" in botany—and given birth to plants rather than leaves. Maybe because their distance from the mother plant was greater, he thought, they wanted to become autonomous so they wouldn't need her immediate support. Trees know more than we do. So I keep quiet, he said when he saw them. In there he found a number of *peltate* and *julianate* plants, and a few *articulate* plants, which screeched like cats when he touched them. Where the wardrobe had been before (the floorboards were a different color because they hadn't been waxed) there was a surfeit of *lycopods*, a nice contrast with their *staminate* flowers.

In his parents' room, which still smelled of used sheets and urine, leaves and plants lived inseparably. The *ophioglossum* in there worried him. These, adder-tongued, shaped like snake-bodied women, elegant and lively, had the habit

66

of twisting themselves around other stems and strangling them with too much love. That's why he tried to restrict them as much as he could. In the bedroom, full of mirrors, there was always a tough contest as to who would surpass whom in height. So the *ectotrophic*, which normally did not grow very tall, had stretched their necks like poised snakes, while the *wing lobed*, with the casualness of a pelican-like American sailor, looked down on them with a certain pity. The competition going on in front of the bedroom mirrors had caused the plants to reach the level of his chest, while in the other rooms they had not yet reached above his knees. And indeed one of them in there, a *thalloid hepatic*, had grown so tall that its palm covered the icon of the Saints Kosmas and Damianos on the wall.

He was forced to be severe with several that tried to go out on the balcony and twist themselves around the railings. He discouraged all such efforts on their part, punishing them as an example, because that kind of thing would put them in danger of betraying themselves and thus making the others pay as well, the others who were trying, decorously and civilly, to get ahead inside the rooms.

The floor lamp, the walls, the electric fixtures on the ceiling, all were covered with leaves. The furniture, dressed in green, looked like sunken ships on the sea's floor, drowned a second time by its vegetation. The furniture could be distinguished only by its mass and by a red or brown strip visible here and there.

In the hall there was too much darkness for anything to grow. But in the kitchen there were some *bryophytes* and *sporophylls*.

One night the lights went out. He thought it might be a general power failure, but he could see lights everywhere in the city. With the help of a candle he examined the wire in the main fuse box. He found it all right. He thought he might have left the bill unpaid, but from what he could remember, the electricity bill hadn't come yet. Then, why was there no light? Dawn brought him the answer: he saw that all the current-carrying wires of the house, without actually changing position or alignment, had become roots. The single wire leading into the phone had become a root, the twisting ground antenna was now a root, roots also the bipolar doorbell wires and the waterproof wires in the bathroom. Then even the water stopped running. The faucet only dripped tearfully; he had to stick out his dried tongue under it to quench his thirst.

One day he found an envelope without a stamp under the door. Before opening it he guessed from whom it was by the handwriting. He read it: "For days now I've been struggling to find you. Your phone doesn't answer. Your bell doesn't ring. The porter says you're upstairs. I'm leaving day after tomorrow for Mt. Athos. I'm with some Germans. Call me *without fail* at 89-64. It's urgent. Kosta."

He heard a noise, he heard a rumble. In his room the supports were falling one by one. The plant was rising like an elephant. It broke the lamp and pushed against the ceiling forcefully. The plaster was falling in white snowflakes. What was it doing? Was it going to destroy the whole top story of the apartment house? Would it have sufficient strength or would it bend and become submissive?

"Kosta, my friend Kosta, you came at a bad moment," he said in his confusion. "I don't have time to see you. I can't. My plant needs me now."

VIII

THE FIRST TENANT in the apartment house to become perturbed by the pressure of the plant was Mme Lebelle, who lived in the penthouse. Her husband was out during the week, came home only on weekends, and Mme Lebelle would enjoy the Greek sunshine every morning by taking her three children to Baxé-Tsiflíki for a swim; in the evenings she would have an ice cream at Floka's; in short, she was living a quiet, contented life when suddenly one moonless night she felt her bed begin to rock like a boat. She jumped up frightened, in her tulle nightgown, her cowlike breasts trembling in rhythm with the whole room. "An earthquake," she thought, and ran to her children's bedroom to see if they too had woken up frightened. But she found the little ones, Jacques, Marilaine, and Pepo, sleeping undisturbed under the mosquito nets, browned by the sea and sun, black-skinned like little devils. "That's funny," she said. A cock crowed. She lay down again, but a new jolt abruptly entangled her in her sheets. Bottles of cologne, lotions, nail-polish remover, boxes full of trinkets and jewelry, were falling off the shelves and breaking on the floor. Her bedsprings were squeaking. She didn't shut her eyes all night. The next day she asked Mrs. Sousamidis casually, as they were coming up the elevator together, whether she'd felt an earthquake the previous night. Mrs. Sousamidis looked at her in amazement. No, she said, she hadn't felt a thing. Nor did the morning papers mention anything about an earthquake, and she read them carefully. But since she herself slept very soundly, it would be better to ask others as well. Mme Lebelle thanked her and continued on up. . . . On the nights that followed, the same thing happened. Her bed squeaked, her body rocked of its own accord. She took sleeping pills, something she had never done before in her life. On Saturday night, when her husband got back, she told him about it. But he didn't take it seriously. And when he left, the nightmarish shaking, at the heart of the lonely night, visited her again. Her husband had told her jokingly that it was just one of her hallucinations. Now she started believing it herself. The pills she took in order to sleep upset her nerves. The unbearable heat and the loneliness—how long it was to the following Saturday!—completed her disintegration. She also suffered a light sunstroke on the beach, and all this, together with her fear of the earthquake, unbalanced her mind; so Mme Lebelle, who exuded health and strength, went to the neurologist on the first floor, Dr. Anagnostaras, to be examined.

What, then, was it up to? What was his plant trying to do? He wondered as he watched it wrestling with the ceiling. What was it striving to accomplish, since even if it did manage to tear down the whole ceiling, it still couldn't soar to the sky like a helicopter or a zeppelin, as he had hoped earlier, because it was now firmly rooted inside the house. He could see it bending like Atlas, struggling to lift the weight of the whole world on its shoulders. "But that's impossible," he told it. "You're struggling uselessly. It can't be done. You were nourished by me, by human flesh, and the dreams of gods are not for us. . . ." Still he couldn't really tell what his plant's purpose was this time. Besides, he'd got used to the unexpected on its part. And he was waiting to see the further signs of its new ambition before venturing any conclusion.

—Crickets. Don't you hear the crickets that have come in through the open windows? The wife of the retired general was saying to her husband in panic. She heard them first and woke him up. But he, an old artillery colonel, like all soldiers of that branch, was a little hard of hearing and couldn't pick up those slight creakings that his wife called crickets, even in the thick silence of an August night. He turned over indifferently on his other side. But Mrs. Exadactylos, who was suffering from asthma and therefore couldn't sleep anyway, wouldn't leave him alone.

—Get up and chase those crickets away, she pleaded, whispering in his ear. Get up. Get up.

—Let me alone, woman, Symeon told her, yawning and stretching. I just want a little more sleep. . . .

In the end she succeeded in making him get up. In his flannel underpants the retired general conducted a reconnaissance of the whole house, found the enemy nowhere, and returned to bed satisfied. It wasn't a fact, then, that he couldn't hear well; his wife was merely having hallucinations. Crickets. What a joke. What were crickets and cicadas doing in town, anyway?

But the next night his sick wife closed the windows and turned on the fan despite her asthma. The heat was churned up by the blades of the fan as though it were pulp. They would both suffocate. What on earth was she hearing?

—Crickets, creaking . . . Ah, Symeon . . . It goes crack-crack. It stops then starts again . . . Crack-crack . . .

Finally, when the sound came closer, the brigadier general heard it too.

—What could it be? he asked her.

—How do I know? she answered, terrified. It's a good thing our little Despina is away (their daughter was at a girl guide camp). The girl would die of fright.

Her husband then accepted it as a matter of honor; he decided to set up an ambush for his unknown enemy the following night, in keeping with standard tactics, and catch him red-handed. When night came, he actually hid behind the armchair, waited, and when he heard the first noise, he vaulted out of his hiding place, turned on the light abruptly, shouted menacingly, found nothing. His ambush failed because the unknown enemy had managed to become invisible as well. He returned shame-faced to his better half.

—Our house is haunted, said the superstitious brigadier general's wife, crossing herself. It's haunted. God help us.

Then Lazaros himself realized what was going on: he heard the fuss in the general's house, saw the roots raising their backs and plunging their sharp muzzles into the floor boards, and he got the point. His plant was pushing upwards, shoving its back against the ceiling so that its feet could go down deeper. It looks as though it plans to pierce through the whole apartment house, he thought fearfully, joyfully. It wants to touch the earth, to take root in its guts; the manure in the barrel isn't enough; it wants to suck at her breasts; the water from the pipes doesn't quench its thirst. He saw it straining itself, the nerves in its neck stretching and swelling. "Courage," he told it. "I'm with you. I won't leave you for a moment."

Nobody spent the night in the Railway Workers' Club on the sixth floor, so nobody heard the creaking.

The high school principal, Mr. Pericles Karmiriadis, was at home alone. His wife and daughters were vacationing at Oreokastron, and he went up there only on weekends. The heat always upset his sensitive nervous system, and he would get to sleep very late. He was correcting the proofs of his new article "On Juvenile Deliquents" when he heard the gnashing of teeth. At first he thought it came from the street, then that it came from the floor above, and when the creaking finally entered his study, he jumped up out of his armchair thoroughly startled. He hopped around like someone walking over live coals, while the noises, playfully, like students giving him a hard time in class, would burst right under his feet. He loosened a floor board on the spot but could see nothing underneath it. Panic-stricken, he started to dash out of the room when a strong "crack" shut the door in front of him. "What Satan won't let me do my work? What the hell . . ." And regretting his swearing, he called on the Lord to exorcise the evil demons that were gnawing at the august serenity of his home.

He himself knew nothing. He imagined only that the roots of his plant were progressing through the walls of the apartment house, invisible, following the electric wires, like travelers caught by night in deserted country following train tracks so as not to get lost. And when he saw the plant sweat, shrink, blacken with rage, he understood that its roots had found some obstacle in the concrete. On the other hand, it would feel relieved when they found an opening through the bricks. "Careful we aren't betrayed," he told it. "Don't crack the walls and let them find us. In the apartments you enter, try to hide deep under the joists, not just under the floor boards." He now took care of it better than ever before. "I would like to have been born different," he would tell it now and then, "so I could be in a position to help you."

Uncle Roupén, brother-in-law of Kevórk Popolián, along with his wife, Yiermoné, a guest of her sister, Sourpouí, was explaining in Armenian his theory about the noises,

73

which, he said, had uselessly upset everybody in the apartment house, since it was all nothing more than the floor boards expanding with the heat and therefore creaking. A fat and jovial man, he was a lumber merchant by profession and, therefore, knew all about wood. Popolián's two grown-up children, Garó and Alice, nephews of Uncle Roupén, were buried in the relics relating to their complicated and dispersed family tree, trying to discover the extent of their relationship to the wealthy Gulbekian, who had died a few days earlier in Lisbon, and what portion of his enormous inheritance was due them. They would stay up late at night and so were the first to hear the noises. In fact they had heard them the night before. They weren't worried. They accepted the noises with their traditional hospitality, as though they were overnight guests. But the two sensitive women, Yiermoné and Sourpouí—kind, plump, always full of tears—got very upset. So Kevórk took the Persian rugs out of moth balls and laid them on the floor. The creaking drowned under them. But the women were still anxious, and that was why this evening, in the wintry atmosphere of the house, they listened with some relief to Uncle Roupén's theory about wood expanding with heat. In spite of this, though, they didn't yet dare remove the heavy Persian rugs.

But Lazaros himself didn't know what was going on. He only imagined that the roots of his plant were still descending, like divers, searching blindly, suffering from lack of fresh air and from the darkness of the concrete. He figured that they would easily penetrate the bricks, pass through their hollows without meeting the resistance they expected, because the house was built of cheap materials. But maybe the wires wouldn't always lead them along the right path. So they might wander aimlessly in the night of their days,

74

wasting their strength and vigor. If they'd reached the fourth floor yet, they may have broken into the apartment of Antonakakis—the former Member of Parliament and his wife were vacationing in Mihaniona—and stocked up on water there. Who knows, he thought, they may even have come out for a breath of air into the elevator shaft, because they knew nobody would see them there. He didn't know anything for sure. All these were his own hypotheses. The plant now let up on its pushing, and he could see, in the area on the ceiling where the pressure had been applied, that the plaster was eroding away as a result of the struggle.

—Down, Box. Quiet, Mr. Plytas admonished his dog, who had started barking at midnight, causing the other tenants to complain. He had brought the dog down from the roof terrace for company. And now that the creaking had entered his house, the dog, annoyed, as though he had smelled thieves, started barking furiously. "Quiet, Box! Down, Box! Shut up, Box!" Nothing would do. Guilt attacked him from all sides. He could hear cries in the night. "You killed her, you . . ." And through the unbearable heat wave, the feel of light footsteps, as though the ghost of his departed wife, who had died on her thirteenth abortion, had appeared to ask about their children. "I sent them off to Arsakli, Popy dear. With their aunt," he answered her. So it wasn't just his sick imagination, as he had thought, since now Box was barking wildly. Her spirit was approaching, it was coming back . . . "Shut up, quiet, down!" The dog's voice was his own, he himself looked like his dog, he could see it day after day in his mirror . . . He couldn't take it any longer. He was nearly going mad. That's why tomorrow he would apply for leave from the Office of the Governor General of Northern Greece.

. . .

He himself came down to buy bread. In front of Mrs. Kalfoglou's door, he saw the maids lined up with buckets and jugs, waiting for water. The water didn't reach the other floors. Only the first floor still had some—and of course the basement, but no lady would let her maid go down to the two whores. So the butcher's wife had suddenly become an important person in the apartment house, and all those who had snubbed her previously were now trying to get on the good side of her so as to pick up an extra bucket of water. She was standing at her door, her sleeves rolled up, her monstrous breasts undistinguishable from her belly, standing there giving out orders and instructions in the tone of a mother superior.

—What about you? Aren't you interested in water? she called as soon as she saw him.

—No, he said nervously, struggling to get through the crowd of maids.

Outside, he took a turn around the building to see if the roots of his plant had cracked the walls anywhere. He saw nothing and relaxed. The roots are drinking all their water, he thought with satisfaction. They're already suffering from drought. Tomorrow they'll be dying of thirst . . . From a distance, in the haze of the summer noon, the apartment house seemed to him an impregnable castle, dressed in the sun's shield. "And yet, your castle is worm-eaten inside and will collapse one day," he said with self-confidence. "Nothing shows on the outside. Not a single crack betrays the termites that are slowly digging through your stone monster." It now seemed to him a lobster—with false armor, antennas on the roof, flag poles on the balconies, other antennas—living out the last moments of its life. "Nothing is revealing my octopus, whose tentacles are twisting carefully around your lobster, preparing to suck in all its meat." He went back happy, the loaf of bread under his arm, its ends eaten away.

—We were expecting the noise again yesterday, but it didn't come. It'll come tonight, Mrs. Ladopoulos, pregnant with her second child, told him in the elevator. Oh, my God! I didn't close my eyes all night, I was so scared. They say the creaking lasts three days. And coming now that (she touched her swollen belly) . . . Has your family come back from the country?

—No, he said, and politely opened the elevator door to let her out.

—They're lucky, said the pregnant woman.

He ran to his plant, fell into its arms. "We're doing all right," he cried enthusiastically. "Your roots have reached the third floor. Courage. We've eaten the best part of the animal. Now only the tail remains. And they're all in an uproar. Amazement grows on the faces of the tenants. While they were pulverizing me with their noises, I never said a word. Now it's my turn. Nothing goes unpunished in this world. That's justice."

But this excess of joy of his didn't last long. For a very different reason, he too became a party to the general anxiety. Would his plant's roots succeed in thrusting through to the earth? Would his plant, which now looked exhausted and suddenly old, have the strength to continue? What if they discovered the roots somewhere along the way? What if his parents came back from Ammouliani? Would the roots have enough time? They must have come across the first worms by now, like sea travelers encountering the first birds, a sign that the shore is near. And they must have taken heart, even if for a moment they'd lost their bearings. But would they have enough time? Inside his apartment the leaves were rustling with the noon breeze coming through the open windows off the bay. They smelled of mint and willow. He again looked at the mother plant, which secretly held, like a dark wasp, so many enigmas. Would they have enough time?

Mrs. Malvina, the midwife, even more superstitious then Mrs. Exadactylos, brought a priest in to perform an exorcism. With a sprig of basil he sprinkled all the corners of the house, generous with the holy water, and exorcized the "devilish spirits" through prayers swallowed up by his beard. As he left with his assistant, he pocketed the payment and the treats. (Down at the entrance the terrified porter, in danger of losing his job, kissed the priest's hand.) But in spite of the exorcism, the noises entered Mrs. Malvina's home and made her cat too playful. Thinking the creaking came from mice, it would jump around on the floor boards, scratch at them with its claws. Without wasting time, Mrs. Malvina, President of the Society of Women Scientists, went up to the other president, the principal, and told him how shameful it was that so many educated people, so many responsible citizens, were unable to discover the source of the evil. Mr. Karmiriadis thought the midwife's protest a just one and called the tenants to a general meeting.

IX

THEY CAME TOGETHER—those who weren't on vacation in the country—one Wednesday afternoon, when the shops were closed. Those who had not yet been bothered by the noises, like the merchant Sousamidis, the psychiatrist Anagnostaras, and the cattle dealer Kalfoglou, also came. Although he was not invited, Lazaros came too, out of curiosity and sadism. He sat in a corner and didn't say a word.

In the beginning it was the principal who spoke, with the ease of both president and host. The tenants had made themselves comfortable in the straight chairs and armchairs, in a semicircle, choosing the area where both fans were blowing (that afternoon the heat had reached its peak), and the principal was standing before them, leaning on his desk as he would on the pulpit of the cathedral during one of his sermons, his crow's eyes shining with the light of Christ out of his brown-fried face.

—Ladies, he said, turning to the only lady present, the midwife (Mme Lebelle had ignored the invitation). Gentlemen! In the first place you must excuse me for not offering you something. My wife and daughters are away in Oreokastron, and alone I can't even manage to make coffee for myself.

—That's all right, quite all right, it doesn't matter at all, two or three people said.

—We haven't come here for a party, said Ladopoulos.

—Gentlemen, Karmiriadis continued, looking up at the chandelier as he would look up at the dome with the Pantocrator in the cathedral. For more than two weeks now we have all found ourselves in a state of emergency. And the cause of our panic remains unknown so far. No one person among us can ignore that our apartment house, in

79

which we live as law-abiding Greek citizens and as brothers in Christ, is in danger of being declared in quarantine. As though we had leprosy or the plague. From what cause? We have lost our peace of mind, our nerves are shattered, and with the added dimension of a canicular heat wave, we have been fully undermined. But what are these creakings which demon-like have entered our homes? Whence do they come? What do they reveal? Have you asked yourselves these questions? I do not believe that their source is to be found in the outside world. It is within ourselves, gentlemen, that both God and Satan find refuge. When we forget the first, the second makes himself heard. And, yes, each of us has forgotten the Lord. We have strayed from His path at an angle of ninety degrees. I speak, as you see, the bitter language of truth, and due to my temperament, I do not like evasions. My opinion, therefore, if you want to listen to it, is this: let us return to the way of the Almighty. Let us become the fertile ground wherein His Word will bear fruit. "He who loses me loses the water of life," says the Evangelist. How else can we explain the lack of water? Diverse books have replaced the Divine Word. The movie theater has replaced the church. We are standing before an open abyss. That's why I have brought along a few copies of the New Testament, which I will distribute to you free of charge, so that in those moments when you gather your thoughts, you may find in these divinely inspired words relief and solace for your tortured, your tormented, souls.

And he distributed the bibles, as though they were the body of Christ. Some in the group took them up and immediately turned them into fans. Others gave them a hurried glance, then hid them deep in their pockets. Ladopoulos alone refused to accept one, saying he had a number of copies at home.

Then, while the president was finishing his distribution,

Mr. Exadactylos took the floor. He was wearing dark glasses, as he used to on active duty when addressing the mustered regiment.

—What our beloved president, our great man of learning, has told us is all well and good, the retired general began, but it doesn't help us to uncover the invaders and their hide-out. I am convinced that these are antinational forces that are acting illegally and, with the methods of guerrilla warfare, are attacking us by surprise. This is neither the first nor the last time that my country has asked me to protect it. I went through the Albanian campaign, I fought at El Alamein, and I covered the Grammo-Vitsi area inch by inch during our civil war. My experience to date can help you, I think, in routing this invisible but no less dangerous enemy. My order, therefore,—excuse me, I meant to say my recommendation—is one and only: a search. A thorough search everywhere. Look through your rooms, your closets, your storing places, your kitchens, your trunks. There's a hidden transmitter in the apartment house, a transmitter made in Russia and sent from there to extend the tactics of the Cold War, upsetting our nerves. Just as during the communist fighting, when our enemy, those blood-drenched dogs, wouldn't let the broadcasts of free Greece reach the ears of the abducted women and children. I can say only this: the enemy is among us. He is hiding in our house. And if we do not uncover him in good time, he may become the cause of even greater suffering. Search, therefore, investigate, and call on me to annihilate him. I'll pierce his belly with a knife. Greece will never die. Long live the Nation! Long live the King of the Hellenes! Long live the heroes of Greek Independence!

He sat down on his chair flushed and trembling. He took off his dark glasses.

—We haven't come here to listen to sermons and patriotic speeches, said the midwife, angered by the vagueness of the men.

—I say that a huge snake has come in through the chimney and is slowly winding its way down, said the cattle dealer.

Plytas was playing nervously with his string of beads. Sousamidis and Ladopoulos had started a discussion about the price of cashmere on the local market. It was hot. The tenants seemed tired.

—Don't get upset, said the neurologist Dr. Anagnostaras, now taking over. We all need to be a little more calm. That's the only cause of this evil. Although personally I myself have not heard this creaking, my specialty puts me in a position to understand this irrational phenomenon which lately plagues our apartment house. We find ourselves confronted with a case of group psychosis. What do I mean by that? Namely, that we're all the victims of autosuggestion. From the telepathic transmission of the electrons in our brains, the expected event is transferred to the outside world and becomes a reality. Gustave Lebon, in his *Psychology of the Masses*, talks about people as though they were communicating receptacles. We are mutually dependent, and each person influences all the others. Let me explain things more simply. When about two weeks ago the French lady from the penthouse came to my office and complained of a strange vibration that shook her bed, I didn't take it seriously. I thought it was an isolated case of neurosis. But then Mrs. Exadactylos, who, as everyone knows, suffers from asthma, also came into the office and asked me for sleeping pills. The wave of insomnia spread through our apartment house like an infectious disease. Someone started the rumor that the noises attack a different floor every third night. And since then everybody waits for their advent. But, gentlemen, as I told you, it is not at all difficult to experience whatever situation you may wish, through the power of autosuggestion. This is a mass psychosis. Nothing else. That is why I brought along—and will distribute to you free of charge—a few miraculous little pills of Belergal, which will bring you the sweetest sleep. Take one after dinner.

And he distributed the pills to the tenants.

—I won't take them, said Sousamidis, who had a secret heart ailment.

—And how, according to your theory, do you explain the phenomenon of lack of water, said the retired general, who had been bothered by the doctor's reference to his wife. Is the water suffering from psychosis too? And he laughed sarcastically.

—If you read the newspapers—the psychiatrist answered.

—I read them, Exadactylos interrupted him. Morning and evening. So what?

—Naturally, being retired, you have time to read all the newspapers, said Dr. Anagnostaras. But you didn't notice that there's a general drought in our town. Besides, you're up on the sixth floor and—

—But it doesn't even get to the first, said the general, biting his lips to avoid swearing.

—The snake is drinking it, said Kalfoglou.

Then the Armenian, who hadn't said a word until that moment, interrupted them:

—Raining outside, he cried with a child's joy. See it!

And they all turned their exhausted faces toward the window, where thick raindrops were glued to the panes.

As they turned their heads, Lazaros could see them all face to face. He noticed how dull their eyes were—eyes that

83

had died over their fires, he thought—how heavily their heads were bent forward. He studied their hands, their sweaty armpits, where the drying salt streaked the material with white stripes, like gendarme chevrons. He watched them gazing stupidly at the glass, torpid, numbed, like cattle watching a train go by. They suddenly seemed to him flies caught in the stone web of this spider city, unsuspecting their fate while struggling vainly to escape it. Then, for the first time, he thought he felt sorry for them.

X

THE TITAN had broken down again on the sixth floor. The porter had asked the technicians to come and fix it, and he was angrily going over to hang up the OUT OF ORDER sign. He had reason to be upset. Not only did he have other worries in his head, not only did he have to act as a policeman for the maids who were quarreling about who would get water first, not only did he have a sick wife who would again require money for doctors, but he also had those outsiders, those railway workers, who climbed into the elevator like animals, when there was a sign saying that it could take only three persons at a time, and so it broke down every now and then because of them. Just as it had today again, in front of their club, on the sixth floor.

Lying naked in his paradise, holding a leaf in his hands, he was thinking that his life was short, that the years went by quickly and that someday he would lie naked in the earth like this; all is vanity, he was thinking, both we our-selves and life itself, only this little leaf is eternal; it will fall to the earth and then climb the tree again as sap, while

84

men fall and never return; men go forever; and Heaven and Hell are a tale for children; the only heaven that really exists is this one that he had made himself; and who knows how much longer he would be able to enjoy it, since everything hangs by a thread, he was thinking, the tender leaf in his fingers, as he lay naked in the partial darkness; and he didn't know why today he had woken up so sad, why there was a cloud covering his heart.

The two technicians had been working for some time on the roof of the TITAN. They tied and untied wires, gabbed a little, waited for a maid to go by so they could tease her. The one who was standing up tightening a nut with his wrench suddenly said to the other:

—Come here and see.

The other man then got up, supporting himself on the cable:

—What's the problem?

—Look here. Is this a cable? Take hold of it and see.

—Sure it's a cable. What do you want it to be? Is that why you got me up here, for Christ's sake?

And he started to sit down again. But the other held him up by the arm.

—It isn't a cable. It's more like wood. Like a root.

—A root? You think this is some kind of garden for that to be a root?

He saw his plant rustling uneasily as though someone had caught it by the foot. "What's wrong?" he asked it. "Why are you trembling like that? Have you guessed that I'm not in a good mood and you're worried? No, our hour hasn't struck yet. Someday, when I'll be somewhere far away, you'll

85

remember me and say . . . But why should we think about that day already? Now we should be happy that we're alive. Look: my cloud's gone away. The sun . . . But what's wrong with you? Why are you trembling? You've started turning yellow with fear. And fall is still a long time away. Think of it: it's a long time till fall. And we're young, children still . . .

—There's another, and another, and another, the technician was saying, groping around the dark elevator shaft where the roots of the plant had come out to breathe. There's a whole mess of them!

The other worker was now quite convinced that they were roots.

—Do you think that's what caused the machine to break down? he asked.

—I don't know. It isn't our worry from now on. Leave everything as it is and let's go tell the porter.

They left their tools on the roof of the TITAN and ran downstairs.

—I can't understand it, my dear plant, I can't share in your anxiety. Why are the leaves of your heart trembling that way? Why have you turned cold so suddenly, tightening your palms into a fist? You're making me very worried now; I can't figure out what's happening. Tell me. You who taught me the seas, you who made me travel to other suns, won't you tell me what's tormenting you? I know. Maybe you're tired of me. But look at our children growing up in these rooms. We didn't waste our lives. Look at the generation that's going to be our heirs . . . Wait a minute. I think I heard something. Noises, voices, human footsteps. They're

86

multiplying. Do you think they've caught on to us? Voices. Footsteps. Multiplying. People. People. They're banging on the door!

The news spread like lightening through the apartment house. A maid heard it first at the porter's. She ran and told her mistress. They found, she said, roots in the elevator shaft. A whole cataract of them falling from the seventh floor, piercing the walls. The mistress rang her neighbor's bell opposite. The news then passed from kitchen balcony to kitchen balcony. It was noon, and all the tenants were having lunch. Some didn't hurry to get up, preferring to finish their lunch first. Others who heard the uproar but didn't know its cause thought there was a fire or that some-one had committed suicide. Since the elevator had broken down, the tenants gathered on the winding staircase and were now coming up hurriedly to see what was happening, whether the root of the evil had finally been found, the cause of their drought, the origin of their insomnia, the secret source of their panic. Even the two whores from the base-ment, Toula and Mary, got wind of the emergency and came out in their mottled robes, kerchiefs on their heads, giggling.

—The game is up, my friend. They've found us out. They've discovered our corner, and soon they'll come into our nest. But what cuckold betrayed us? What bastard? What fairy? What bugger? . . . Let them bang on my door. I won't open it . . . Who? What punk? What son of a bitch betrayed us? . . . Lazaros isn't here. Lazaros is dead. Let them break the door down, let them come in on their own. I won't open it for them . . . But who, what stool pigeon, what asshole, what clip-artist, what shit-heel, what pimp? So you had reason to be trembling. You sensed the danger before I did. Knock as much as you want to. I won't open up. I won't usher you in with a "welcome." Animals! Ah, the game is up, my plant, my woman, my Atlas.

—Lazaros, Lazaros, come on out.

—Maybe he isn't in there.

—He's playing deaf on purpose.

—But why are you all against him?

—Because he won't open up, that's why.

—We have an obligation to search the house.

—Lazaros doesn't look like a bum.

—Lazaros, my boy, come on out.

The porter was trying hard to open his door with one of the passkeys he carried on a ring, but he was too flustered to manage it. In the meantime, behind him, the tenants kept moving up. They pushed, they crowded, they wanted to see, wanted to find out in a hurry what was happening. The people in front were being crushed; they were shouting to the others to stop shoving and squeezing. The pregnant woman fainted from lack of air, and they took her into the retired general's apartment to bring her around. The whores screamed hysterically when someone touched them. And the porter was trying one key after another, holding a whole bunch in his hand, but none of them wanted to fit. And all the while the line of frantic people grew longer. It now reached to the middle of the fifth floor. They howled, they screamed, they roared, they raged.

—We lived well, we prospered, we had an unforgettable summer. That's more than a little. We shouldn't be ungrateful. We came to know the light, the sea, the clouds. What

88

else is there? Maybe we wanted to know too much and so think we've known nothing. Maybe we wanted to do too much and so think we didn't have time for anything. No, it's better this way, in the stress of our youth rather than in that slow death of deterioration . . . I still remember the spring. Your first flower pot, and you in the moonlight. Your body bound to the night. My desire a knife in the air. And the sea a broad bed where we gave ourselves to each other. Now, tree, hold my sorrow. And you, sea, drown my tears. Your words, you say, will be born within me like sea gulls on deserted islands. Only from now on, water will always taste of the pipe for me . . . But I have no regrets. We lived well, we prospered, we had an unforgettable summer, my plant, my woman, my Atlas.

Finally, the porter opened the front door and the first wave of people rushed inside. They all managed to fit, even the maids. As they entered, though, the sight they saw silenced them. Some of the women even took off their shoes so as not to trample on the green world. Amazed, they gazed at this garden, at the leaves, at the unusual disposition of the house, wondering inside themselves how it was possible that such a paradise could blossom in their barren apartment house. It looked like one of the hanging gardens of Babylon. And how cool it was in there! Two or three children wailed because they wanted to see. Their mothers told them to be quiet as in church. But the shorter people at the back didn't understand what was going on. Why had everybody fallen dumb as though a sorceress had stolen their voices? Those in front hesitated to move ahead. Their nerves, taut like wires, now softened, became roots, like the ones entangled in their feet. Toula cut a red flower and put it behind her ear. "But where is he? where is he?" someone whispered timidly.

Naked as he was, Lazaros had hidden in his bedroom out of shame. He climbed onto the barrel and wrapped himself in his plant as in a sheet. And there he waited. Through a small opening in the plant it was possible to see without being seen. And he felt good behind his green shield.

But the ecstasy of the intruders didn't last long. After the initial amazement came second thoughts. Maybe this was partly because the principal got caught up in the roots and fell flat on his face. In any case, as the daze dispersed, they remembered the creaking that had kept them awake so many nights. It had come from the very roots they were now admiring, foolishly, like small children. Maybe they had already gone down deep. Maybe the whole apartment house was in danger of collapsing any moment. They had to be repulsed immediately. What, then, were they waiting for? They didn't have a second to lose. And once aroused by words, they sent their reluctant wives away, armed themselves with knives, penknives, hatchets, axes, and any other weapon they could find, and got down to the job of destruction.

—They're now slaughtering the *articulate;* hear them scream, Lazaros murmured to himself from his hiding place in the plant. Now they're approaching the *gymnosperms.* I hear the *ophioglossum* in trouble. They're probably slipping through their fingers. It's your turn, *julianate.* And you, *wing lobed,* get ready . . . I can't hear them. They must be in the other room. Here they are again. They're cleaning out the *spirals,* the *lanceolate.* They're now slaughtering my *lobed, serrate, orbiculate* dreams. It'll be our turn afterwards. Get ready. Oh, how cool your embrace is; the one thing I'll be sorry to lose, my plant, my woman, my Atlas.

His bedroom door gave way suddenly. Through the opening he saw the familiar faces of the tenants as he remembered them from the meeting of the day before. There were the butcher, the merchants, the retired general, the high school principal, the doctor, the civil servant. It was the general who was supervising the liquidation operation. The men were sweating, and green splotches stained their shirts.

—What a monster! God!
—It looks like Bucephalus.
—Christ and the Virgin.
—Look how furious it's getting. It's sprouting thorns. What do you think, Kyr-Babi, can you take care of it?
—I've taken care of bulls and you think I'm going to be frightened by this palm tree?
—Use the ax.
—The hatchet's sharper.
—We've left the main body of the enemy for the last.
—Get back, everybody, so it doesn't crush you.
—Where's that young bum hiding?
—I'll tell his parents about the whole business when they come back.
—Gentlemen, this delinquent generation!
—Come on, Kyr-Babi, let's not waste any more time.

He saw the cattle dealer spit on his hands and grab the hatchet. At first he could see only the top of his body; then, as the man came nearer, only his head, only his eyes, nose, and mouth. In the end, he could see only his black mustache, which enveloped him like a bandage made of darkness. The first blow of the hatchet shook him. The second staggered him. Kalfoglou had caught the plant in his hands and was struggling to bring it to its knees. It was a fierce battle, giant against cyclops. Lazaros fainted.

When he came to, it was night. Opening his eyes to darkness everywhere, he thought the black mustache of the cattle dealer was still in front of him. Through the broken window a little moonlight entered, and a draft formed in line with the open door of the balcony. Lazaros stirred. There was a lake around him. How could I be in water? he wondered. He couldn't remember anything. He ached to the marrow of his bones. He tried to get up, slipped, tried again, moaning. On his feet finally, he saw the skeleton of his plant prone on the floor, immobile, in a death spasm, rigid and white under the light of the moon, like the remains of a mammoth. Of its robust flesh only a membrane was left. The rest of its body had turned to water, flooding the floor. "And the waters prevailed, and were increased greatly upon the earth." He saw the barrel floating like a buoy. "And the Arc went upon the face of the waters." He looked again at the skeleton of the plant: the spine was split into sections, the ribs too had snapped, like gutless bows, shreds of skin hung loose: the frayed ends of a trodden flag, its pole cast away. "And all flesh died that moved upon the earth. And every living substance was destroyed which was upon the face of the ground." The room seemed empty to him, enormous without the plant that had filled it. "And all in whose nostrils was the breath of life, of all that was in the dry land, died." A knot formed in his throat. "And Noah only remained alive upon the waters."

He looked at his watch: it had stopped at twenty to three. He was hungry.

XI

THE FOLLOWING DAY, the following days, he finished off on his own all that had been left undone by the sweeping fury of the tenants. His family would be returning from Ammouliani any moment now, and he didn't want them to find the house in that kind of mess. With a penknife he unhinged the roots that were still left in the corners, in the walls, in the door lintels and window casements. This way, though, bits of furniture came loose along with them, plaster fell, joints cracked. The floor looked as though it had been plowed. Furiously he went after everything that was left over. He didn't want anything to remain behind that might remind him of what had been. He had always been repelled by cheap sentimentality and tears. Instead of bending and breaking after what had happened, he became more insistent. He took a sensual pleasure in the destruction. He threw the remnants into a large basket; but he had trouble getting the skeleton of the plant out of his room. It wouldn't go through the door. He struggled, he broke it up. No luck. Then, one night, he threw it down into the street from the balcony. But in the morning he saw it caught up in the electric cables like the skeleton of a flying kite. Then he brought in a cleaning woman to mop up the house, to wax the floors; he brought in a carpenter to refinish the furniture, a mason to plaster the walls. He put the furniture back in its place. The house looked new.

He thought he had finished with the weeding but he suddenly discovered, under his bookshelf, as he bent to pick up his slippers, a small leaf, all green, all alone. It

93

disturbed him. He didn't want to look at it. But the thought of it left him no peace. What could he do with it? He became demonic. He burst out swearing. How did it get down there? How had it survived so much destruction, so much liquidation. What did it want? What did it mean? Why was it playing the innocent? His first impulse was to grab it, to crush it in his hands, to wring it. But he lost heart. He didn't have the courage any longer for that kind of thing. His hands didn't dare. On the other hand, if he let it alone, what would that prove? Hope? He didn't want any hope. He wasn't desperate, yet neither did he want any hope. So? His hands trembled with indecision. He buttoned a button, unbuttoned another. I don't have the courage to start from the beginning, he thought. Once in a lifetime, once only . . . His fists started tightening furiously with hatred, with thirst. I must strangle it, he decided. It has no place in here. No place at all. I must kill it. I will be honoring the memory of my Great Plant if I strangle it. I don't want any hope. Once in a lifetime, once only . . .

He bent down and uprooted it, pulling out the full root like the nerve of an aching tooth. But he didn't have the heart to throw it away. Carefully, with feeling, he pressed it between the leaves of a heavy book so that it would keep its shape, its form.

XII

HE WAS ASCENDING NOW, going up Apostle Paul Street again. He crossed the "boundary," the streetcar tracks, and entered the other world. It was September. The night sweet, as though in spring. But as he passed in front of the Rotunda, he didn't smell the scent of mimosa. He was climbing. He moved on hurriedly. He ran.

94

He didn't want to go anywhere in particular. He had escaped from his castle in order to clear his mind. At home that evening they were entertaining the two dried-up ladies of the Council of the School for the Blind. He couldn't take them. His family insisted that he stay. That they all have dinner together in the warmth of their family hearth. They were right. He should have stayed. But how could he tell them that however well he understood them, it was no longer possible for him to live under their code.

Suddenly, as he reached St. Demetrios Street—full of people, girls, young men, songs, shouting—an idea flashed through his mind: to go to the young girl's house, to find her, to speak to her. He wanted to talk to someone human, to tell all, how it began, how it ended. To tell her how he had stolen the flower pot with the plant from her courtyard one night in May—Ariadne was the name he had given her so that she wouldn't be completely abstract in his mind—how the plant had later grown of its own accord, kept him company a whole summer, and then how people had become jealous of their happiness one day and had killed it, so that he was now alone again, more alone than ever before. "You know," he would say to her, "whatever you tell people, they always think only of what is theirs. And since the plant was yours, I think you'll be interested in hearing its story."

He tried to imagine what expression would come into her face as he told her all this: would she laugh, cry, feel sorry for him? Unable to imagine it, he remembered that he had never seen her face. . . . So he was telling lies. In the end, he was fooling himself. He wasn't going there to talk to her. He only wanted to see her, to see her face. And why now? How come it hadn't occurred to him all this while? How had he let so many months go by without longing for her? And tonight, why tonight in particular was he all

95

aflame to give a form, a shape, a face, to the anxiety that tortured him?

He climbed hurriedly in the rhythm of his thoughts. He passed Kassandrou Street, turned right at Ioulianou. A recollection of his *julianate* leaves passed through his mind. They're gone now, gone, he said to himself. He felt no bitterness at all.

He paused for a moment outside the neighborhood movie house, which was showing a double feature, as usual at the end of the season. They were announcing the opening of the indoor theater "very soon." "A change of program twice a week." He passed in front of the Turkish Consulate, and the guards outside it looked at him suspiciously. He was afraid that it might get dark, that he might get lost. He turned into Chrysostomos Street. He was close now.

But what was this that suddenly appeared in front of his eyes? What sort of square monster, all black, where night lived? Was this really Ierissos Street, or had he made a mistake again? He looked: this was it. But number 17 didn't exist. Nor did the iron gate exist, nor the courtyard with its small flower bed, nor the two-storied house with the orange light in its windows. What was this seven-storied monster rising before his eyes? Scaffolding with girders, the hoist down low, the cement mixer motionless in the middle of the road among piles of gravel and sand and cement. A sign hung over its heart like the horseshoes that Gestapo soldiers wore:

PAPADOPOULOS

Civil Engineer

And another:

96

FELIZOL INSULATION

And another:

NO ADMITTANCE EXCEPT ON BUSINESS

Out of the distance came the voice of the yoghurt vendor advertising his sheep's-milk yoghurt. The voices of children chasing each other in the twilight. The barking of a dog. He didn't bother to ask the woman opposite, who was promenading in front of her window with her breasts hanging out. He didn't bother to ask her where Ariadne's family had moved. Let's go, he said to himself. We're finished here too.

He was now on the wide dirt road that passed by the rabies clinic above the Evangelistria cemetery next to the Jewish graves where the young couples moved silently. He saw the Fair grounds below, a magic city, with its multicolored lights, its advertising signs, its Luna Park; a wheel with airplanes nailed to its spokes was turning, all alight, in space. The clamor of happy people reached his ears, and the voice of the megaphones: "The young lady in number six should be more careful. The gentleman in fourteen should hand in his ticket . . . Come on in, ladies and gentlemen, come on in and you'll see the most famous magician in Europe: Maurice the Illusionist." Fireworks started bursting above, showering the lawns of night like fountains. But another voice, heavy, full of longing, now reached his ears. It was coming down from above, slowly, as though it brought with it the weight of the whole world:

"Night has come to Yiadi-Koulé"

97

The voice was calling him. He turned, gazing up at the old castles, the Acropolis, the seven-towered walls, the Vlatadon Monastery, the prison of Yiadi-Koulé itself.

"The world outside enjoys the good life"

Unwittingly, he started climbing. The voice drew him on. He didn't resist. It was full of static, wrinkles; it was hoarse, unwound, yet warm and human. He climbed on. He was rising toward it.

"And I sigh, I sigh night and day
inside my jail"

Like a sleepwalker he continued along the outside edge of the wide dirt road. The voice pierced straight through to his heart.

"Come, mother dear, before they condemn me
Cry, mother dear, to make them release me"

He turned and cast a last glance toward the world he was leaving behind him: he could see the new castles of concrete, their dark loopholes, their symmetrical ramparts, hiding the view to the sea where the sun had definitely set.

"My crime is not a grave one"

No, he would never go back, never. No, he would no longer bear the guilt of a crime he didn't commit. He would go there where he couldn't find other monsters, beyond, behind, far away, beyond the poles of the Public Power Com-

98

pany, behind Yiadi-Koulé, farther away than the hill where
they held executions every morning.

>*"But the bars are a heavy burden,*
>*the jail's a burden too"*

He would go there where he would find the sun in its
dawn, on the ridge of the mountain, and he would throw off
his clothes, he would go naked into the sun, he would go
naked into the prison of the sun, into the yoke of the sun . . .
The voice stopped calling him, and he found himself
alone among the old deserted castles.

THE WELL

TRANSLATORS' NOTE

THE *variations from the Greek text in "The Well" are the product of collaborative effort on the part of the author and the translators.*

THE WELL

It wasn't a well exactly. It might better be called a reservoir. But this wouldn't be exact, either, because it didn't quite look like a reservoir. It was in fact something in between these two, with characteristics of both, something hermaphroditic. Such as it was, undefined, unique and strange, it drew the interest of all the inhabitants of the region. The simple-minded peasants called it a monster. But was it really a monster, or was it merely their ignorance of it, their fear of studying it at close quarters, that established the name?

Its opening was large and square, shaped like a room. Its walls, whose whiteness contrasted with the dark water that stirred in its depths, were of solid marble. The square void between the walls was crossed by various water pipes that eventually emerged above ground. A series of ladders descended from the surface to a wooden platform that served to support the complex machinery for drawing up the water: wheels, gears, pulleys, arms, crossbars, levers. This entanglement of metal, which seemed the rough draft of an iron labyrinth, was directly connected by a system of belts to the motor shed, a shack standing on the northwestern side of the well, housing the pump motor and other machinery once used in irrigating the property. This, in short, was the substance of the well that looked like a reservoir or —small difference—of the reservoir that looked like a well.

But the simple-minded peasants had their own image of it. For them, its history went far back into the past: when God decided to create Man on Earth. At that time He destroyed all the monstrous beasts that roamed undisturbed over land and sea, changed them into stones, rocks, islands. The latter was the fate of an exceptionally large mammoth crab, whose shell became what is now called Thassos, one of the prettiest islands of the Northern Aegean. Even today, they say that a visitor to Thassos can make out its prehistoric anatomical structure: two facing promontories— the capes of St. Anthony and Kefala—which were once the giant claws; the shore that stretches between them, which was once the greedy mouth; the sandy beach, an atrophied tongue; a group of rocks off shore, teeth that fell out; finally the well, which was the pharynx of the beast—one beast, they say, that has never forgiven Man for its destruction and still tries to snare people with the lure of water in its esophagus, snare them so that it can gulp them down as a posthumous revenge. According to the peasants, that's why the ancients called it Hades, or Hell, which for them was the world of the dead. And from constantly saying "he went to Hell" or "she went to Hell," people in the region—often toothless from the impure water they drank, so that they tended to swallow words and syllables—eventually ran things together so much that "went to Hell" ended up "well."

In our day and age, shortly before the second world war, the well fell into the hands of the Omega family, along with the farm that Mr. Omega purchased to serve as his country estate. He knew about the history and alleged dangers of the well; but with the marble slabs he used to line it, with the motor he placed beside it to regulate the flow, with the numerous pipes and wheels he brought in to control it, with the trees he planted around it as a cover, he succeeded in changing it dramatically, transforming it from the remnant of a paleontological monster into something valuable for the farm. And he was about to fence it in so there wouldn't be the slightest danger to visitors when the war broke out, forcing him to abandon his plans. All he had had time to complete was a series of three terraces going down to the well, in this way breaking the sharp downhill approach.

The Omega family lived in Salonica; but they would move to Thassos for the best part of each summer to vacation on their estate. It was a large piece of property, situated exactly opposite Mt. Athos and near the fishing village of Poto. Half of it was covered by a forest of pine trees and half by various orchards, a vineyard, and a vegetable garden. On the dividing line between the two, a good distance from the well, stood a small house with a red tiled roof and some large, astonished windows with low awnings for eyelashes. Mr. Omega had once hoped to build a grander house by the sea, but again the war had frustrated his plans.

This year the family reached their country place later than usual: it was already the beginning of August. They had arrived late in the afternoon with the caïque *Haido*, on the regular run from Kavalla. Since the house had been closed for two years, the first thing they did was remove the dusty furniture for cleaning, as though taking flesh off the fragile body of a mummy. Out came the table, the couch, the chairs. They strung hammocks between the pine trees, set

up the camp beds. Then, having little on hand to eat, they
went out to a taverna in Poto, leaving Malamo, their young
maid, to do the sweeping and cleaning. When they came
back, they found her touching a match to the kerosene
lamp. There was a sudden pool of light in the dense darkness. Moths gathered around the lamp's chimney, stupidly
knocking their wings against it. As they prepared for bed,
Mr. Omega brought up the problem of getting fresh water.
He told Malamo that she would have to go to the well early
the following morning. It would be her first, her most important job of the day. And since she didn't know the way
there, this being her first time on the estate, he suggested
that Thanos go along with her.

—She'll get lost alone, the father said to him in private.
And she has so much else to do tomorrow . . .

—And you've got to teach her not to be afraid of the
place, the mother added. You're a man now. There's no reason why you shouldn't take her and— Well, anyway, you
go along with her tomorrow so she doesn't get lost.

Thanos didn't dare say that he was still as terrified of
approaching the well as he had been since early childhood.
And all night long, in his dark room, the camp bed he was
lying on rattled like a human skeleton.

—Is it a long ways yet? the maid said.

—Don't be in too much of a hurry to get there, Thanos
said, pausing in the middle of the path.

Malamo, who was walking barefoot behind him, her
head bowed as she concentrated on avoiding stones and
thorns, almost ran into him.

—What did you say? she stammered.

—Just that, he answered curtly. He who hurries
stumbles . . .

. . .

Malamo continued behind him on the narrow path that coiled snake-like under the green apricot trees. She became silent and apprehensive; all her efforts to start a conversation with Thanos had been unsuccessful. He's not in a good mood today, she thought. He probably didn't sleep well last night. And she knew from bitter experience what was in store for her if he really were in a bad mood. He would use any excuse to vent his anger on her, to give her hell until he saw tears in her eyes. That alone would make him ease up, even turn him tender. She had learned to start crying immediately. But today things had not yet reached that point; if she said another word, they might, so she decided to keep her mouth shut despite her curiosity about their destination.

A good thing she stopped asking questions, Thanos said to himself as he pushed aside the branches of the apricot trees that were blocking the path. Because otherwise . . ." Fragments of the nightmare that woke him last night were still in his mind. "Help! Help! We're drowning!" "Run, villagers, we're drowning!" He could still hear the agonized cries. And he recalled that as Malamo fell into the well, she didn't drop suddenly and disappear, but she went down slowly, like a race horse in a slow-motion newsreel—almost nonchalantly. Yes, that was the way she looked as she disappeared, still holding her bucket and pail.

Malamo's curiosity about their destination wouldn't let her mind rest. What kind of a well could this be? she wondered, studying the heavy bucket lined with cement that she was carrying in one hand, then the pail—swinging like a basket—that she was carrying in the other, a pail whose coiled rope was so long it filled the inside completely, even ran over the rim a bit. Her curiosity had been first awakened the night before, while she was alone in the house cleaning up the kitchen. A little boy, black with smoke like a miniature devil, had passed by her window and stopped to talk. He was returning from Theologos, he told her, where he was learning to be a blacksmith in the shop of an uncle, being an orphan, and, anyway, he warned her not to go near "that well," because people here said it was haunted, and they called it a "monster" in Poto, so many accidents had happened there, animals and people drowning. "Go to Bambakies, over there, see, beyond the stream. The road is straight and the water good for drinking, only there are some sheep folds around there and the sheep dogs might bark at you, but you shouldn't be half as afraid of those dogs as of that well of theirs." She was on her own, without her employers around, and the boy was talking her language, yet she didn't believe him. She said if it were really haunted, her mistress wouldn't send her there, and so he'd better run along now and not come back through the property. But her curiosity had been pricked further when they'd told her last night that Thanos would accompany her because she didn't know the way there and ought to be guided. What kind of a well can it be if you need to take a guide along? she asked herself. She turned her head to look back toward the house, to get her bearings, but the apricot trees had blocked it out. She walked on silently into the unknown.

And then, Thanos mused, trying to piece together the fragments of his dream, when I saw her fall, what did I do? That's right, I felt sorry for her and tried to get hold of her, bent over the rim and caught her, then felt that I was sinking with her, still in slow motion, so that I had time to shout: "Help! Help! We're drowning!" Yes, I was on top of her, pressing against that old cotton dress my mother gave her to wear out here in the country, and I could feel her young body wriggling with fear under me, and it was warm, like village bread just out of the oven, and she cried out, saying that I was feeling her up, and I told her that we were drowning, and she said she'd tell my mother, and I said she wouldn't get a chance to because very soon we'd be in the next world, and then . . . then our old gardener, Barba-Sotiris, came out of the motorshed and looked down at us laughing, and I asked him to throw us a rope, and he said the black hole was dragging us down, that he couldn't go against the black hole, and he asked us to give his love to his dead wife, Panayiota, and Malamo started shouting, and I told her to shut up, and she said "Shut up yourself," and we wrestled as we sank deeper and deeper, yes, that was the worst part of it: the well was sucking us in, yet we were fighting as though we were still on earth . . .

Whatever kind of well it is, I don't care, Malamo said to herself. They had emerged from the green tunnel of apricot trees into the almond orchard; the sparse branches and yellowing leaves ahead allowed a view of the sea, of a few houses on the edge of Poto, and of the *Haido* at anchor, resting there all white like a sea gull with folded wings as it waited for the passengers from Theologos who would soon arrive by bus. It was still early; the sun hadn't yet come out from behind the cape of St. Antony, but its rays were now extinguishing the light of the moon and the last star. All was quiet, still asleep: the sea and mountains surrounding them, the inhabitants, the birds; the only sounds that

could be heard in the crystal calm of that August morning
were the whistling of a shepherd gathering his sheep, and
the bells of the flocks returning to the fold for milking.
Whatever kind of well it is, I don't care, Malamo repeated to
herself, reaching for an almond and cracking it between
her teeth. It had been two years since she was last on
Thassos, the two years she'd been working as a maid in the
city—two whole years, and this was the first chance she'd
had to feel the sacred soil of her island under her feet; they
had become soft in the big city, and they were now sensitive
to the thorns and burrs she came across, but it didn't really
matter to her, she walked barefoot on purpose, just as she
used to before she'd left her village. She couldn't see it from
here, it was behind those mountains on the other side of the
island, but, anyway, she would be going there for the feast
of the Virgin, the fifteenth of August, her mistress had promised her that, and she would see her family and friends
—oh, she'd missed them these two years—and they would
see how much she'd grown, how pretty she'd become. She
breathed in the cool morning air coming down the ravine, air
sweet with the scent of pine and thyme. The almond trees
seemed old lovers calling her, arms open, to come up and
embrace them. She felt fully content now, warbling to herself joyfully like the partridges on the hillside opposite.

The almond trees haven't yet been relieved of their
almonds, the irrigation trenches are plugged up with dirt,
the olive trees are half dead, there's phylloxera on the grape
vines, the vegetable garden and the melon field are being
smothered by thistles, and there isn't a single scarecrow
among the pear trees to ward off the crows. It's obvious
that the farm isn't getting any attention at all. The earth
itself hasn't been plowed for years, Thanos mused as he left
the heavy-shadowed apricot trees and came out into the

clearing. His mind turned back to the golden prewar years, when he was still a child: the water would be pumped up from the well into the reservoir in the forest on the far side of the farm and from there it would spill down into the irrigation trenches and flow on as far as the house when free and, when not, into the numerous furrows along the way, guided by Barba-Sotiris and his wife to serve the whole estate. There was green everywhere then: in the gardens, the vegetable plots, the melon fields. The place was a delight to the eyes, a paradise. There were bottles of insecticide hanging from the olive trees, the vineyard was sprayed with sulphur this time of year, there were scarecrows in the pear trees and the fig trees, and the earth looked eager for plowing long before October . . . Then the war and the Occupation: the Germans used the trees as machine-gun targets, his father lost all his money . . . What is once spoiled is spoiled forever, he said to himself. And during the civil war the guerrillas stole the motor from the well, and then that poor old gardener seemed to lose his senses when his wife, Panayiota, departed—God rest her soul! . . .

—Ouch! Malamo said behind him.

—What's wrong?

—It pierced my foot like a nail.

She abandoned the pail and bucket to pick at the thorn in her heel.

—Who told you to come out here barefoot?

—Is it still a long ways, Kyr-Thano?

—No, we're almost there. But we've got to keep moving.

He had very nearly forgotten where he was going and the fear that went with it; but his voice—strange even to himself—now gave him away.

The path went along the slope of the hill, then rose abruptly to its ridge before twisting down, snake-like, toward the well. Thanos stopped on the ridge—which was shaped like the second hump of a camel—and stood there waiting for Malamo to limp her way up to him. The sun was about to emerge above the cape of St. Antony, and the row-boats were now ferrying the passengers out to the *Haido*. When Malamo came up behind him, he turned suddenly and said:

—There, that's the well.

—Where? asked the maid excitedly, seeing the end of her torture.

—Down there. You can't really see it from here. It's hidden by the trees and the oleander. See that dark shadow beyond the mulberry leaves and the marble projecting from the flowers? That'll tell you how large it is.

—Christ and the Virgin! Malamo said under her breath.

—We're lucky we can't see the full chaos of it, Thanos said with the same sensation of horror that ran through his body every time he faced it.

—Then it isn't really a well at all but a reservoir, the young girl said.

—No, it isn't a reservoir. The reservoir's in the forest. It's a real well, because the water comes into it from below.

He's talking again, Malamo said to herself, relieved. With new courage she asked:

—Why don't we go to Bambakies, Kyr-Thano?

—What do *you* know about Bambakies?

—I heard there's a small well there, said the young girl shyly. Not very deep, with some olive shoots around it. A well like all other wells, with good drinking water . . .

—Who says so? That's where they water the sheep and it tastes milky.

—A boy came by the house yesterday and . . .

—I get it, Thanos said. The villagers have been after

you already. They don't like us very much. They're jealous. But you belong to us, not the village. And for your information, the water from our well is incomparably lighter and more digestive than the water from Bambakies. It may seem a bit brackish to you at first because it's close to the sea, but you'll get used to it.

Malamo made a move to start off again. Thanos grabbed her arm.

—Where do you think you're going? I haven't explained things to you yet. Drawing water out of our well isn't as easy as milking a goat. There are dangers, obstacles. Every detail has its significance here.

As though to cast light on the mysteries ahead of them, the sun rose at that moment above the pine-covered cape of St. Antony, its rim perforated by pine needles. At the same moment, the *Haido* started up its engine, the roar of it shattering the morning stillness. Then the sound of the anchor being raised. The last rowboat left the caique's side for the pier. Handkerchiefs fluttered, good wishes crossed the water both ways. The white ship moved off, tearing the satin of the unwrinkled sea.

—You can get the best over-all perspective of the well from up here, Thanos said, gaining confidence with the coming of light. But don't stand so still. Move around, like me. Walk a little. When we go into action, your body should be warm and supple, your members loose. If you get numb from standing still, it'll be dangerous. Anything hard—a stone, for example—will fall into the well straight and true, if you see what I mean. Now give me your hand. Let's loosen up a little. In fact, let's go over there and eat a fig or two. They're fresh and sweet in the morning. That's better. You remind me of a baby learning how to walk.

113

—Kyr-Thano, let's not take too long getting there. My mistress will be furious.

—You're very conscientious and I'm happy to see it, Thanos said, reaching up for a fig. But don't worry about being late today. My mother will understand. She won't care how long it takes us because it's the first time— Now what's the matter? Why are you staring like that, for God's sake?

—That sign down there, Malamo said almost inaudibly.

Thanos came over beside her to look. At the foot of the slope there was a tilting post with a sign on it that said DANGER—DEATH in faded red letters.

—That's something new, Thanos said. It wasn't here two years ago. Our gardener, Barba-Sotiris, must have set it up there. The Germans used to put up those signs around their mine fields to warn the local shepherds. And I guess the gardener thinks that death lurks around the well . . .

—Why should he think that? Malamo said, now staring at him.

—Because he lost his wife to the well.

—What do you mean, lost her to the well?

—Just what I said. She fell in and drowned.

—Fell in *this* well? Malamo said. How?

—It's a long story.

Malamo was still staring at him. He decided he'd better tell her.

—It happened some years ago, Thanos said. During the winter, February, I think. Anyway, it was very cold. Only the gardener and his wife lived on the property. Everything was fine. The farm was productive, and she was about to make him a father. She had come down to the well with a pail to fill the trough with fresh water so she could water her sheep. Sotiris was in Poto playing cards at

Aristophanis' café. It was dark when he returned to his hut. He didn't find his wife waiting for him as he expected. "Where's she running around at this time of night," he thought. Then he heard the sheep's bell approaching from the direction of the forest. "There, she's coming," he said to himself with relief. "She must've gone out to water the sheep and night caught up with her." He then called out: "Panayiota! Panayiota!" No answer. He called out again: "Yiota!" Still no answer. Only the sound of the sheep's bell coming closer. Then he picked up the lantern and ran like a madman toward the well, constantly calling his wife's name. They say his voice has stayed hoarse since that moment. Anyway, when he reached the well, it was deserted. He lowered the light over the rim but could make out nothing in the darkness except icicles everywhere—it was the heart of winter, remember, and bitter cold. He spent the night there, waiting for dawn. Then, with the first rays of light, he saw her left slipper on the rim of the well . . .

—My God, said Malamo. How did she fall in?

—Some say she tripped over one of the bedeviled obstacles in front of the well, others say she slipped on the ice. But the most plausible version is that she got entangled in the rope she was lowering and that dragged her down.

—And she had a baby in her belly, sighed the girl.

—That isn't the worst of it. The worst of it is that her body was never recovered. They searched everywhere in vain. Some divers even came over from Theologos and went down to the bottom of the well in diving suits. They found everything you can imagine except her body.

—Where did the body go?

—That's the problem. The gardener's built whole theories around that phenomenon. If one had time, one could sit and listen to all of them. He maintains, for example, that there's a secret passage in the well that leads to that mountain over there, the one with a white shrine on it. He claims his wife reached that shrine through the secret passage and from there her soul flew up to heaven like a dove. And now every woman he sees reminds him of his wife. Even my mother. He's a sick man, a harmless madman. But I haven't told you the significant part of the whole story.

—What's that? Malamo said, half afraid to hear.

—There's no proof that the woman drowned. Since her body didn't turn up, we can't be sure she fell in.

—What happened, then?

Thanos stepped up to the ridge of the slope.

—Let's hope the gardener hasn't been listening. He lives in the motor shed right down there, and he has an uncanny way of hearing anything said within a mile of the place.

—So what happened, then? Malamo said in a whisper.

—Well, gossip has it that the woman ran away with a lover she had in Theologos, Snoth the tailor, ran away because she was a lot younger than her husband. And supposedly Snoth and she are living together happily in the Peloponnese . . .

—Then how come her slipper was found?

—That's one source of the gossip. They say she left it there on purpose so people would think she drowned. So her husband wouldn't go after her with the police. Understand?

—No. Because if she really wanted to fool him . . .

The sound of a window opening in the motor shed below cut Malamo short. The gardener's head suddenly appeared in the frame like a ghost's head in a house of horrors.

—What you told the girl about my wife is all well and good, young master. But you forgot to mention that the pail which fell in ahead of her became a flower pot at the bottom of the well and a jasmine plant grew in it. Because my beloved wife loved jasmine very much. She would always . . .

—Malamo stood there mesmerized by his deep, otherworldly voice, mesmerized without hearing a word he said. It was his face that held her conscious attention: one of his eyes, she saw, was injured, so that it seemed a lump of red earth in gray soil; his good eye, though, had a strange intensity, glistening as though moist from a tear permanently suspended there. His elongated beard made her see him for a fraction of a moment as a monk, perhaps from Mt. Athos across the bay. But the worn remnant of a rural policeman's uniform that he was wearing brought her back to reality. The old man suddenly raised his hand; his fingers seemed to flutter like a bird. The spell he had cast over her broke as the window was shut abruptly, and there was silence again—deadly silence. The pail and the bucket stood motionless on the ground beside her. No leaf stirred in the trees. No bird split the air.

—Well, now you've seen him, Thanos said, trying to look nonchalant as he glanced at the sun, which was climbing the sky like a steady kite. The cicadas in the olive trees planed its rays, but the vineyards still felt their full weight. And the sea jelled like yoghurt.

—Why don't we go to Bambakies, Kyr-Thano? Malamo pleaded. Nobody drowned there . . . And we could have gotten ten buckets of water by now.

—Just because something unpleasant happened in the past—if it actually did happen—doesn't mean that we have to be afraid of the place forever. Of course, it's true that the well, being an empty space—a vacuum, so to speak—draws things into it. Not only the insects and butterflies that pass over it unsuspectingly and become food for the huge spiders that walk around in its depths, but also the birds, rabbits, and other animals that go there to drink and, deluded by the reflection of water on the marble, tumble in with a splash. The song that goes "Ding dong bell, pussy's in the well" originated here. That's why there are those three cement terraces down there near the sign post; they are supposed to break the speed of any unknowing creature who might race down to the well from up here. Their usefulness is immense, since they act as a barrier against the magnetic force of the well . . .

—No, no, no, young master, came the interpolating voice of Barba-Sotiris as the window in the motor shed opened again. The terraces are three in number but indivisible and consubstantial, like the Holy Trinity.

At the mention of the Trinity, Malamo crossed herself instinctively, a habit she had acquired from her years in parochial schools.

—He thinks he's an authority on all matters relating to the well, Thanos said quietly, ignoring the gardener. He considers himself its oracle, its official guide. As far as I'm concerned, he's only a mortician and nothing else. But I avoid contradicting him because he's oversensitive on this subject. The truth of the matter is he constitutes one of the obstacles that you have to learn to bypass out here . . .

—Why is his one eye bloody? Malamo asked under her breath.

—Once, in the good old days, he was struggling to repair the motor and a lever suddenly snapped, almost gouging it out. And now, wherever he may be looking, that eye always fixes on the well, as though it doesn't want to lose some mysterious communication with it. But let's move on down to the first terrace so he won't be able to hear every word we say. . . . Come on, what's the matter with you, anyway?

—That cloud, Kyr-Thano. See how it's swelling!

Behind the mountain range of Psario—which covers the whole of Thassos in folds—Thanos saw a huge cloud suddenly appear, buttery and white like the wing of an enormous sea gull.

—Haven't you ever seen a cloud before in your life? he said.

—It's going to rain.

—That's a heat cloud, silly girl. It's not going to rain.

But a second one, also enormous, now began to emerge from behind another peak like whipped egg-white.

—It's going to rain, it's going to rain, Malamo cried gaily.

—I hope it doesn't rain. Because if it rains, we won't be able to do a thing.

—Make it rain, the maid said to the sky. The bees won't die, the olives will lose their wrinkles, people will have money for the winter . . .

—Then that's one more reason for hurrying, Thanos said. Now come along, for God's sake.

But they had hardly taken two steps down the slope before Malamo stopped again.

—Kyr-Thano?

—What's wrong now?

—Don't you hear them?

—Hear what?

—The cocks crowing, Kyr-Thano, the cocks . . .

It wasn't only the roosters that were creating a disturbance at Poto; they served as an alarm that set off all the other animals. Thanos could hear donkeys braying, sheep bleating, dogs barking.

—What's gotten into them? he asked Malamo.

—It's going to rain, Kyr-Thano, I told you. They got wind of the storm.

He looked up and saw that things had suddenly turned serious in the sky, just when he least expected it. Dense black clouds were descending from Psario, like a street riot swiftly taking on the muffled sound of destruction. Those clouds would soon cover the sun, now blazing with full intensity as though living out its last moments.

Malamo's face was luminous joy. It would finally rain, she told herself. Her troubles were over for the time being. With the rain water they could gather, they would get along for that day at least. As for tomorrow, God would provide. She would come here alone, and alone she would have nothing to fear. She thanked the Almighty who had heard her prayers, and she waited for rain with the same anticipation as the thirsty earth she stood on.

The animals at Poto had calmed down. Another roar could now be heard, one that seemed to emerge from the bowels of the earth.

Thanos' face darkened the moment the clouds covered the sun. He felt somehow vulnerable in the sudden darkness that enveloped the world. The semblance of night that now covered him recalled his recent nightmare, and he again heard cries echoing in the dark void, cries that knifed through him deep inside somewhere and that awakened other cries, sharper still, cries buried for years: "Quickly . . . Quickly . . . Air raid . . . To the shelter . . . Run . . . Blackout . . . Help . . ." And he saw his fellow tenants in the Salonica apartment house emerge from their doorways and run that night of the Occupation, run in panic as the sirens screeched outside and the dull roar of approaching planes filled the sky, run still dressed in pajamas and slippers, tripping and falling over each other in their desperate descent to the shelter.

He started down the embankment as the first thunder and lightning exploded in the distance. . . . Just as then, he said to himself. Exactly. Using the same tactics, they hit the outskirts first: Doundoular, the Old Station, the Upper City; and then the bombers moved in closer, aiming for the harbor.

—Malamo, he called hysterically, what are you doing up there? Take cover, for God's sake. They're coming in.

—I will when it starts raining, Kyr-Thano, the girl answered.

—It'll be too late when it starts. Get on down here while they're— Quick. Inside the motor shed.

A flash of lightning blinded him. And a long rumble, curling over on itself, sounded above him. He looked up: the clouds were coming in very low, like fighter planes set to strafe. And the first dense drop of rain hit his shoulder like a bullet.

—It's started, it's started! he yelled at the maid. Are you coming down or do I have to—

—I like the rain, Kyr-Thano. Oh . . . Ah . . .

And she received the raindrops with an erotic smile, as though they were kissing her.

Thanos calculated quickly, saw that he could still make it to her in time, and ran up the slope. A flash of lightning suddenly ripped through the sky in a wild zigzag and penetrated the sea. In his blind panic, Thanos picked up the pail and wore it on his head like a helmet. With his free hand he dragged Malamo along behind him.

—Leave me alone, Kyr-Thano. Leave me alone. I don't want to close myself inside. I like the rain. I'd rather get soaked—

—If you think this is just rain, you're crazy, Thanos said, pulling her along forcefully.

He turned around to look a last time. Between the tree trunks in the distance, he could distinguish his father running in the direction of the house with a folding chair under his arm. He recalled that during the whole Occupation his father had come down to the shelter only once: at the time of the big bombing, when the Catholic church was burned down and half the town was licked by flames, when a bomb had exploded outside their house and the pressure of air coming into the shelter had nailed him against the wall, when he had wet his pants out of fear and knew for the first time in his life what fear really meant.

—Come on, for God's sake, he said to Malamo, who was still resisting him like a goat.

—I love the rain, the girl said. Leave me alone.

—I'm responsible for you, I can't leave you exposed like this. You're young and can't understand how . . .

More lightning and the roar of thunder as the earth's bark burst with raindrops, the leaves of the fig tree peppered the air with noise, the sea raised murky waves, and the wind blinded them with dust.

As they entered the motor shed they seemed to be moving into the calm and stench of the hold on a ship floundering in rough seas. Barba-Sotiris didn't seem at all bothered by their presence. He was sitting on the dirt floor cross-legged like a buddha, his arms supported by his knees, his back turned to the door. His look was fixed in front of him, where there was some kind of dark hole in the floor. He didn't even take the trouble to turn his head.

As soon as Malamo found herself inside the low-ceilinged, tight little hut, she felt sick from the reek of kerosene. She picked out the old bogeyman sitting bent over, then a mouse that ran to hide under an empty case, then winged cockroaches besieging some remnants of food on the floor, finally whole caravans of ants on the walls, whose corners were rounded smooth by cobwebs. In the center of the room stood something that looked like a coffin, covered with patchwork rugs. She went to the far side of the room, where the old man was sitting, and thrust her face against the closed window, trying to breathe some fresh air through a crack in the pane.

Thanos couldn't stand up to his full height inside the shed, so he sat down on an upended oil drum and took the pail off his head. The familiar smell of kerosene which had soaked the walls during the period the pump motor was working brought him to abruptly. His recollection of the shelter, of the bombing outside, dissolved completely, and he listened to the rain that had already begun to drip in through the wooden ceiling. Then he wiped his misted glasses with a dry handkerchief and looked around him: there was the camp bed, the spirit stove, the ancient muzzle loader, and, in the center, the base of the one-time motor covered with rag patchwork. Only he didn't remember those posters hanging on the walls, and so many insects grazing along the floor and casually climbing up the gardener's hunched back. He was curious to see what Barba-Sotiris was looking at with such concentration; stooping forward, he discovered the hole through which the belt used to move, joining the motor to the machinery in the well, and, bending over further, he saw the water pipes crossing the darkness of the hole, forming something like a human skeleton. He sat down again, holding his shirt free to let it dry. He could hear the rain outside growing heavier. The steady drip from the ceiling forced him to move a little to his left.

The absolute stillness of the place was finally broken by the gardener, who took a tin box out of his pocket with trembling hands, pulled a pink cigarette paper free, laid some tobacco along it (losing half in the process), rolled the cigarette between his fingers, and brought it up to his lips to seal it. Then he put the box back in his pocket and pulled out a lighter with a long wick. He lit up, taking care not to burn his beard, and took a deep drag. But the smoke he exhaled, instead of rising, descended to disappear inside the hole.

As the lighter flashed, Malamo turned around and saw the ghost move; the fright of it made her press against the windowpane all the more forcefully. The crack in the glass allowed enough fresh air to keep her from the same vertigo she had felt on first smelling the asphyxiating kerosene. Yesterday too, aboard ship, though the sea was calm, she had almost vomited from the smell of the engine. Her mistress had given her some cologne and a piece of lemon to chew on, but what really brought her around was seeing —as the ship approached the island—the whitewashed houses of her village spread over the slopes ahead like a herd of sheep. She alone knew how much she had yearned for Rahoni during the past two years. And she again started counting the days left before the fifteenth of August. Today was the eve of the feast of the Savior, Sotiris. Tomorrow would be the sixth. Ten days left until the Assumption. As many as my fingers, she said to herself. I'll tie a string around them for each day that goes by. And she remembered that her mistress had called her "golden-fingered" when she finished her work quickly. She wanted to earn the name more than ever now so they would give her time off to go to Rahoni. But Thanos was holding her back; he was a problem, all right, apparently bent on making sure they never got water out of the well. She was especially annoyed with him because— Something started crawling up her leg and she stabbed at it with her free foot.

She's scratching herself, Thanos noticed. The sight of her bare foot rubbing against her leg excited him. Till a minute ago she was fixing her wet hair. Now she's scratching herself and looking at the rain. She's pleased that it's raining, she's happy to be alive, she knows she has hair, knows she has feet. For her, rain is rain. Double dash and period. Rain equals rain. While for me . . .

LET US NOT SEEK RESPONSIBILITIES:
WE MUST ALL BE CAREFUL

Hell, something's confused in all this, something's not right, he said to himself, no longer looking at Malamo. Last night during my dream I got excited just like this; I was holding her, feeling her warm little body flutter like a frightened bird under that old cotton dress. I envy her. Yes, that's it. I envy her for being uneducated, simple and unknowing. I envy her for being happy. I can't enjoy things

any more. I envy her for seeing things as they are. I got
things confused again; my mind turned to— Malamo's
simple; I can't be after all they've taught us, after all we've
seen, after . . . Here in the country she finds herself in her
element. She fits in with the trees, the goats, the shepherds.
And she's the only girl around. In town, things were different. I envied her there too, but I could always lord it over
her with my knowledge. All the mechanical things around
her she didn't know about gave me a means for exercising
my superiority. But here I've lost my armor. I'm naked.

PEDESTRIAN, WHOEVER YOU MAY BE, BEWARE:
EVERY TIME YOU GO AGAINST THE RULES
YOU ARE PLAYING WITH DEATH ITSELF

Yes, thats it, he went on, without really giving a second
thought to the sign on the wall. I'm violating the rules.
With all my heart I'd like to make a quick confession to her,
tell her: "Malamo, you take *me* to the well. I don't have the
courage to go alone. Come, take me by the hand. Ever since
I was a child, I've been afraid of it. Whenever I planned to
come here, I always made sure to have company along. Now
they've sent me here to guide you. But I can't, I tell you I'm
afraid—how can I say it?—ever since I was a child . . ."
And instead of this, what do I do? Exactly the opposite. I
tell her lies, pretending I know all about it, I try to scare her
as much as possible so that I feel more at ease myself. And
the result? We don't progress, we don't move one bit closer
to it . . . There, I've found the clue to the knot; now the
other half remains: how to disentangle myself.

MY AIM AND DUTY ARE TO PROTECT YOU.
NOTHING ELSE GOVERNS MY THOUGHT.

ALL MY EFFORTS, EVEN IF THEY MAKE
YOU LOSE PATIENCE, ARE DIRECTED
TOWARD PRESERVING YOU FROM THE
DANGERS YOU MAY ENCOUNTER WITH
EVERY STEP YOU TAKE.

And the gardener may well have found peace behind the blinkers of his madness, Thanos thought, concentrating for the first time on the traffic posters. He's settled down. He lives with the hole for company, the tunnel that joins him to his beloved deceased. For him the well is a world that has been lost forever . . . But what happens to those of us who are not yet mad and who bear a heavy burden of unwanted knowledge? The pride and egotism that sprout from its seed to distort everything? After such knowledge, what forgiveness? So the well is no longer a well, nor is the rain any longer rain . . . Oh, to see things simply, as Malamo does, her back turned to all this as she watches the rain grow in strength . . . Oh, to be simple . . . But how, how can I now turn back?

ACCIDENTS FALL INTO THREE CATEGORIES:
MINOR, SERIOUS, AND DEADLY

Thanos, Thanateros, Thanasimos: Deadly, Deadlier, Deadliest; if my name were an adjective, that's how I'd be declined. And beyond the superlative remains the same question: how can I disentangle myself? Only two means exist: to pretend I'm sick and return home with her, or to speak to her openly, tell her the truth come what may . . . The truth . . . Our property deteriorates year after year. It's collapsing like the old bourgeois world. In a few years it will no longer exist at all . . . It will return to the people, to the poor peasants from whom it was taken, or it will be sold in lots to rich tourists. Yet how did I react when she suggested we go to Bambakies for water? As though she had mocked the value of my private fortune, my inheritance. I should go to Bambakies for water, I whose father had created such a magnificent well, a well that— The motor doesn't work any longer, but nobody seems to be particularly concerned. As though things were still as safe as they used to be before the war, as though the world weren't ready to blow up from one moment to the next . . . Now that I'm safe inside this place and self-composed, I can think straight, I can find the right words to . . . I've learned to live alone inside four walls . . . It's outside that I get confused, that I mix up my words, that nature frightens me . . . I imagine a scorpion under every stone; I see a snake in every tree . . . Nor do I know any way of approaching Malamo . . . If I make a pass, she'll say: "I'm your maid, I'm not right for you . . . Go on and find some vacationing lady, someone your mother would approve of . . ." Simple . . . Simple . . . But isn't my wanting to be simple merely the beginning of new complications? And what conclusion emerges from all this? Simply an impasse—and a voice saying: "Thanos, stop thinking; thinking eats at a man like a maggot." Yet this voice, yes, this voice itself is a thought.

He gazed at Malamo—who was drumming her fingers against the windowpane absent-mindedly—and he felt like getting up, going over to her, telling her: "Forgive me for everything. It's all my fault, I know it." But if he did, what would come of it? How would it help? Relief for a moment maybe. The problem, the root of his division between action and thought would remain unaffected. By giving charity to one poor man, do you really lighten the burden of your world-wide guilt? And he couldn't possibly talk to the gardener. He began to feel that he would burst from asphyxiation. All the while he'd been getting wet without realizing it. He turned around, changed his position, then saw an enormous sign on the wall beside him:

THERE ARE WELLS EVERYWHERE

He could see a centipede stretched full length under EVERYWHERE, as though underlining it.

There's a terrible stench in here, he thought, irritated. It stinks like a sewer. Must be that hole. The old man probably eats over it. Probably uses it as a toilet . . . And the rain doesn't seem about to stop. It's raining, raining. Oh, if only I'd been born different! Not a human being, but a tree, a bird, a breeze. If only I could live without thinking, die without remorse. If only I were a sponge at the bottom of the sea, so that a diver could uproot me someday and make me serve to wipe the dirt, the smell, the kerosene off humanity. We live in a marsh and howl, we live only to sink someday without knowing the reason.

Malamo had forgotten where she was as she traveled through other times, a day with a rain storm like this one when she had found herself alone on the open threshing floor and, having nowhere to hide, crawled into the hollow trunk of an olive tree, large enough to seem a whole hut inside, and there she found a small goat, abandoned and alone; she took it in her arms and caressed its forehead, and the goat rubbed its tender horns against her. How carefree life was in the village! She almost felt sorry she'd gone to the city to work as a maid. Suddenly, as she stood there reminiscing, a swallow came and pecked at the window. It startled her. She saw the swallow's eyes full of fear and its wings heavy with rain. It had no place to rest in the thunder and lightning that were struggling to uproot the sky. Without asking anyone, she opened the window and let it in.

The sudden gust of air that came in through the open window, bringing some rain with it, roused Thanos out of his torpor and inspired the gardener to turn his head and stare at the young girl with his good eye (his maimed eye remained directed toward the hole). The gust lifted the patchwork rug off the motor, uncovering sections of rusty iron and a pressure gauge that looked like an old clock gone dead. Malamo forced the window closed against the wind, then turned around only partway to avoid facing the old man. Along with three human beings, there was now a bird inside the tiny motor shed.

What followed occurred so quickly that Malamo didn't have time to realize what had happened. The swallow, apparently happy to have found a roof, flew around at first from corner to corner, hoping to find a dilapidated nest, everywhere spotting the cobwebs of spiders ready to catch him in their trap, always escaping, dodging this way and that, playfully slicing through the webs with the scissors of its tail, suddenly stopping dead still as though nailed to a void, then sinking gradually, so that it seemed an invisible thread were drawing it down. Malamo saw it flap its wings and screech, descending lower all the while, but she thought it was merely maneuvering to catch a fly; then, in a matter of seconds, with a quickening fall and tiny inarticulate screeching, it disappeared before her eyes down the hole.

The gardener laughed, Thanos stood open-mouthed, Malamo burst into tears.

—Where did it go, Kyr-Thano, where? she kept asking between sobs.

—I don't know, Malamo. I didn't see what hapened, how it got trapped like that, where it disappeared to so suddenly.

He got up to console her.

—It went down the hole, young master, Barba-Sotiris said, stroking his beard with satisfaction.

—What hole, Kyr-Thano? the maid whimpered.

—Don't listen to him, Thanos said, caressing her hair. Your swallow isn't lost . . .

—It went down the hole, the holy hole, the gardener bellowed. It was caught in the whirlpool. The well breathes, creating whirlpools with its breath. If she wanted to save it, she should never have opened the window for it. Now that one's gone too, gone down the hole.

Malamo's body shook with her sobbing.

—It isn't gone, Thanos told her tenderly. Swallows are the only birds that don't drown when they fall into water, because the good Lord turns them into fish . . . Once upon a time there was a little fish who was bird from the waist up and who was madly in love with a little bird who was fish from the waist up. So the fish-bird kept saying to the bird-fish: "Oh, why were we created so that we can never live together? You in the wind and I in the wave. What a pity for both of us!" And the bird-fish would answer: "No, what luck for both of us. This way we'll always be in love because we'll always be separated." Come on now, Malamo, look: it's stopped raining outside. You mustn't cry any longer.

But as they started to leave the motor shed, the old man blocked their way with his trembling hand, which was holding up a photograph.

—There she is, he said. That's my Panayiota. She also

131

disappeared down the hole, which is where we'll all go one day. Look at her closely! See how pretty she was!

—Just shut your trap! Thanos yelled at him, furious. And get your Goddamn arm out of the way.

And he quickly opened the door. He was now holding Malamo by the hand—which burned as though she had a high fever—and since the pail was in his other hand, he couldn't close the door easily. He just had time to hear something like a moan, like a muted cry, emerge from deep inside Barba-Sotiris.

The earth outside was now rich with the fragrances that come after rain. Malamo breathed in, as deep as she could, and the breath was like balsam to her lungs, sullied by the stench of kerosene. The rain not only made colors more vivid but wakened scents that had become dormant in the heat. The perfume of mastic, of thyme, of willow, of linden came into her and purified her heart. She ran, light, skipping, like a wild animal recovering its freedom, without glancing back at the prison behind her. She stopped finally at the top of the ridge to gaze across the landscape below. Outside the property and beyond the ravine, on the country road that joined Poto with Theologos, villagers were going by on mules that they had dressed up in their best blankets and decorated with amulets. The men—in clean white shirts, holding their shoes in their hands—walked along in front, singing. The women—in their local costumes, kerchiefs covering their hair—stayed in the rear, knitting as they walked. They were obviously on their way to celebrate the feast of the Savior. "Oh, if only I could go with them," Malamo sighed, her joy turned melancholy.

Thanos caught up with her near the fig tree; she was kneeling on the ground beside the bucket and pail, digging up earth with a stick to see how deep the water had penetrated. From that height it seemed as though a new day had started. The earth had turned dark and was now steaming. The wet twigs on the ground had reddened strangely. Beyond the property, in the neighboring ravine, a new-born stream of water roared. The torrent coming down the gully crossed the marshland to the sea, dragging along a pile of wood that had been ready for loading, so that Vangelis, from Poto, had to set out in his boat to gather it up again. The land breeze had now changed to a northwester coming off Cape Kefala, as though the wind had turned to the sea along with the sun. The clouds had dispersed one by one like a crowd after a political demonstration, and the black in them had moved on to the cone of Mt. Athos to robe it in a priestly cassock. A ship on the weekly run passed by at the rim of the horizon, leaving a trail of smoke between the parallel capes of St. Antony and Kefala, which lay like supine lions before the throne of Psario. Disparate rivulets of water descended on all sides toward the well, as once upon a time all roads led to Rome in its decline. Only the cicadas in the olive trees remained as they were, humming on as always.

—Kyr-Thano, Malamo said, look at the rainbow! They say the angels weave it in heaven using the sun as a shuttle! Is that true, Kyr-Thano?

—True or false, we don't have time for fables now. We've got to get water. The truth, if you want to know it, is that the rain delayed us too long.

—The rain was golden, Malamo said.

—As far as we're concerned, it was disastrous.

He had been kind to her in the motor shed and she had expected him to go on being so. But now he spoke to her even more harshly than he had earlier. She suddenly felt something biting her thigh. Hurriedly raising her skirt over her knees, she put some spit on the bite with her finger.

Thanos stared at her dark-brown legs; he had never

133

imagined they would be so shapely, so tender. He didn't say a word until Malamo covered them up again with her skirt.

—Now, he said quietly, empty the rain water out of the bucket and follow me.

They came down the slope together and stopped on the first terrace. From here their horizon was limited; they could see only a segment of the sea. The sun hung from the branches above them like an overripe fruit. And Malamo, to her sorrow, lost sight of the rainbow.

Thanos moved down to the second terrace so he would be on a level with the maid.

—We're closer to the wall here, he told her. In fact, we've entered its magnetic field. This is the anteroom, so to speak, the antechamber, a few steps away from our final destination. That foot path through the oleanders will take us there; the gardener planted them in order to beautify what he calls the road to death, like the wreaths in a graveyard. As you see, the path looks straight, level, attractive. But it isn't so at all. There are three obstacles along it that only the Devil could have placed there. . . .

—Where are they?

—I knew you'd say that. It's exactly what I expected you to ask. And you can't imagine how it encourages me to find that you're paying attention. So I'll tell you first of all that the obstacles are not fully visible to the naked eye. Secondly, they would be nothing at all if encountered far from the well. In any case, since they are more or less invisible and more or less contiguous— Now what's wrong again, for God's sake?

—I want to relieve myself.

—Can't you hold it back?

—I've been holding it back for an hour now, Malamo said.

—All right, go ahead, then. But I want you to know

134

that it'll be your fault if we never get water, and the minute we . . .

But Malamo had already gone. Thanos followed her with his eyes. The thought of what she was going to do excited him. He decided to do the same. But where? Here he might rouse Barba-Sotiris' anger. Back there was where Malamo . . . He moved off toward the property gate, but at that moment a truck appeared down the road, loaded with villagers going to the festival at Theologos; they waved to him, called out to him, but in the roar of the truck motor he couldn't hear what they were yelling. Turning back to his left, he found himself confronting the path with the three obstacles. He was now trapped on all sides. Glancing down, he saw a slug slithering along the wet ground. It had no shell, no protection, and it moved the soft fleshy horns on its brow from right to left searching for a passage among the impregnable rocks that surrounded it.

Malamo soon returned. Thanos saw her skipping along gaily, sprightly, a stranger to his agony, a non-participant in his fear—and he felt jealous again.

—Now, I hope you'll keep your ears wide open and listen to me, he said, wiping away a late raindrop that fell off the mulberry tree overhead as a bird stirred in its branches. I don't ask for more. Just your attention. Now, the three obstacles I was telling you about consist of the following: first, an iron hook right in the center of the foot path that leads to the well; second, the southwestern corner of the well, projecting into the path like a wedge but largely hidden by the oleander; and third, the earth-colored roots of the fig tree arching dangerously above ground.

—And what's so dangerous about them? Malamo asked.

135

—Well, they may not be so dangerous by themselves, but the point is, the three obstacles are arranged so that it's almost impossible to avoid one without tripping over another. That is to say, if you go to the left to avoid roots, you'll fall against the wedge-shaped corner of the well, and if you step right to avoid the corner of the well, your feet will get entangled in the roots, and if you try moving down the middle between these two, you'll trip over the hook, which is a little beyond them and exactly in the center of the path.

—Then why don't we get there some other way?

—Show me another way and we'll use it. Unfortunately, that's the only approach there is within the boundaries of our property.

—Then why don't you just get rid of the obstacles?

—That's out of the question. Barba-Sotiris guards the place like Cerberus. Among other things, he believes that the fig tree is joined to the well inseparably, that the two constitute a virtually complete couple married for centuries now. It's a marriage, he says, of the Upper and the Lower world. The roots of the fig tree go down into the well to play with its water like lovers do in bed.

—Christ and the Virgin!

—As for the corner of the well, he strongly objects to altering it in any way. If we round it off, he rebuilds it in the shape of a wedge so that it matches the other three corners which complete the square marble trim around the well. He says the well is his wife's grave and should therefore be as symmetrical and beautiful as she was.

—What about the hook?

—The hook. I'm glad you remembered the hook. That's another matter entirely, having nothing to do with Barba-Sotiris. Since we don't have an icebox here, we use the well as a natural and inexpensive means for preserving perishables. We tie one end of a rope to the hook and attach a basket full of whatever needs cooling to the other end, then suspend the basket in the well. So the hook is essential.

—Then what are we going to do? Malamo asked. How are we going to go through all these obstacles?

—That's the problem. They can't be surmounted by normal walking. You either have to hop over them in series or take them all together in one long leap. Because the important thing is not to go *through* them but *over* them. . . .

A door suddenly opened and closed. Barba-Sotiris emerged with his ancient muzzle gun. The image of him dragging his feet along the ground, elongated like a shadow on a wall, terrified Malamo. Thanos rushed over to confront him by the gate.

—Forgive me, Barba-Sotiris, if I unwillingly insulted you earlier. Tomorrow is your nameday and I wouldn't want you to think that—

—The well is profound, young master, the old man answered hoarsely. It has full knowledge of forgiveness.

As Thanos turned to leave the old man to his thoughts, he suddenly heard his mother's voice calling him from the top of the hill—a voice soft as her caress, distant as her world.

—Coming! he shouted back, his hands forming a loudspeaker over his mouth.

He crossed in front of Malamo on his way up.

—Don't tell her it's my fault, the young girl begged him.

—It's neither your fault nor mine. The rain delayed us.

He found his mother wrapped in her black shawl standing against a telegraph pole on the edge of the apricot orchard.

—What have you been up to all this time? she asked him as he arrived out of breath.

137

—I've just been explaining to her how—

—Your father's furious. And I myself—to tell you the truth, I've been worried. Where were you during the rain storm?

She fingered his shirt to see if it was wet.

—In the motor shed.

—I see. I mean I understand how difficult it is. Only try to go a little faster. I keep having to make excuses for you with your father.

She avoided his eyes as she spoke. Thanos watched her silently.

—Here, she finally said, smiling. I brought you a sweater so you won't catch cold. And a flashlight so you can see the depth of the well.

Thanos took them from her indifferently. Still smiling, she said:

—Just be careful you're not influenced by the maid's village dialect. It's really quite vulgar.

Thanos watched her disappear behind the apricot trees —tall, aristocratic, slipping away from him like a ghost.

He came down the hill dejected. He came down like a car with its motor turned off, propelled by gravity. Fear always got me by the knees, he thought, trying to react to the feeling of paralysis that now took hold of his joints, so that his body seemed close to dissolution. It always got me by the knees and then progressed through the rest of my body. He fiddled with the long, tubular flashlight trade-marked LIGHTER SWITCH, turned it on and off, tried its four different colors. Yellow-red-green-white. Always the same combination. How boring. He started to put on his sweater but it made him too hot. I rejoiced with my hands, feared with my legs. Up to that point, he had held to the vague hope that he wouldn't reach the well. Maybe something, maybe Malamo . . . Now there was no emergency exit left. And all the bridges behind him were burnt. It was as though he had been given a shove toward the precipice, the cave of night. He came down trying to recall some daring act he had committed in his life, some significant act from which to take courage and strength. He searched, reviewed the past, found nothing, recalled nothing. He had let life go by, allowing it to touch only his outer skin. With the cunning of cowards, he had managed to avoid its rapid current, managed to avoid the curving fall of its cataract that dives down from above to behead itself on the rocks. He had always remained safely beyond reach. The cataract had passed him by without touching him; only the mineral salts in its spray had penetrated inside him, causing a whole cave to grow over the years—like that cave he had seen in Edessa—full of stalactites and stalagmites, forests of stone trees and thorny shrubs, with a dark passage between them, treacherous and hollow, where his fear now circled violently, like a bat in the night.

—What did my mistress tell you? the warm and comforting voice of Malamo suddenly spoke beside him.

—She gave me this flashlight so we could see down the well.

—Aren't we going back?

—Certainly not. Let's get going. Are you ready?

—I've been ready since early this morning, Kyr-Thano, the young girl said quietly.

Two yellow-black fig peckers, flying impetuously toward the fig tree, veered sharply to the right as they spotted the couple standing under it and headed for the pine trees. A weary sea gull passed high overhead searching for food.

. . .

Thanos led the way, stepping down to the third terrace, approaching the path carefully, then searching the ground ahead of him with his foot before each step, as though clearing a mine field. He reached the turn with the three obstacles and stopped short. Their arrangement seemed to him a triangular trap, their individual shapes grotesque, horrifying: the roots petrified serpents coupled in a deadly embrace, the hook a monster's claw emerging out of the ground. He braced himself, then turned to help Malamo cross ahead of him, offering her his hand as an acrobat might before the *"salto mortale."* Malamo took it, then let go. Barely glancing at the ground, she skipped over the obstacles in three short hops. Thanos stood there gazing after her. Then he braced himself again, drew in his breath, vaulted over the obstacles in one long leap. It was too easy. As he took Malamo's hand to guide her along the side of the well, he felt almost disappointed. He let go of her hand to turn on the flashlight and gradually directed the beam down the well. It picked out a jumble of metal, pipes, drains, a ladder, pulleys, wheels. No water showed; however directed, the light failed to strike anything that cast back a reflection and so was lost at an indeterminate depth. As they moved on, he could feel the well's dampness begin to encompass him. He reached the hand pump on the far side and finally relaxed.

—What was all that scrap iron in the well, Kyr-Thano?

—See what I mean? Thanos answered. There's a whole factory in there. And we have to get the water with our bare hands. Even this hand pump doesn't work. Everything's broken down now, Malamo, everything's useless.

He started lowering the pail slowly, careful not to bang it against the sides of the well and dent it, handling it like a delicate depth-measuring instrument. Malamo followed the descent anxiously, and as she saw the rope getting shorter and shorter and the pail still not reaching bottom, she became frightened at the thought of having to bring it back up full.

The rope ran out and the pail still hadn't reached water.

—Strange, Thanos said, holding the knot at the tail end of the rope. Especially since we cut this rope to the measurements of the old one, even added a couple of extra lengths. I can't understand it. Hold me by the ankles, I'm going to make one last try.

And he lay on his stomach across the marble trimming. Malamo held him tightly; she could see him lower his arm into the well, then watched half of his body disappear, like that of a fisherman straining to make his line reach.

—Everything's going wrong today, Thanos said, pulling back and gathering in the rope. How could the water level be so much lower than it was two years ago?

—So what are we going to do now? Malamo asked dejectedly, seeing the efforts and agonies of a whole morning about to come to nothing. Are we going back home without water?

—No, Thanos said. We can't go back empty-handed.

—Then what are we going to do?

Thanos hesitated.

—I'll go down into the well, he said on an impulse— out of boastfulness rather than courage.

—You'll go where? Down inside? And you aren't afraid?

—Me afraid? I've never been afraid of anything in my life.

"Like one for long prepared, like a courageous man," he continued:

—There's a metal ladder going down partway over there. I'll give it a try. The rope should reach from the foot

141

of the ladder. But your help will be of great consequence in my effort. You'll hold the flashlight for me from above. Right?

—Sure, Kyr-Thano, Malamo said, no longer hiding her admiration. But wouldn't it be better to—

—Forget what would be better or worse. The way things are, this is the only thing to do. Understand? You just give me enough light so I can see where I'm going.

And he got himself ready like a diver before a deep plunge, tying his shoelaces tightly, taking a few deep breaths, securing his glasses, picking up the pail after slowly filling it with the rope, casually glancing at a fishing boat heading out to sea, taking a second to listen to the sea splash in the arms of the rocks along the shore and another second to listen to the taverna radio in Poto playing at that very moment a folk song about the girl Yierakina falling down the well.

—What a goincidence, he turned and said to Malamo, who was bending over the rim of the well to see how far down the metal ladder went.

And then he took his first step into the void.

He wouldn't go down too deep. He remembered that the ladder had nine rungs, because as a child he used to go down it occasionally with Barba-Sotiris when something wasn't working in the pump mechanism. But that was a long time ago. Why did I say "goincidence" rather than "coincidence"? he wondered. He paused for a moment on the third rung to think it over. Malamo asked him if something was wrong; he answered that all was well. Then he remembered: a family friend always pronounced the word that way as a joke, and they would all laugh. But now it didn't seem funny enough to make even an idiot laugh. His mind drifted back to the house: they would be sitting at the table now, expecting him to arrive with fresh water at any moment. They don't know what I have to go through, he thought. When I explain it all later, they won't believe me. I'll suggest that they come here tomorrow and try it themselves with the same piece of rope. We'll see how much water they get.

Above him, Malamo was handling the flashlight carefully, casting the beam on each new rung below. On the fifth rung he slipped. The dampness has made moss grow on this thing, he thought. But since his head was still above the rim of the well, he felt reasonably secure. Even if he were to fall, he could still grab hold of the rim and Malamo could reach down to bring him safely back above ground. At the sixth rung his head came level with the rim. The real descent began from here on; he was now entering the well substantially. It's the head that counts, he told himself. The body is of secondary importance. The shepherd counts heads. And the ostrich, in face of danger, first of all hides its head in the sand. He leaned back and looked above. Though he could see almost the full extent of the sky, the sun was missing. He could hear the sea snoring by the shore, and in the distance, an announcer's voice on the taverna radio listing missing persons for the Greek Red Cross. He kept his ears taut; it was the last human voice he would hear before finally descending into darkness:

Maria Kaftanzoglou, nee Devlotoglou, from Proussi in Asia Minor. Disappeared in 1922. Please contact her sister, Eleni Sotiriadou.

Alkibiadis Giokas, from Villia in Attica. In 1948 Alkibiadis set off for America. Has not been heard from since. Please contact his niece, Venetia Gioka.

*Ioannis Karakostanoglou, from Proktion, district
of Komotini. Missing since 1947. Please contact . . .*

Kostoula Sarantavga, nee Balouktsi, missing . . .

The fate of the following people is unknown . . .

He moved down to the next rung. He was calm and
collected now. Unafraid. Now that he had decided to engage
in significant action, courageous action, he believed he would
succeed. Besides, there was really nothing terrifying about
it. He had three more rungs to go, and then he would let
out the rope again. If the pail hit water, he'd fill it and they'd
go back home. If it didn't, they simply wouldn't get water
today. In the last analysis, it wouldn't really be his fault.
The rungs were becoming more and more slippery with the
growing dampness as he descended; he held on tightly to
the railings with both hands and tested each rung with his
foot before easing his full weight down on it.

On the last rung, the ninth, he sat down, letting his
legs dangle over the void below, holding on to the railing
with one hand while he slowly let the pail down with the
other. He soon reached the knotted end of the rope without
the pail having touched water. Again he bent down as far
as he could without result. Malamo, still holding the flashlight, seemed to understand what had happened and called
down: "Come on up, Kyr-Thano, come on up." Her voice
circled the well, went up and down the ladder, bounced from
one side to the other, so that his ears filled with echoes, then
disintegrated like bread in water. In the last analysis, it's
her fault, he thought. Just because I want to show off to her,
I'm playing heads or tails with my life. As he sat there
hunched over on the ninth rung, unable to move, he made
the great decision. It might be pure madness, it might be

144

silly, it might be catastrophic egotism, it might be wounded pride—there was no time to think, to analyze his feelings calmly to find out what it was that was now pressing him to go down deeper. No, he wouldn't go up as the girl wanted him to. He would cross over to the other metal ladder opposite and try to descend from there. And quickly, immediately, while the impulse was still hot, while the flashlight remained lit. But before starting off on his new descent, he glanced up at the sky, now squared as in a distant window. He could make out the wake of a jet plane that had long since passed overhead.

The only way of reaching the other metal ladder— the one that came down from the motor shed through the gardener's hole—was by means of a thick pipe that he would have to cross hand over hand. The distance wasn't great, but the pail would be an impediment. He thought of tying it around his waist, then decided to wrap the rope around his shoulder so it wouldn't snag on anything and let the pail fall against his back like a knapsack. The pipe he had to cross, once the central water main, was surely heavy enough to hold him. Besides, he didn't weigh more than 130 pounds. The beginning was what was difficult, he said to himself as he got ready. Malamo was still holding the beam in front of him, illuminating an assortment of objects around him, a wheel, a belt, several pulleys, two dormant gears with teeth meshed.

He clutched the pipe tightly with both hands and let himself hang from it, then began to move across the void hand over hand, his body thrusting forward with each change. The pipe proved to be rusty and hurt his palms. What if I get tetanus out of this, he thought. Below him, he knew, the void was waiting for him. But he could no longer see anything down there; the darkness seemed dense and unbroken, and he felt as though he were swimming in

145

the Black Sea. The gardener will be completely startled when he sees me come out of his hole, he said to himself. Because if I manage to fill the pail, so that I have only one hand free, I won't be able to come back this way and will have to climb this second ladder through the hole to the motor shed.

He was about halfway through his air-borne journey when a thrust of his body caused the pail to slip off his shoulder, so that it hung loose from his right arm. That arm was now completely useless, and naturally he couldn't go on with only one. He tried to get the pail back over his shoulder, without success. He began cursing gods and demons, all wrath, and as punishment for his blasphemy, the pail he was trying to flip backwards struck him in the face. He felt something warm dripping from his nostrils. "Blood," he said. It reached his chin and continued down his neck. He touched some with his tongue; he could tell it was blood from its sweet-salty taste. "My nose is bleeding," he said aloud without meaning to, and heard the phrase repeated all around him: "My nose is bleeding. My nose is bleeding. My nose is bleeding." The blood on his neck slid down to his chest. I mustn't talk out loud, he said to himself. Then again, if that's the way things are down here, I'll say something that will bolster my courage. And he shouted: "I'm not afraid." At first it echoed as he'd said it, but then the "I'm not" was mysteriously erased and from all sides, as though a thousand people were shouting back at him, came the words "afraid, afraid, afraid . . ." Well, that gimmick didn't work out too well, he told himself.

When he finally succeeded in getting the pail back in place, he moved on hand over hand. The blood had now reached his belly and was tickling his navel. I'm a hero in spite of myself. I'm like those who tremble at the thought of war, yet turn daring under fire. It was a hard struggle, but

146

he finally reached the other ladder. A wave of relief cooled his body as he stepped onto it. He wiped himself with the edge of his shirt and put his head back to stop the bleeding. Tomorrow all my bones will ache, he thought. I'm out of training, completely out of training, impossibly and unacceptably out of training. I've completely neglected my body. With his head back he studied the sky. From this new position he was certain he could see a falling star go by and he just had time to make a wish: that I get water! But then he began to doubt that it was a falling star. It was probably just a firefly, or a satellite sent to the moon. No, it couldn't have been a falling star. After all, it's daylight outside.

The blood stopped dripping, cooled, dried up. He turned around and looked at the distance he'd covered hanging from the pipe. Unbelievable! Now he was more or less in the heart of the well, halfway down, at least so it seemed from the flashlight beam, which struck his legs at an angle. He couldn't remember ever having gone down the ladder that now awaited him. Nor did he know how many rungs it had. I hope the pail finds bottom from down there, he reflected, because if it doesn't, this whole business becomes inexplicable. And with the pail in his hand he cautiously began his descent.

The new ladder plunged him into new darkness. The deeper he went, the heavier the atmosphere around him became, until he found it difficult to breathe. The air he now inhaled was very different from that above ground; here it was full of foglike particles—a thick black liquid that soaked his clothes. It's a good thing I'm moving, he thought, otherwise I'd freeze down here. The new ladder proved to be even more slippery than the old, and some rungs were missing, so that he would sometimes have to stretch until it hurt. Every time he encountered a gap like that, he would think he'd reached the bottom, yet there was always another rung at the limit of his stretch. Since there's another, I'll go down another, he would say. The flashlight beam had become weaker, more diffuse, like a searchlight in fog. He looked up; Malamo now seemed very far away, and the square sky minute.

Something caught his ear. He stopped, listened carefully: a whisper, a voice. He tried to stretch his hearing through the silence that spread around him as densely as the darkness. "Come . . . Come . . ." The sweetest of whispers caressed his ear. "Come . . ." Who could it be? he wondered. Nobody. I'm not mad yet, thank God. "Come . . ." If I believed what the gardener has to say, I'd take it to be his wife calling. "Come . . ." I've got it, he said suddenly, relieved. It's the remnant of Malamo's voice calling me earlier to come back up. It descended into the depths of the well, reached the water, and is now returning effaced and trembling. He coughed loudly, and his cough dug holes in the night around him. Then he listened again; he heard nothing. I wiped out the voice with my cough, he said triumphantly. And he continued his descent. Over him the darkness added layers to its trap door. He was now far from the earth, from the world, from humanity. What I wouldn't give for a dog's bark, for the sound of a cicada, for . . . He stopped the thought short. Nobody's forcing me to go down. I'm doing it of my own free will. I have no complaints about being abandoned . . . He stretched his leg taut like a cord, searched, found no rung. This must be the bottom finally, he thought. Let's see if the rope reaches.

That was all he needed at this point—for the rope to get caught! He tugged at it, tugged again. The pail was safely in his hands, but the full length of rope was dangling free, snagged at a depth he couldn't determine. It must have come unwound while he was descending the ladder and now . . . A loose rope is worse than a snake, he said to himself. It was a loose rope dangling from another pail that got entangled in the feet of the gardener's wife. Nonsense. There was nothing for him to be afraid of; he was on to the well now, fully familiar with it. Only it was no longer easy to communicate with Malamo. His voice turned to pulp long before it reached her. Nor did her voice reach him. She anxiously moved the flashlight beam back and forth, then in a circle. He signaled her not to worry, then, following the path of the beam, tried to discover where the rope was caught. Oh, why wasn't he more careful, why did he always get himself into trouble like a bungler! He cursed the damned well. Why did it need all this machinery if the motor wasn't working? They should simplify the whole installation, throw out all that wasn't necessary, leave only the ladders. He'd suggest it to his father tomorrow, yes,— that is, if he lived until tomorrow. It then occurred to him to abandon everything and return to the world, to the earth's joyful surface. But how could he face Malamo? He tugged at the rope again with all his strength, so that he slipped and nearly fell. It can't be caught on anything metal, because I felt it give a little. He studied the situation again and discovered that he was pulling against something so heavy as to be just movable. Bending down as far as he could, he spotted what looked like a rope ladder just within reach to the left of the last rung. That's where the rope must be snagged. I'm pulling against the rope ladder. I'll have to go down and free it. I can't leave it like that, only six feet under me.

His nose began to itch. Someone must be thinking of me, he said. But who? He tried to remember the faces of his friends. He saw them, boys and girls, lined up in front of him in the melancholy sequence of portraits in a provincial gallery: all far away, in their separate frames, with empty eyes and hands that couldn't help. There was Lakis, Lucas,

Yannis, Marietta. Pavlos, Pantazis, Popi, Aliki. But which one of them? Which one? His nose stopped itching. That's better, he said, now I can get on with my job.

He eased over to the rope ladder. He recalled that when his fishing line would get caught, he would hold it between his fingers as he went underwater and let it guide him down to the rocks where the hook was snagged; he decided to follow the same procedure now. But the rope ladder wasn't as secure as the metal ladder. He swung back and forth on it like a sailor in the rigging of a ship during a squall. He moved across the void like a pendulum. His feet twisted around. His waist buckled to a right angle. He was descending with the same sensation in his groin that he knew as a young boy when falling from a height. He found himself fully horizontal at one point, and something fell out of his pocket to land below with a dry sound. It must have been the key, he thought, or the change I got from the boatman who rowed us ashore yesterday. He looked up. Malamo seemed like a bent-over willow tree. Weeping willow tree, he thought. And the face of the flashlight now seemed the moon. Only it kept changing colors. She's playing with it, he said to himself, because she's bored waiting for me . . . And he started declaiming: "Yellow, the color of hate. Green, the color of hope. Red, the color of danger. White, the color of despair." The flashlight finally settled on white.

The rope ladder was making him feel nauseated, and the darkness now stuck to him like coal dust, so that he felt as he once did going down a coal mine in Belgium, three thousand feet under the surface of the earth, moving from one deserted tunnel to another with the polluted air striking him as he walked stooped over trying not to hit his head on the support beams—he could still remember the small roots emerging from the walls—walking until he reached the place where the miners were at work, mostly

Italians, naked from the waist up, black with coal dust, so that only their teeth and the whites of their eyes showed, at work with drills, hatchets, shovels, loosening coal from the earth's entrails and pitching it onto a belt that ran under their feet like a black stream, bent over double because there wasn't even room for them to stand up, and he remembered that one of them with huge blue eyes had looked at him reproachfully, so that he couldn't help wondering what two blue lakes such as those were doing inside the earth's impenetrable sanctuary, amidst the noise and asphyxiation—certainly God's inferno could be no worse, he remembered thinking, or thought now, remembering . . .

He was confused. It seemed he was still in that coal mine, listening to the drills, now working alongside those men, bent over, working along with them at the very moment the short-circuit occurred that had drowned them all like mice the following year, one hundred and sixty workers dying because they couldn't breathe, their lungs bloody, buried alive in a standing position because they didn't have room to lie down, in the tunnel, beside the black stream, three thousand feet under the earth—and he started to compose his funeral oration: "Unforgettable friend, you left us too soon. But you had the courage to dare what is beyond daring. You had character, you had values, values lacking in the young men of our times. You left a void among us that surely cannot be filled. And we shall stand as faithful guardians of your memory, Thanos. May the earth that covers you be light, may it be light!" No, they can't say that, he thought with indignation. Three thousand feet of earth can never be light. They're lying. They must take that sentence out of my obituary immediately. What obituary? Where was he, after all? I'll be going up again soon, and when I get out of here I'll eat yoghurt made of goat's milk, and tomorrow I'll go over to Theologos and find some pretty girl on vacation so I can live, yes, live through an unforgettable summer . . .

But the rope lader wouldn't stop swaying. He finally had to hold on to something solid or fall. He stretched out his hand, found a wheel of some kind, grabbed it, and clung to it for all he was worth. But the wheel started turning, turning and groaning. The well began to fill with noise as the wheel apparently set off another wheel further back, and that one also started groaning. Gears were now shaking off their rust like a monster waking. Other wheels started moving, creaking demoniacally everywhere; the well filled with echoes, wailing, cries, the sighing of metal—the void serving to magnify the clamor—as pulleys, containers, belts, springs, regulators, a whole world woke out of its long sleep. And he had thought that nothing functioned, silly man that he was. Then suddenly in the midst of this pandemonium he felt something brush against his face like the touch of a bird's wing or maybe a spider—more likely a bird's wing, because it kept returning sporadically. The swallow must have woken up with all the noise. He would feel it touching his neck, then his ear, then his cheek. He cringed, finally started yelling with all his strength. He shrieked like a bird winged by the bow, screeched like a rabbit caught in a trap, howled like a dog bitten by a snake, screamed like a woman in labor—all together shaping a sound that was wild, anguished, endless.

Malamo heard his lamentations from up above, feared that something she couldn't see, something horrible had happened to her master, and started running back toward the house as quickly as she could to warn her mistress and bring help; but then it occurred to her that it might be too late by the time they got back, so she stopped short and, after a few moments of deliberation, decided to go down into the well herself. She was light, and agile enough from climbing trees to manage it easily. Besides, now that someone else was in there, she wasn't nearly as scared. And picking her way with the flashlight, she started down the first ladder, found it much simpler than she had expected, saw the water main as nothing more complicated than the branch of a tree, swung her way across it hand over hand, and started down the other ladder without a second thought.

Thanos saw a light descending, a white light, desperately white, striking his eyes so as to blind him.

—What's happened? Why were you yelling like that? the maid called down to him as she reached the last rung of the second ladder.

—Is that you, Malamo? Really you? Give me your hand. I'm so dizzy. I need a hand, your hand, a warm, human—

—I can't give you my hand. I've got to hang on with something. Take hold of my foot if you want.

Thanos struggled up desperately until he could reach her foot, caught hold of it tightly, brought it over to his lips, kissed it with passion, with gratitude.

—You did so well to come, Malamo. I swear I'll never forget this, never in all my life.

—Why were you yelling, Thano? Malamo asked, dropping the "Kyr" for the first time as far as he could remember.

—I'll tell you all about it. I'll tell you everything. I want to calm down first, to stand still a moment. It's so good to be like this, with you near me, so good!

And he gently tightened his hold on her foot.

Malamo searched the darkness below with the flashlight. The beam—so much stronger now—illuminated the wooden platform that held the bulk of the well machinery just below the rope ladder.

—Let's go down there, she suggested. So you can rest.
—Down where?

—The platform, she said, pointing below him.

He helped her down to the rope ladder, and with two of them to keep it stable, the ladder proved no great problem. He tested the platform with his outstretched foot, found the planks less waterlogged than he expected, eased on to the edge of it, and sat down with his legs dangling over the void. He reached back to give Malamo a hand; she took it and lowered herself carefully until she was sitting beside him. Then she turned the flashlight on his face.

—You're covered with blood, Thano.

—The pail did that. It's caused all the trouble. I was getting ready to let it down when I saw that its rope was caught, so I tugged and tugged at it but it wouldn't come loose, and then I went down onto this rope ladder to try and pry it loose, and while I was swinging back and forth a bird came along and flew around me like a hen, licked my face with its wing, pecked at me with its beak . . . I think it must have been that swallow.

—It couldn't have been, the young girl said. That swallow became a flying fish. You said so yourself. It must have been a bat.

—Maybe, Thanos said, edging closer to her. Anyway, I got frightened. I've been afraid of bats ever since I was a child, because they get into your hair. They say that white attracts them. Maybe my white shirt . . .

He didn't try to pretend any more. His nerves relaxed now, he let himself go into the maid's embrace. It calmed him further; in fact, ever since that morning what he really wanted was to become her charge rather than her protector. He started fondling her with his cold hand. He was jealous of her warmth, wanted to steal it. Only he couldn't tell exactly what he was touching. He would ask:

—What am I touching now?

—My leg.

—Now?

—My neck.

—What's this?

—My dress.

—This?

—My hair.

He made himself snug against her side, comfortable as he would be beside a clay stove. Malamo could feel that he was frozen like a corpse and didn't try to stop his hands. She tried to edge away a little and said she hoped they'd start back up soon. She didn't like staying that long in the heart of the well, the navel of darkness.

—Just a little longer, so I can calm down completely and get my strength back, he begged her. I can hardly raise my feet . . .

She felt sorry for him, as she did for all the maimed, lame, and blind. By instinct she placed him among those not favored by nature.

Thanos had begun to feel his blood run through his veins again; he'd reached the critical point of a snake coming out of its winter hibernation, of a stalactite melting; he felt thoroughly content with the purring of her belly under his head, with the waking of his senses near another's warm flesh. He was starting to fall asleep when her voice, full of fear, roused him.

—Look, Thano, look up there . . .

He bent his head back and saw the shadow of the gardener pass across the mouth of the well.

—Don't worry, he reassured her. He comes around at regular intervals to look down the well for his wife.

—The old bogeyman! He'll drown us, just as he drowned his wife . . .

They both followed the progress of his shadow, tightly

155

embraced, like two communicating vessels of fear that have finally reached the same level. Suddenly the well filled with the sound of a voice. Barba-Sotiris was calling out his wife's name from above. Malamo stiffened; in her panic she started digging her nails into Thanos' back. She didn't want to see the ghost. He found himself on top of her without realizing it. He could feel her young body wriggling, her shortened breath licking him, her fingers goading his blood, her little voice stirring the fire. He was blazing now. And the gardener's voice wrapped them in a cloud, so that nothing could be heard any more, neither his moan, nor the squeaking of the boards, nor the girl's crying. A last spasm, a lunge, a death rattle, and it was all over. Malamo opened her eyes without seeing a thing. Thanos had slipped down beside her.

—Thano . . . she said, completely drained now, scratching herself with her free hand. She pointed the flashlight below her and saw that she was besieged by mosquitoes. They were biting her savagely, driving her mad, so that her nails drew blood in their scratching.

Thanos lifted the pail and the rope came with it.

—It's broken free, he said gaily to the maid. And he started lowering the pail carefully over the rim of the platform. This time the pail touched bottom. But it didn't touch water. He pointed the flashlight over the edge and discovered that the bottom of the well was all mud, mud that looked like pulp. He could see eels slithering through it, and voiceless toads bounding along the surface. A cloud of anopheles mosquitoes, woken up by the light, rose suddenly upward. He told Malamo to look too.

—It's gone dry, he said, embarrassed. Completely dry, Malamo. Our famous well just doesn't exist any more.

The maid gazed over the edge as though she were peering into a newly dug grave.

—And now what are we going to do? Thanos said. What are we going to do tomorrow?

—Tomorrow? Tomorrow we'll try Bambakies.

Thanos let the rope slip from his hands; he saw that it too became an eel, slithering through the mud.

—Let's go, he told the young girl. There's nothing more for us to do here.

Malamo followed him. As she swung onto the rope ladder, new waves of mosquitoes rose under her skirt.

THE ANGEL

TRANSLATORS' NOTE

THE *translation of "The Angel" is based on the second edition of this work, published in Athens in December 1963.*

THE ANGEL

FIRST DAYS

*"I SWEAR TO KEEP FAITH in the Heavens and in the
Unsubstantial Archbishop of Angels, obedience to the System, Laws, and Edicts of the Government of the Dead, sub-
ordination to those holier than I, executing their orders
promptly and without objections;*

*To defend the Swords with faith and devotion to the
last drop of my light, never to abandon them nor separate
myself from them;*

*To follow the Angelic Laws to the letter and in general
to conduct myself as a faithful and self-respecting Angel."*

You TOLD ME to write you wherever I might be, in whatever corner of the world. Well, I'm not in the world, but
I'm writing these letters anyway, with no hope of ever sending them to you, because there's no mail from our star to
your earth. But it's the only thing that can still give me
some relief, and I'm glad that, here in Heaven, they haven't
deprived me of this harmless mania of mine, and that there
is ample paper in the P.X. The others think that I'm doing
tomorrow's homework. Let them think so. Besides, while I
was alive, didn't the others always think things about me

that were far removed from the actual truth—I mean my personal truth? Didn't misunderstanding always dog me like my own shadow? And here in the School of Reserve Heavenly Angels, believe me, my love, there's much less misunderstanding than there was in the narrow glass bowl of our city. Here we're all made equal under the leveling law of death: men and sub-men, educated and illiterate, rich and poor. We're not distinguishable from one another in the uniform dress they've issued us. Maybe later, when time has passed and this panic that now tightens our hearts has gone . . .

One of our group just passed by me and said: "Writing your girl again?" I shook my head negatively. "But you won't see her again, buddy," he added as he left. You see, he doesn't know. Like all the others, he thinks we can still correspond with the earth, as they told us in the study room day before yesterday, the first afternoon we arrived up here. Saint Abbacum was on duty, and at the end of the study period he told us: "Now you can drop a line to your families. But only a line, d'you hear? Any letter longer than that will never leave the School. And write that you're well and everything's fine. No complaints. Is that understood? You have three minutes' time. Now get moving." So I wrote you then: "I'm well and doing fine in Heaven. Don't worry about me. I'm well, I tell you, I'm well." And I put it in an envelope with my new address on the outside:

> *Reserve Candidate Angel*
> *Angelos A. Angelidis*
> *6th Company*
> *S.R.H.A.*

Yesterday they let us write seven lines. We were in the study room again, busy arranging our desks. Saint Abdiu was in charge and he seemed a softer touch than

Abbacum. He didn't dictate what we were to write. He just said: "The maximum is ten lines. If it were in my hands, I'd let you write as much as you wanted to. But it's a rule of the School. You have until seven o'clock. It's now ten of seven," and he looked at his watch. So I wrote you then: "Maybe you still don't understand how I died so suddenly, how I left you. No, my love, it wasn't your fault, you didn't kill me. For God's sake, don't think I want to put the blame on you. It's my fault for not having spoken to you sooner. But I didn't want you to know my weaknesses. I wanted to be as you imagined me, as you wanted me to be: young, handsome, and strong, able to do as I pleased. Yet . . . The clouds that separate us sometimes become mountains now, sometimes look like the foaming sea. I'm above the clouds and—how can I say this—I feel so differently now! It's always clear on our star. Always clear. Boundless blue sky. I'm inside the sky, and I'm well and doing fine. Only the sky's so empty . . ." Then I sealed the letter and gave it to the guy in the first row who got up to collect them.

And today the same thing happened again. At the end of the three-hour study period, which was taken up by the distribution of regulation booklets, they gave us fifteen minutes for correspondence. And I wrote you: "In my deadness you are the secret hope of my resurrection, because from the time I died, the thought of you sustains me, fills me, gives me the certainty that I'm not completely dead. Only each of us here will have to lose his body. And I'm very afraid that you might be lost with mine, because you were the first to know my body and that's why my flesh will always be bound to your memory. How can I get lost, then? How can I lose you? What would the whole of Heaven mean without your face, without your voice, without the memory even of your warm body? Oh my world, I may not be able to see you any longer, I may know that I won't see you again, but believe me, I can't acknowledge that we're separated, because I carry all of you within me, and my body is your prison . . ." But since I'd become too sentimental, against my will, and since I knew a letter like that would hurt you, I tore it up as the guy came by to collect it and hid the pieces in the book of regulations for the "Swordbearers' Platoon."

But a little later this afternoon, during the hour between study hall and the evening meal, a precious hour that we all dedicate to arranging our belongings in our kits according to the plan they gave us and to polishing up our swords—everything here is done according to plan, and absolute uniformity is expected from all of us—an angel of the senior class came into the barracks and asked to see me. I stiffened to attention immediately and the others did the same. (It's a rule, you see: when one of the seniors comes into the barracks, we have to snap to attention.) He gave the others the stock phrase "Look alive, look alive, keep at it," and stopped in front of me, gazing at me silently with a smile that seemed at times ironical, at times sadistic. I gazed at him too, trying to figure out quickly who he was, what he wanted from me, to see behind the implacable mask he was wearing the features of some former earthly acquaintance of mine. "Are you Angelos Angelidis?" he finally asked me, full of sarcasm. "Yes," I said, lips closed, still standing at attention. "Follow me," he commanded, and we went out, he in front and I behind.

When we'd found ourselves alone and he'd made sure nobody was looking, his expression changed abruptly as though he were lifting the mask to show his real face. Yes, it was Yannis. You know him. The one we saw so often at the university running around with the blond girl whom everyone called your twin. It was my friend Yannis, all right, only a lot thinner, bony, almost transparent. "Yannis,

I'll be damned," I cried, ready to wrap an arm around him. "Shsh," he whispered. "Don't give yourself away. Besides, they call me Saint Akepsimas here." And putting his tough mask on again as he saw some seniors approaching, he said: "Come along with me, on the double."

From him I learned, among other things, that our letters never leave Heaven. "It's a trick of the Administration," he explained. "They know the psychological state of the new arrival's and they always let them write home the first few days. The freshly dead, like you, never completely accept their new condition. So, to avoid too much initial reaction, they let them live with this illusion a while. Later, after some time's gone by, you'll see that you don't need to write anyone. Life up here is such that . . . No, they'll never prohibit any of you from writing. You yourselves will get tired of waiting for an answer that will never come. You'll resign yourselves to the fact that you've been forgotten. That's what happened to me . . . Only don't tell this to anybody or I'm a goner. There are stool pigeons everywhere. God hands out extra duty right and left."

"I don't know anybody to tell it to," I answered.

We talked about a lot of other things I won't go into now. The important point is that what he had to say reassured me rather than upset me. I now knew that the only means of tyranny left—correspondence—no longer existed. And I already feel freer writing you letters that I know you'll never receive, now that I don't have to weigh their consequences with the thought that you might read them; just as I feel infinitely more alive now that I'm dead; just as I also feel you're infinitely more mine now that I don't have you at all, rather than when I only half had you or half saw you. A strange thing has been happening to me since I died: instead of losing my memory as I feared, I find my memory ripe with you; instead of finding myself unprotected in the darkness of this other world, I'm flooded by your light; instead of losing you, I've actually found you, whole and indissoluble, more alive than when we made love and you said to me: "Deeper, Angelos, deeper." I've never been deeper inside you than I am now. And I'm grateful to the clouds that separated us, to the sky that uncovered you to my eyes.

But all this is another story that maybe you'll understand better as I myself understand it more clearly, because for the time being at least I can only see it as a miracle. Besides, why should I be upset by Yannis' talk, since even while I was on earth I could never write you? That one time I dared to send you a note, didn't you get into trouble at home? And then we were on the same planet, think of it, living in the same atmosphere. So, why now? . . . And when that classmate of mine came by and said "Writing your girl again?" I laughed inside. How could he know, poor devil, that his letters still weigh down on our star!

Our star is naked. Inexorably. I would call it bald, but these boulders that surround us have never known even the roots of a single tree. Red stones turning black under a sun that burns very close to us; sharp rocks that knife through our bare and untrained feet. But they say it was chosen on purpose among so many others because the plan is to have us fly one day, make our flesh lose its density, our bones their rigidity. That's why they force us to run all the time. How can we fly if first we don't become invulnerable to falling? That's why the ground on our star is so inhospitable.

The deeper we move inland, the more we see of rock bedded in rock; hill ridges looking like jagged metal; mountains whose stone seems granite. At scarce intervals on this

THE ANGEL

wild, brutal, arid surface, a small scalding valley of sand appears, embracing the feet of the mountains like foam around rock islands.

Our star is soundless. Dressed in the silence of primeval lava, it echoes our groaning as we emerge from the camp limits to get acquainted with the anomalies of the terrain where drills will later take place, they say. Our soles bleed like our hearts. Oh, when will we stop being nostalgic for the tenderness of earth, when will we become like this earth under our feet, when will we too turn hard as granite?

Some say it would have been better if they'd left us down in the cemetery, privates within the ranks of death. What use did we have for the high offices of Heaven? There at least we still had some contact with worldly things. At night we could see the lights of cars moving along the highway. On Sundays relatives and people dear to us would come and decorate our graves with flowers, light up our extinguished lampions.

The only good thing about the School is that, situated as it is on the edge of the star, it opens before us that immensity of space where, during the day, we see planets circling through the chasm with that mysterious shared understanding they have, and at night all the impetuous motion of the Milky Way is near us. We ourselves are not yet allowed to go too close to the edge. Only the seniors have this privilege, and they assemble during their free hours in a place they've named Romance, where they wait for the moment when the clouds beneath will break so they can see segments of the lost earth. There must be some magic— besides the vertigo—in surveying from there the depths or the heights, which are one and the same thing, as our star turns on its axis, soundless and naked of feeling.

· · ·

167

I'm trying to get acquainted with the new barracks, with the new faces. Inside, the barracks is monotonous: bunk beds in a row, square windows that look out on the building opposite, where the other company is housed. From my window I can also see the dome of the Administration Building. Ours is a two-story structure, very cold. Walls. Stairways. I'm in the room to the left of the stairway. In the beginning I got confused and went into the room across the way, where the other platoon is housed. I felt equally at home there; I thought I was standing by my bed, even started putting my kit in order. Everything is so foreign to me still and so uniform that it doesn't matter where I am or who I talk to. In the passage that divides the sleeping quarters, on the upper floor are the offices of the Saint and the Overangel, who's a candidate in the senior class, very demanding and full of himself. He walks with his head high, believes in ideals and in the mission of angels, both of which he tries to transmit to us. The third room looks like a storeroom and always remains closed. Opposite that is the washroom, consisting of a row of misconceived faucets that whistle by themselves. And then the door to our quarters.

To get inside, you have to report in smartly, with your hand glued to the circle of your halo: "I have the honor to report to you, Holy Barracks Chief, that I request permission to enter the barracks." And the barracks chief, who is a 1st Underangel in the senior class and has his bed next to the door, gives you a nod of the head as though to say "Pass." He's the one who received us with a lot of tough talk and had us moving on the double when we first arrived at the school still dizzy from our trip on the Lighted Nebula. Now he's a little more casual, but he continues to hold us under the threat of his loud mouth. Some of the boys forget to report in, so he makes them report in ten or twenty times.

And all the while the others gather outside wanting to come in, and then there's a whole chorus of angry voices, which just seems to make him that much happier with himself. When someone reports in quietly, he yells: "Louder, you meathead! I want to hear the windows tremble!" But some just aren't made to shout by nature, and the more they try, the more their voices turn weepy, screechy. "I have the honor . . ."

I'm trying to get to know my neighbors. But they're all afraid, difficult to get close to, and they don't have time for talk. During the one free hour of the day, they work, put things in order, clean up. Distrust has muzzled their mouths, fear has narrowed their eyes. So many new faces have created panic in the hearts of all of us. And the shouting, the orders, the threats . . . My ears buzz constantly. Only after lights out, when that stunted angel sounds his dissonant bugle and the camp sinks into darkness and sleep, only then do I find a little time of my own to think about you, to bring you near me, to bind together the fragments of our lives, the moments—but my weariness is such that sleep comes too quickly and under its heavy cape I forget you.

The morning we reached our star we found the school empty and thought that was the way it would be, but that afternoon the candidate angels of the senior class, coming back from their exercises, burst in on us like hungry wolves, yelling and howling, ready to tear us to pieces. They caught us under the showers, naked, crammed in twos or threes, the water either boiling hot or freezing, the soap vanishing the second you dropped it; they caught us there, trapped,

VASSILIKOS

unarmed, and began tormenting us: "Your name . . ? Address . . ? Father's name . . ? What's your profession . . ? What's your relation to So-and-so . . ?" And while the water alternately froze and scalded, the defenseless nude had to answer. "Look alive, look alive, resume washing," the senior would then say, and move on to another victim.

That first day was full of surprises. We must have reached the school just before noon, and after they divided us up in the central courtyard according to our educational level, two Holy Saints, Patapios and Onisimos, who seemed to have had previous altercations, started choosing among us. They spoke angrily to each other, and if Oversaint Pausikakos hadn't been there, they would have started fighting. "I want this one for myself," one would shout. "But you took that tall one," the other would answer. "Yes, but he was a high school graduate, while you took two university men, one after the other." "Calm down, calm down," the over-saint would say. "They're all the same. They're all equally dead." Onisimos finally chose me for his platoon, while the one man I had got to know somewhat during the journey and therefore would have liked to be with found himself caught in Patapios' net. They then counted heads, and since both platoons proved to be equal in numerical strength, they handed us over to our respective leaders, who goaded us into running, barking alongside us. "There's no walking around here, you jerks. On the double, on the double . . ." And so, with our packs dragging behind us like sins, we ran through our first tour of the unknown school. Someone in the column tried to talk to his companion, but Saint Baruch's voice lashed out at him: "No talking while in ranks, you deadheads!" There was only one of us who wouldn't run, wouldn't follow the others; he held back at the end of the column, limping, his two packs hanging between his legs like overinflated testicles.

Our first stop was in front of the church, where we were to light a candle to the memory of our former selves. The wind was blowing. Stopping suddenly, still wearing the clothes that were suitable for a cemetery but much too hot up here, we started to sweat, and there was a lot of mumbling about catching our death of cold in the drafty air around us, full of the odor of stars perhaps as exiled and infertile as ours—each of us forgetting that there is no second death. When we remembered this fact, everything changed. Even the air changed, becoming a strange animal that licked us with its breath, sneaked inside our trouser legs and our open collars, sniffing our armpits, our bodies, which still held a human odor, warm as they were from their recent death.

From the church we went to our platoon quarters, where, standing on the front steps, Holy Saint Onisimos was waiting to receive us. He looked us over for some time, silent, impenetrable, studying us to see if anybody was moving while at attention, and then said in his hoarse voice:

—At ease. D'you hear me, all of you? Even the ones in back? Good.

He smiled, then moved a step higher, dark and sinister like a curse. His voice echoed against the opposite building and returned to strike us in the back.

—From now on, he began, you'll have to deal with me. I don't yet know what kind of rascals you are, what you did in your other life. Your papers will arrive from the archbishopric soon and I'll look them over carefully. But whatever sinful past you may have had won't influence me in the least; I won't take it into consideration at all. Where life ends, death begins. Where the earth ends, Heaven begins. You are therefore blank sheets of paper to me, but—

171

You! he shouted at someone near the back. What are you daydreaming about? What's your name? Yes, you, the thin one pretending not to understand. No, next to you, the one without glasses.

—Reserve Heavenly Angel Candidate Harilaos Haralambidis, came a voice from behind us.

—Well, Haralambidis, we're not going to hit it off, are we?

—Why, Saint? What have I done?

—Shut your mouth! Now, I want to make myself clearly understood from the beginning, because where there's understanding, there can be no misunderstanding. There's still the odor of human breath in your mouths, and you're still untrained dead under my absolute power. You'll be judged by the conduct you show in this School, in this building, through which many classes of candidate angels have passed ahead of you. So I can say that I know you before I've even met you. I can already spot a few of you who think you're wise and know everything. You don't know anything, I tell you. You're deadheads, you're blind. We'll open up your eyes. I don't care how much studying you did in your lives. Up here you're empty skulls. I demand that you pay absolute attention to what your superiors tell you and that you show blind obedience. I will punish any insubordination mercilessly. And be sure to take care of the equipment that the service has entrusted you with, apply yourselves conscientiously to your studies and exercises. You nonentities, I want the 6th Platoon of the 42nd Class to rank first in the School, I want us to take the 4th Platoon (he gestured toward the building opposite, where his opponent, Saint Patapios, would at that moment be saying the same things to his own men). I was never the saint of a platoon that came out second. I'll make hash of you if you don't do better than they do, I'll beat you to a pulp like octopus. There'll be no favors. Only those who are sick—I mean those who are suffering—will be relieved of duty. Laziness and sloppiness will be punished by confinement. I'm fair, and I'll hand out K.P. to all of you equally. No one will have cause to feel left out. Your fat guts will shrink and your fat chests. There won't be any flesh left on you. So that later, when you become full-fledged angels and go to serve in the battalions of Heaven, you'll remember me— remember me fondly. Are there any questions?

—Atten-shun! yelled the Undersaint, and we all stiffened as Holy Saint Onisimos started down the steps imperially.

Then, leaving our things there for the time being, we moved on to the doctor, who examined us to make sure that no one of us was alive, and from the doctor they took us to the barber, who shaved our heads, and then they gave us our uniforms and halos, and finally they hustled us into the showers to remove our cemetery odor. And that's where the candidate angels of the senior class found us, that same afternoon, and finished the job of harassing us.

They came in exhausted from the exercises, thirsty, hungry, blackened by the dust from the black stones which grated their feet all day under the sun, on which they'd lain face down, on which they'd fallen during the short practice flights they'd attempted. They came in singing wildly, singing a rousing hymn that helped them to stay on their feet, tearing the closed-in silence of the camp with their savage voices, stopping with a sudden *crack*, their swords at their shoulders (we who were getting ready for the showers watched them fearfully through the window), and then, with the Overangel's order "Loosen the straps," they dashed into their barracks to remove their

173

heavy halos, their weighty bronze wings, and all the equipment that bound them tightly into the warring armor of an angel.

They fell upon us, after a while, like carrion birds. Our lingering human odor stung their nostrils. It seems they had long since forgotten how a human being smells, and though they kept coming closer to us, they couldn't sate themselves.

There was no place for us to hide. They smelled us out everywhere. Their eyes were wild, their questions dictatorial in tone, as though we ourselves were responsible for coming up here and depriving them of the joy of being the only inhabitants of our star. But we soon found out that underneath it all they didn't really hate us; on the contrary, they were immensely happy to have discovered new arrivals more recently dead than they were, so that they could ask for news from earth, so that they could find out what had been going on since they themselves had died.

Each one of them would look for an old acquaintance, a classmate, a fellow townsman, a fellow countryman, someone at least who would know someone else and so could give news of the world, even if indirectly. Their thirst smarted their eyes. But if it was difficult for them to recognize us the way we looked—our heads shorn, in new uniforms—it was quite impossible for us to figure them out at first. Their bony faces had already begun to take on an angel-like coloring. Their eyes had become bigger, their voices shriller. And not even from their walk could we recognize old acquaintances, since they hardly touched the ground with the soles of their feet.

They pursued us in the same way during the days that followed. Only the barracks itself was relatively quiet, and that's where my friend Yannis, Saint Akepsimas, found me on the third afternoon—the third afternoon away from you.

. . .

It was on the evening of that first day that they crammed us into the narrow dark assembly hall, where the school God was to come and talk to us. The Undergod stood at the door waiting nervously for His arrival. We heard "atten-shun" again, and the school band played our anthem. Then the hall suddenly filled with light. God and all His stars came in. His halo shone blindingly, so that we couldn't look Him in the eyes, and with heads bent, we listened to His sweet, lulling voice:

—As Commander-in-Chief of the School and the Star, I heartily welcome you to this honored Institution, where you have been called, like all those who came before you and all those who will come after you, to spend a portion of your posthumous life. Unfortunately, your apprenticeship will be short, considering the vast number of things you should be taught. But the needs of Heaven are so great that they do not permit us a greater expense of time for your training. The School employs the best personnel to be found among career Cherubim, Seraphim, Oversaints, Saints, and Martyrs. I assume that none of you is unaware of the fact that you are the chosen among the hosts of the dead, selected for the office of angel on the basis of your qualifications and the recommendation of the Archbishopric. Here you will learn how to fly. With the wings that will be given to you shortly, you will experience the joys of space, when—bodiless, immaterial, and fully equipped—you will float in the light. You will also become accomplished antagonists of the Devil, a former Angel who betrayed the ideals of Heaven and who therefore knows our system and our weaknesses. That is why you must become perfect: skillful, invulnerable, full of self-sacrifice, courage, faith, and purity. He is not mightier than we are but much

175

more cunning. Your work promises to be difficult; Space these days is under attack from all sides by the Devil, it is under siege to the point of asphyxiation; its very foundations are becoming satanically sapped, and it is on you, Reserve Angels of tomorrow, that the hopes of Heaven hang . . . Yet all of you will not graduate. As your Saints will have told you, we are not interested in who you were. But cases of disobedience, insubordination, and delving into the past will be very severely punished by me. Apart from this, I will be with you like a father and give you my love, because love is the law of life beyond the grave. And when you enter into the harsh struggle to annihilate Satan, you will remember the School as a place in your dreams. So, long live Death! Long live Heaven! Long live its Saints, Angels, and Martyrs! Long live Supergod!

We applauded at the end of His speech and shouted in unison: "Long live . . ." but apparently we dragged out the "live" too long, because the Undergod reprimanded us, saying that we were not at a political demonstration and should shout "long live" sharply, vigorously, with finality. Then he told us that applause is forbidden in Heaven. Darkness surrounded us once more, and, stiffened at attention, we breathed with difficulty.

Our exit was torture. We heard: "Get moving, get moving, I want to see some hustle around here." We pressed through the narrow doorway all together, twisted our elbows, sucked in our stomachs, racking our bodies, which still weigh upon us and which we will soon have to lose.

Faces become more distinguishable in the barracks as the days go by. They're uncovering themselves. Eyes look all around, find other eyes. A hand stretches, a voice asks: "D'you have any brass polish left?" "Go ahead and take it,

but give it back to me when you're through." "How can I
write 'I will not salute again without my halo' three thousand times?" "I think Holy Saint Onisimos overdoes it."
"Keep it low, I think that guy over there is the Undersaint's
boy." "Did you get a letter?" "No. You?" "Nothing yet."
"They say nobody has." "What on earth's happened to those
people down there, anyway?"

Faces come out from behind the mask of fear. Shy
voices are heard. Each one of us is trying to find someone
he can talk to.

Asimis has already become a sty in the eye for the
seniors. He's the one who refused to run from the very beginning, saying he'd twisted his ankle. He spends his free
time in the latrines smoking. A senior caught him there
once. Rumor has it the following occurred. The senior,
frustrated because he hadn't managed to find a fellow
townsman among the new arrivals, would catch unprotected dead after dark and torment them in out-of-the-way
corners. So they say he was lying in wait for Asimis, who
sat there surrounded by the crap of others, smoking bliss-
fully. "Your name?" the senior asked him. "Look, buddy,
shove off, will you, please?" Asimis replied. "How's that?"
the saint bellowed, furious. "You impertinent slob, you . . .
Look, d'you know where you are? Who you're talking to?
I'll show you, you meathead. Just start running . . ." "My
ankle hurts," Asimis said cynically. "Run, you bum, and
we'll see what's hurting . . . Who's your barracks chief?"
"Somebody." "Who?" The senior knew by now that he'd
bought himself trouble, unfamiliar trouble. "Saint somebody," Asimis repeated, nailing the senior with his big,
almond-shaped, diabolic eyes. "So you refuse to give me the
name of your holy platoon commander?" "You asked about
the barracks chief, Saint," Asimis said, without moving an
inch. "Shut your mouth, wise guy," the senior said, reaching

out to grab his arms. Though Asimis is thin as a skeleton—
nobody could possibly be afraid of him—he moved so
sharply, shoving the guy back so furiously, that the saint
stood there stunned. "Take your goddamn hands off me,"
Asimis said, and spat on the ground.

This scene was reported to us by somebody else who
was in the latrine at the time. According to this source, at
that moment another saint from the senior class happened
to pass by, and our friend the sadist called him over to help.
"Saint Boniface," the sadist said, trembling with confusion.
"Saint Boniface, this mug here, this fish-face refuses to
follow me and . . ." "What's that?" the other said, coming
closer. A victim like this one was precious to the seniors, a
delicacy to relieve their boredom. "He refused? The mug.
Leave him to me, Saint Basiliskos. I'll murder him. Your
name?" he asked Asimis, bringing his face right up against
his nose. Asimis wiped his mouth. "Your name?" the saint
bellowed, furious now. "Asimis Asimakis," he said indifferently. "Is that how they taught you to report? Jerk.
Idiot . . ." The second saint was getting violent. "He insulted
me," the first saint started yelling, "I tell you he insulted
me," and his shouting brought in other seniors who smelled
a party. Asimis was now surrounded by a team of maniacal
candidate angels who kept asking him in turn: "What's
your profession?" "Who's your barracks chief?" "What's
your excuse for living, you deadhead?"

Asimis apparently stared back at them disdainfully,
chin high, then moved off calmly, making his way through
the crowd of them as though they didn't exist; he came into
the barracks, where the rest of us were feverishly preparing
for the next day's inspection, and sat there casually without a word. After a while the Overangel burst in, looking
for Asimis Asimakis. He ordered him to pick up his locker
and shout "I am Atlas"; Asimis said he couldn't because

he didn't have that much strength. Then the Overangel ordered him to jump like a rabbit with his sword between his legs; Asimis refused on the grounds that he wasn't a rabbit. "You bum!" the Overangel shouted, out of his mind. "Come again, Saint Prick?" Asimis said very calmly.

The word he'd used went through the barracks like an electric shock. The Overangel raised his hands and said: "Tomorrow morning you'll be put on report because first of all you refused to obey an order from your superior, secondly, you insulted an officer holier than you by the use of disrespectful and indecent language, thirdly— Attention!" The order roared through the barracks. "All of you are going to pay for this man. You're to go outside and run round the building fifty times. Quickly, on the double . . ." He turned to Asimis. "You come with me."

The faces are becoming distinguishable. In the lower area of the barracks there's Manolis Farcos. Tall, with a giant's body, and dark-skinned, you'd consider him the perfect specimen of an angel. The Devil would merely have to look at him to be terrified. The funny thing is, though, that Manolis trembles with fear. He's scared of everything imaginable. In the beginning he was afraid he wouldn't be chosen to become an angel. When he was chosen and came to the school, he wanted to leave the very first night. "I can't take it, I can't," he'd babble in his sleep, then wake up to ask what he'd been babbling about. The second night he just couldn't stand it any longer. He got up secretly—without saying a word to anybody and taking care to avoid notice by the guards—dragged himself to the edge of the camp, and tried to escape by jumping over the barbed-wire enclosure. His cry trailed through space. And they brought him back in the morning. He'd landed on a cloud, and a

179

guard spotted him at daybreak. A winged patrol went over and picked him up. He was with us again, more frightened than before, having now realized the futility of escape; and through his unsuccessful attempt, we too came to see clearly how complete our isolation actually was.

The faces are shedding their masks. There's Melanidis, constantly washing, always worried because he's slowly losing his paunch. And Paulakis, who never goes to the latrines alone, who keeps track of everything he gives out, like a housewife, and who waits impatiently for the Saturday bath; he has a large mouth, eyes like wine, and at night he asks those next to him to tuck him in. And Telis, who's always silent, circulating among the various cliques in the barracks to pick up gripes that he can report to our Undersaint. We've caught on to him now; the moment he gets close, all talk stops or else the conversation turns to wings. And Planis, who was silent at first but whose tongue has now loosened up so that nobody can stop its wagging. And there's Karakostas, who snores every night and, when there's a full moon, babbles deliriously; he sleeps with his eyes open, and their whiteness is nightmarish in the darkness, like that of a corpse whose eyes haven't been shut. And Myrrodatos, who can't stop masturbating, and night after night . . . Many have got up enough courage to bring out their secret relics: a picture of their girl, or of their fiancée, or of their mother, or even of themselves, so they can remember who they were.

The first clouds are vanishing. At the same time, the barracks is becoming a microcosm, with the bunks too close together, the aisle too narrow for forty candidate angels. There isn't room enough for all of us.

. . .

Yannis comes over in the afternoons and takes me away from the asphyxiating barracks. Crossing the treacherous ground of our camp together, we sometimes run into seniors—seniors who haven't yet sated themselves with the blood of recruits—lying in wait behind rocks. Yannis won't let them bother me; he's my patron saint. We've found a unique hiding place on the west side of the camp, there where they have the horizontal and vertical bars set up, the trenches, and the ropes. We slip into the pit under "Tarzan," a long rope hanging free, knotted at the end so the trainees can cling to it. The rope's used for one of the preliminary exercises that's supposed to strengthen the shoulder blades, where the wings will be added later. We sit on the straw and other dirt at the bottom of that pit, where no one can see us, and we talk. Only our time together is short, so Yannis is always in a great hurry to find out, to have me tell him once again, all that's happened since he died—the ways in which our city's changed, and most of all, news of the girl he loved.

—So she was alone, right? Completely alone? he asks me every time.

—Yes. And she walked with her head lowered.

—Where did you see her?

—On the street in front of the university.

He was asking this question for the thousandth time and I was answering it for the thousandth time, as enthusiastically as I did the first. Then he realized that I didn't feel like going over all I'd told him, and we changed the subject.

—So they've really removed all the streetcars from our city?

—Yes, before I departed, the new buses had taken over.

—The streetcars had their charm, though, Yannis said,

lost in memories. Remember when we were boys how we hopped free rides on the coupling bar at the back, and the conductor would come at us and—

—They're tearing down the old houses, and all you see are enormous apartment buildings sprouting in their place. You wouldn't recognize the city if you were to turn up there again.

—I'll turn up there again, I'm sure I will.

—When? How?

—I'll turn up there again. I've learned from a reliable source—but please keep this between us—I've learned from someone in the administration that after they officially give us the rank of angel and before they announce our transfers to the battalions, we've got a whole day in which we're free to stay here without belonging to the school's forces, without having to muster or anything else. That's when I've decided to take off, fly down to earth, land in our city, on her street—see her even if she can't see me, talk to her even if she can't hear me, cool her with my wings even if she thinks it's just a breeze or air from the fan. Yes, I've got it all planned. I'll do it no matter what happens. Nothing's going to stop me. My passion to caress her is so intense that I won't even care if my presence brings her no joy. I've been very uneasy recently, Angelos. I mean, since you arrived. I thought I'd forgotten her completely, that I'd succeeded in getting her out of my system. You proved to me that it wasn't so. From the moment I saw you and you talked to me about her, I changed. I'm now as careful about my wings as I am about my own eyes. To tell the truth, I never cared about achieving a perfect record in the service. From the very beginning I didn't want to become an officer. And I hated the wings they gave us. God, how they disgusted me! They were the means for separating me even farther from the earth. And I made fun of the others who were so proud of them. But now . . . anyway, you, Angelos, you can understand me. We both had girls, they even looked alike, and we made love to them in the same parks, on the same streets. Though the Holy Saints tell us mockingly: "Your girls have forgotten you, they must have picked up new prospects"; and though love for most of those here has turned to hate, I refuse to give in. Before my final exile to the frontiers of Heaven, I would like, even if only for a day, to live near her, to breathe the air she breathes, to become familiar once again with her walk . . . And so, my friend, the deeper my secret hope becomes, the more secure I feel in my silence and the less I feel the need to complain, to express my indignation. The knowledge I gain is like that left us by dreams. Our tongues are bound by the inexplicable things we dreamed, and though we can't talk about them, we recognize that they have made us wiser, more knowing. Here at the school everything is forbidden territory: what we once were, what we experienced, our beliefs, even our sorrows. But the one thing they can't take away from us is the right to dream. And even though we become more transparent every day, so they can study us better, they still can't interfere with our dreams . . . Now that I've found a function for my wings, I take care of them, I shine them, I look after them like— But what have you got to say, you who've covered the distance from our earth more recently than I have? D'you think I can make it there and back in one day, without any stops, or will I get lost somewhere in the middle?

—You'll make it, I told him, since you want to so badly.

—Good, Yannis said, his eyes burning.

—But what's the point of making it? So you'll see her. But she won't see you. You'll— And, besides, by then maybe . . . What I mean to say is, we're dead, and the Second Coming is a long ways off. Everything's over as far as those below are concerned. It's here, in the indifference of space, in this void, that we have to find the solution, find our liberation. Going back is always a weak move, because it doesn't lead anywhere. I think the only thing you'll accomplish will be to hurt yourself uselessly, while—

—Tell me, he suddenly cried out, and his voice resounded in that empty grave. Did you see her with somebody else, by any chance, and you don't want to tell me?

—No, no . . .

—I want to know the truth. Do you hear me? The truth. And he caught me by the throat, his face even more ferocious than when he was wearing his mask.

It was my good luck that someone came up at that moment and, grabbing hold of the "Tarzan" rope, started swinging from one rim of the pit to the other. We could see him hanging over the void without his seeing us, moving like a pendulum over our insoluble problems, over our hearts, a distorted human form against the dome of Heaven, which had now begun to darken. We remained silent until he left. For some time after that the thick rope swung back and forth like a bell clapper that has nothing to ring, like our counter-balanced hearts which also couldn't find their place in Heaven and rest peacefully.

Yannis was probably deeply hurt by what I had to say, but I felt the need to say it because for some time I had decided that returning was no solution, that no one can live forever by ignoring or avoiding his fate, which rests in the truism that nothing ends without containing in its end the beginning of something else. And I've felt this beginning ever since I died: a light behind the mountain in whose dark ravines we have become lost. Behind the mountain, on top of the mountain, there must be a light that will liberate us. The streets and the trees, the parks and their benches, the buses, the rooms and the elevators, are all obstacles because they fracture light, divide it, fragment it, I felt dimly that above these objects, beyond the world of surfaces, deep beneath the shell of what is seen, the light must be indivisible, and I was heading toward that light. What would be the meaning of a return to matter? What meaning could it have, since matter presupposed, even caused, death? When you die you have to find a new route rather than return to the narrow confines of a city that knifed you, of a tree that betrayed you, of a neon sign that pierced you like an arrow. Because I knew I could never be invulnerable. Yannis' scheme of returning invisible disgusted me, terrified me. I couldn't express my feeling to him then because I myself wasn't clearly conscious of it. So he probably misunderstood me and got angry.

But this wasn't the only reason he stopped coming in the afternoons. Basically we had nothing to say to each other. For Yannis, Heaven was just routine. For me, it was all a beginning which forecast my liberation from the burden of my flesh. Besides, we didn't agree on anything that had to do with our city and our love life. His nostalgia, a result of his having died without any awareness of a final separation, of a final first death, made him romantic. He wanted to go back. For me, the city was a monster which became more distorted day by day, changing in relation to the bay, so that, from the horseshoe it once was, it now seemed a noose tightening around the neck of the sea . . . So he stopped coming, and I had more time in the afternoons to devote to myself and to search the crowded barracks for a friend, someone who might at least become a friend.

· · ·

Asimis is still paying for the obscenity he let loose at the Overangel. The seniors have written his name inside their halos, and they come in teams, in gangs, and take him out. The first thing they say to him is: "So you're the fish-face who had the nerve to call the Overangel a prick?" And from the way they say the word, you realize how much they've missed it, how much they delight in repeating it, with the excuse that somebody else said it. Asimis follows them out with obvious boredom. We don't know what they do to him once he's outside. And he himself doesn't tell us anything. He replies to whatever we say to him by repeating: "That's one way of looking at it." This phrase has become the slogan of the barracks.

Among all the rest, who increasingly reveal an annoying conventionality the more they emerge from their shells of fear, who talk about the exercise, the credits, the star, as though identifying with these absolutely, who've become parts in the immense machine we serve without having gained any perspective about their deaths, without having done anything to shed new light on our condition, anything to explain our difficult position in Heaven, and who execute every order without a murmur, trying to court the favor of their superiors—among these, Asimis strikes me as the one man I might have something to say to, the one man who might have something to say to me, if only he wouldn't remain so distant, if only he too showed that he needed a friend.

It happened one evening when they were putting on a ridiculous program of entertainment in the assembly hall. Next to me in the darkness sat Asimis, hunched over, smoking despite the rule against it. At one point I heard him suddenly say to me:

—Let's go outside and save ourselves from this disgusting nonsense.

Crouching, we passed unnoticed between the rows of benches.

—Got any cigarettes? he asked the moment we found ourselves outside in the night.

—Half a pack, I said. That'll be enough . . .

We moved into a hollow in the ground, right under the southern star. In the distance, the silent buildings were lit up like castles.

—We're in the same company, I said hesitantly, in the same platoon. I watch the way you behave, how you act during exercises and in the barracks, and to tell the truth, I don't understand you . . .

—I'd be surprised if you did, he said, lighting a new cigarette off the butt of the old one.

—Not because your attitude strikes me as strange—we all share the same feelings to some extent—but because I wonder where it's going to get you.

—To the end, he said curtly.

—Which is what? That of going back where you started from?

—Not at all, he said calmly, as though used to the kind of frontal attack I had adopted to feel him out. The end I have in mind will prove that we all live and grow and die yet still find ourselves in the Trap.

—What trap? Satan's trap?

—No. *The* Trap. It's a theory of mine that would take too long to explain.

—Go ahead. We're in no hurry.

—Well, let me try to simplify it, Asimis said, taking a long drag. Do you play chess?

—I did once.

—Then you know that all the pieces, from the pawns

to the kings, have a restricted territory in which to move.
They can't take a single step outside their little pattern of
squares. And when the game's over, the opposing black and
white pieces end up in the same box. Follow me?

—I think so.

—Anyway, I always kept off the board, refused to play
their game.

—You're lucky, I said. Have you ever been in love?

—Are you kidding? I've never loved anybody in my
life.

—Well, at least you must have had a girl down there,
so you know . . .

—Sure I had a girl. All she did was talk about marriage. As a matter of fact, I've kept a souvenir of our relationship.

He brought out his wallet. I expected a photograph.
What he produced looked like a segment of dried snake skin.

—The rubber from our last act of love, he said, lighting a match so that I could see it clearly.

—We're cut from different cloth, you and I, I said. You
don't seem to believe in anything, while I believe in—

—You've got me completely wrong, Asimis said. I believe in a great deal. I always have. While on earth, I once
belonged to the secret Party of Satan. I served him with all
my energy. You see, I believed that since God didn't exist, I
had to . . . Anyway, I was a fanatic at the time. Then I
discovered the Trap, so I gave up the Party. The other members still think I'm a turncoat, an apostate, just as these people do up here. And I can't play their game, either. One
way or the other, we're all caught in the Trap, so the
only thing left is to sacrifice yourself for the sake of your
ideas.

—That's very Christian, I said. At heart you're really
just a traditional—

188

—Not at all, because Christ's sacrifice meant something. At least for others. Mine would mean nothing. To sacrifice yourself for the idea of the Trap is still another facet of the Trap, only on a higher level. Supergod and Satan, the Angels and the Hosts of Hell, Earth and Heaven are merely opposite facets of one and the same thing. And I—

—Kill it. Someone's coming.

We watched a shadow cross toward our hide-out, then move on to the latrines. Asimis lowered his voice.

—The point is, he said, in holding contrary extremes, like the chess box, I'm going to get in trouble with the authorities here. I know that. Here you have to belong to one thing, and I can't belong. I can't be like Saul who turned into Paul and thought he'd accomplished something, when the only thing he'd accomplished was to move to the other side of the Trap. And all the while they'll think I'm against Supergod, so they'll punish me, condemn me finally. And when they do, it will serve no other purpose but to convince me that I've reached the peak of the Trap, which is to let yourself be condemned knowing that you're still in the Trap and that your sacrifice has achieved nothing.

—Well, as far as I'm concerned, I said, you've got to believe in—

—As far as you're concerned, Asimis said, still heated, you've never inhaled hashish, you've never been disillusioned by ideas, you've never . . . God, how attractive Satan once seemed! His ambition to conquer the world, to bring down the monarchy of the Church, to divide the income of fat archbishopric priests among the poor. And then I had to find that Satan has his own fat archbishopric priests, as well as . . . The point is, one way or another, both facets belong to the Trap.

—That isn't the point at all, I said. The point is that in life one finds a mathematical progression toward death, whereas in death one finds an opposite progression toward life.

—Progression toward what life? Asimis said coolly.

—Toward the absolute, unconditional acceptance of light. Which will occur only when I lose my body, when I can soar off to liberate myself in Space. So I just wait patiently for the wings they're going to give us.

—That's one way of looking at it, he said dryly.

—You're being sarcastic, I said.

—No. It's just that I never paid any attention to my body. It was always merely a skeleton that followed the dictates of my brain. Anyway, the light you say you believe in may turn out to be as disturbing as too much darkness. As far as I'm concerned, there's no way out of the Trap, and that includes your light. The only thing left to us is the joy of not betraying our ideas while knowing that this stand will be of no use whatsoever, that our . . .

He went on, but I turned away to gaze up at the stars that covered us; they looked to me like a net. Asimis' voice was heavy, off-beat, mysterious, seeming to come from lower depths. His mixed character, his contradictory traits, appealed to me at first, but now I began to feel completely detached from him. He was indifferent to what I wanted. What he sought was foreign to me. The burden in my case was this weighty body that I carried with me and that contained a heart. For him the burden was his brain, contained in a net of encephalic nerves that became his trap. My trap, if I wanted to find one, would be the sick heart, the betraying memory. Asimis was in a sphere where ideas took on the texture of flesh—so real were they for him—around a skeleton of unbreakable bone. My flesh always became an idea, and my skeleton an abstraction of the light.

. . .

190

During the following days Asimis and I exchanged a few words now and then during the smoking breaks between exercises, but we always refrained from saying anything relating to that discussion of ours. Yet even slight communication between us didn't fail to come to the attention of Holy Saint Onisimos, who called me in to his office one day to talk to me "privately."

Close up, Saint Onisimos looked quite different from the picture of himself that he offered each morning during the company's muster, standing at the top of the steps intimidating us with threats, bombarding us with curses, distributing punishment lavishly; close up, his ferocity assumed a face, he seemed more human, except that his eyes were just two blank holes.

I had knocked on his door, heard his hoarse voice say "Come in," opened the door with shaking knees, started into my "I have the honor . . ." only to hear him cut me off: "All right, all right, at ease," and now I stood in front of him, rigid, gazing at an icon of the Crucifixion on the opposite wall. He started out by talking about his village, and just as I was beginning to feel somewhat relaxed, he suddenly asked me:

—What's your personal opinion of Asimakis?

—You mean Asimis Asimakis? I said, stalling for time.

—Yes, that pock-marked character, he said, shifting in his chair.

—He's smart, I said.

—Cocky, you mean.

—Why do you ask *me*? I said.

—Because all of us have to help the school in its difficult task. Of course the administration will reward you accordingly.

That made me catch on fast: he'd called me in to worm

information out of me, to make me disclose details, and
hence all that phony sweetness at first.

—I've heard he advertises the fact that he doesn't believe in the existence of Supergod, the Holy Saint said. Is
that true?

—No, I said.

—No he doesn't believe or no he doesn't advertise it?
he asked me, frowning.

—Both, I said.

My hate for the Holy Saint was beginning to glow.

—Do you happen to know that in real life he was an
existentialist?

—It's the first I've heard of it.

—And that he even belonged to the following of one
Simon the Existentialist?

—I don't know a thing.

—So, do you think he's the right kind to serve as an
angel?

—You're the one who knows the answer to that, I said.

—I'm asking for your opinion, he said, angered. What
I think, you'll know soon enough. I want your opinion.

—Then he's the right kind.

—In other words, you agree with him? You also believe in his theories about space?

—What theories are those? I asked.

—Come on, Angelidis, you're his closest friend. Are
you afraid to tell the truth? We don't plan to hang him. I'm
asking you for his own good. He himself told me—he was
in here just before you—he himself told me that you're the
only one he respects in the platoon. That's why I called you
in. To see how much you respect him.

—My respect, Holy Saint, has nothing to do with the
service, I said.

—Very well, then, he thundered, and jotted something

down on the pad in front of him. You think he's all right. You think he's qualified to become an angel. Sign this, and he handed me a sheet of paper.

—What is it? I asked, picking up the pencil.

—A statement that during the trial you'll act as a witness for the defense.

—The trial?

—We're sending him up before the Heavenly Court Martial. You can expound your views more fully there.

I signed.

—But you won't get very far, he said sarcastically. Here's the evidence of his guilt, and he flung a heavy folder on the bare desk. His papers, he said.

—From the archbishopric?

—No. From right here. We found them in his desk. Instead of studying, he's been writing this nonsense.

And leafing through them nervously, he read me a few random sentences: "My joy, you've taken wings . . . Heaven and our crap are one and the same . . . To be a fanatic is to be a coward. To be un-fanatic is to be courageous. When I piss and shit on our star . . .

—And a lot more of the same, all in an incomprehensible language, the holy saint added.

I was flabbergasted by the news. The same thing might happen some day to my own papers . . .

—I don't want any new demons in my company, said Holy Saint Onisimos, standing. I want my company to come out first, and I'm not going to permit Asimakis to bring it dishonor.

—And when is the trial? I asked.

—You'll be notified in due time. Dismissed.

As I was about to open the door:

—And four days on restriction for failing to salute before leaving, he bellowed as though blaspheming.

. . .

The news that Asimis would be sent up before the Heavenly Court Martial spread quickly. Most people now avoided getting close to him, as though afraid they might become contaminated. The recruit who shared his double bunk asked to be moved. Our kind Undersaint no longer stopped in front of him during inspection. Even the seniors no longer went after him; on the contrary, some even tried to give him advice. "Don't be stupid," I heard one of them say to Asimis. "Maneuver, use influence, sign a confession of repentance. Otherwise they'll crush you like a worm." Rumor has it that his trial is set for the feast day of The Three Suns. Amidst all this, Asimis remains the still eye at the heart of a hurricane.

THE FIRST NIGHT ON GUARD DUTY

Junior Syllabus

1. *Science of Forgetfulness*
2. *Hierarchy of Thrones and Powers*
3. *Structure of Angel Platoons*
4. *Combat Strategy against Satan*
5. *The Nature of Hell*
6. *Maintenance of Sacred Equipment*
7. *Spaceology*

The cosmic space that surrounds us absorbs me more and more. Though spaceology is not one of our major subjects, I find that I spend all my time on it, now that studying has become my one preoccupation. And I'm always discovering new facts that tell me something about you. Did you know that your earth is rained upon daily by an invisible dust made up of meteorite particles, and that the air you breathe contains, among its other properties, this silver dust of infinity?

I departed from your earth, I broke the inexorable law of your gravity, I conquered the attraction of your volcanic core that remained and always will remain unexplored, I escaped the languor that every contact with your body brought me, only to reach this star which has its own atmosphere, its own gravity—in other words, only to fall once again into something I want to escape. So I don't study space just out of curiosity regarding the composition of air or the dangerous relation of comets and planets to the motionless constellations which number myriads; I study because I'm searching to find the solution once and for all, the final solution, that which doesn't involve separation, or the first death, or you and me, but something else, something beyond us and our weaknesses. You know about the light, as I do. But it must be something else again to feel it rolling through your veins, flooding you, to be alone there bathing in its cataract, in its timeless span, a speck of dust in its ray, which sets out from infinity to end in infinity.

I say: I fled, I escaped. But life here begins to get complicated again; I begin to have ties again, and it's this that I most fear. I shudder for every lost moment away from you. That's why I don't see Asimis often, though he's always eager to see me, that's why I've cut myself off from all the others. What meaning would the other life, the new aspiration, have without the knowledge that experience is useless? Every tie has its bindings, so I've turned in on myself like a hedgehog, projecting black quills that I hope will someday become rays emanating from my luminous core. Through this identification with light, and wearing the wings they will soon give us, I hope to conquer our star's gravity and find your more integral self, your purer self, there—find you with all the hair you cut off one day, find your voice in the immaculate silence . . .

How can I explain to the others here that I've passed beyond the clouds, that I'm above the lighting and the rain, that all the battles have been won and lost, that the only thing left is for me to approach not the quiet sun but the spotless light, which is without beginning and end, indivisible, inchoate, ubiquitous, self-created. To become a participant in the light . . .

Space doesn't interest me for what they tell us it is: a battlefield against Satan. If I enjoy studying it, I do so because I find our lives in it, your life and my own, though in their final abstract form, which is the only state I'm interested in conquering, that or nothing.

I know, you'll say that I'm asking for too much, more than even this third heaven can give me, and that my body

—the root of my disunion, that which first bothered me like a feeling of remorse, of guilt—my body is a thing I'll always carry with me. Maybe. But I can still hope. Besides, without this hope even death would be impossible.

Our star doesn't have seasons. The only thing that changes in time is its relation to other stars, and this in infinity saves its few inhabitants from the monotony of repetition. We're here during only a small segment of its elliptical course; we leave long before it completes its cycle, a process that takes years. Night and day change rapidly. And our contact with the moon is unique: we don't depend on its light alone to brighten our nights, and its shapes are various. At times we see it as a triangle, at times as a hexagon. A full moon means that we can see all thirteen of its angles.

The end of training for each class begins when the seniors turn over guard duty to the juniors. In keeping with School custom, there is always a mock funeral for old Demos, who, as the folk song has it, was "a mountain klepht for forty years and never had his fill of sleep," and that same night, after the funeral, the juniors take over.

I was sound asleep, dreaming of Tito, when I suddenly heard: "Wake up . . . Wake up . . . Guard duty." It was the barracks sentry shaking me by the leg. His voice got confused at first with the voices of the police guarding the intersections in my dream, with the sound of armored tanks passing by—their lugs scarring the freshly laid asphalt—with the backfire from the police motorcycles scurrying up and down the streets trying to assure Tito's safe passage through our city. And you on the sidewalk opposite me, the two of us separated by the river of steel flowing between us . . . The agony of possibly not seeing you that day, since time was passing and Tito had yet to appear, was still with me when I woke. I got up shivering, pulled on my heavy

tunic, picked up my sword, and went out. The guardhouse
was by the supply depot, on the edge of the school grounds,
near the boundary between our star and infinity. Not a bad
place to be on guard duty, I thought as I walked with the relief Underangel through the biting cold. The man I was
relieving gave me the password and the code numbers. The
guardhouse was warm inside. The duties of the guard and
the schedule of rounds were tacked on one of its walls.

The first night I was on guard duty something strange
happened to the moon: it started hiding inside its own body.
A part of it covered itself in darkness. The remainder started
turning red. In the absolute silence of that night, near the
barbed wire that surrounded the supply depot, with the fear
of darkness all around me—every shadow was suspicious,
every noise—trying the whole time to keep the password
and the code numbers straight in my mind. I saw my whole
life unfold before me, come at me in enormous waves, en-
gulfing me, and I couldn't explain it all: one part always
remained dark, like that covered by the moon's eclipse; another part always remained clear, open to new horizons;
and in the fever that had caught me up, in the whirl of
multiple moons, I saw why the moon had bled without anyone's having wounded it, and then I understood love for the
first time.

Lord, don't ask me for an explanation.

This is how it started: as soon as the other guard left,
I lit a cigarette and reread the instructions on the wall:
"A guard is responsible for the area he takes over . . . He

does not smoke, does not sing, does not make noise of any kind . . . He does not lean on his sword . . . He does not stray from his territory . . . He does not leave his post . . . He does not . . . In case of fire he shouts: 'Fire! Fire!' A guard who is insulted arrests the insultor."

I could remember the instructions more or less. What I kept forgetting were the password and the code numbers. The man I relieved had given them to me on a small piece of paper, which I had trouble retrieving from my deep pockets because my fingers were frozen stiff. I decided to learn it all by heart. The password was Holy Saint Zoe. My code number was 11, that of the patrol leader 32. And I kept repeating: Holy Saint Zoe, 11, 32. Holy Saint . . .

I hadn't quite woken up yet. I kept shivering; and I spent my time watching the other stars moving through infinity without ever colliding, leaving behind multicolored wakes of smoke which surrounded me like fog—and which made me afraid I might not see the patrol if it happened to pass by. I tried to catch a small purple meteorite that sailed by very close, but it slipped through my hands, leaving soot from its wake on my fingers. I became so distracted that it wasn't until our orbit took us out of the starlit harbor into infinity that I realized the password was your name. And then on the prow of our star, before the sea of night, your image came to me as you yourself once came, more alive now than in my dream, holding a bag of popcorn and sunflower seeds.

I want you to understand me. Until that moment, until that apocalyptic night, I had never been alone. Not that I had forgotten you or that I had become so involved in the problems of others. But I had never felt the security of isolation. And the barracks, even when it was empty, always held the odor of the others. When we slept, somebody would always snore, somebody else would talk in his sleep. And it was as though you were waiting for the moment when all the remorse, the worries and torments, the asphyxiation and panic, the sour taste of separation would have drained out of me so that you could flow into my empty cistern as clear young water and strangely fill me to the brim. You drowned me, spilling over everywhere. Your light flooded me—your love. I felt a sense of fulfillment such as I hadn't yet experienced since the time I died.

That's why I now love guard duty. And while the others gripe when the Overangel sends them out on watch at a time that cuts their sleep in two, I, on the contrary, prefer that part of the night which neither begins with sundown nor ends with daybreak. And I can hardly wait for my turn to come around again.

So, with a starlit mind, I saw my whole life before me, and I began to pick up the first strands, the ones I thought had got lost in the darkness, events that one forgets because they're painful, and then the net started unraveling of its own accord. I was startled by the many loose ends I found, by the many tangles. But I always managed to follow the right thread, with you as my only guide:

I

FRAGMENTS *from the period before I met you. Recollections of the enslaved heart. Learning in hidden schools. The fear of the Turkish Gennesars. Amiable Ali Pasha. Visions of a quick liberation. The Friends of the Revolution. Palaion Patron Germanos Street. The first banner: our youth. Blood and assassinations belong elsewhere. A candle that secretly burns in the night of our Occupation, giving joy to my body. A thick pencil that records my guilt at not going off to fight in the mountains but remaining instead in the city, my head slavishly bowed to the conqueror, making compromises to eke out my survival. Then the borrowed clothes. My alleged existence. My altercations with the others. Who are you? I'm alone. The Friends of the Revolution disbanded. The dreams collapse: the revolution that can never come from outside, the independence that must remain beyond the reach of all born slaves like myself. And then you. You. After so many battles, so much useless searching, so many lost days, you coming to me with laurel in your hand, speechless like the sky.*

"Light struck and the young man knew himself."

I turn, I return, to the first period, to our first flight, when, having nowhere else to hide, we found that boat on the shore by the undiscovered sea, on the dark beach where the seaweed smelled of rotten egg, just beyond the seaside cafés, and there your hands searched my face and you said "So much mist, Angelos, so cold," and as gently as possible you dissolved the mist from my eyes with your fingers, bared my face of the fog adhering to it like gauze to a wound, and you told me that I had legs for walking, arms for embracing the horizons, and a mouth for kissing the dawn, until a fisherman came down and ordered us out from under his boat, and then, with matching steps, we started walking through unknown neighborhoods, and you said "Our two bodies are joined in paradise, my limbs have already taken on the music of yours," and you were full of fire, because I knew you before I met you, and both of us had been locked up in the prison of that city, and this was the first night we

*had fled our separate cells, so that it didn't matter where we
went, since it was enough—isn't that right?—that we were
walking together on this level stretch which didn't go anywhere but whose horizon opened broadly, so that it seemed
we were closer to the stars, the night immense, and then
at the brook: "I'll be too heavy, you won't be able to lift me,"
you said, and I told you that you were like a feather in my
arms and that it was your absence that had been heavy so
far, and finding ourselves on the main road again, I said:
"Are you tired? Shall we take the bus?" "No, no," you answered. "Only, Angelos, I'm afraid I'll just be an episode in
your life," and I laughed, tried to kiss you, and you pushed
me away gently, saying: "Why do you think it's so funny?"
and then we walked on in silence, exploring the darkness
that the Public Power Company refused to illuminate more
thoroughly, until you stopped short: "God, here we are already," as we reached your neighborhood, and I realized
that somewhere in that vicinity we would have to separate,
yes, now, and then, limbs suddenly weak in a corner formed
by the meeting of two walls, your face upturned, you suddenly surrendered to me as though hypnotized, and your
lips had the taste of bitter almonds and banana, your breasts
cushioned my mooring at your quay, and in your ear I
found the small labyrinth that led me to your swooning,
how long, how many hours until you finally said: "I'm late,
I'm late, I'll get in trouble at home," "Just a little longer,
wait, I want to tell you something, it's important," "Angelos,
this isn't going to happen again," and you left, angry at
yourself, you left me standing there dumfounded, in that
corner full of enormous shadows, and I waited until you
disappeared before walking down to the bus stop, my feet
dragging as though they were paralyzed, your six parting
words heavy like the foreboding of a storm, and I with the
sour taste of ending before we had even begun, born as we
are with the sperm of death within us, and all night long I*

thought about the unsailed sea, the boat, the seaweed that smelled of rotten egg, the level stretch that went nowhere, and of all your words the only thing that remained was your last sentence, more mysterious than an oracle, heavier than the coming of a storm, wrapped in the taste of bitter almonds and banana: "this isn't going to happen again."

I turn, I return, to that first period, even before you let your hair fall free, when your house was right at the crossroad, there where the streetcar line separated from the bus line, where I used to wait for you to come out, needing to see you, wanting desperately to find you—October nearly over and the threat of winter close—waiting for hours and hours surrounded by the death rattle from the streetcars as they dragged themselves cursing along their tracks and the fumes exhaled by the buses, a pipe from Mt. Athos between my teeth, sometimes pretending to read a newspaper at the stand, sometimes pretending to wait for the bus, unable to see you, not even at your window, since I didn't know your house well enough to distinguish it in the confusion of others around it, just as I didn't know you very well at that point —consider how much time we needed to really know each other, how many centuries—and my agony grew until you were more necessary to me than crutches were to the lame beggar on the street corner across the way, since the flight of our one evening together hadn't allowed me time to tell you anything when I wanted to tell you so much, and waiting there, I devised many ways of entering your sanctuary before I settled on using the mailman . . .

—You shouldn't have written me. My father got hold of your letter. He tore it up. The sketch you enclosed was torn along with it. I kept the pieces, though, and I'll put

them together. My parents have been suspicious since the day before yesterday, when I came in late. The mud on my shoes betrayed me.

—But where can I see you? You've disappeared completely. I tell you I couldn't wait any longer. Where will we meet? I want to see you every day.

—At the university. Now that classes are about to start—

—Yes, but until they do start?

—I'll let you know.

—When? I want you to tell me now . . . Let's get out of the rain, under the tree over there. Why are you so quiet? What are you trying to hide from me? And why did you tell me "this isn't going to happen again" as you were leaving last time? Is there someone else? Is there—

—Yes. It's too bad, Angelos, too bad for both of us.

"I drink canned juice and dream of fruit"—that's how it began, the poem you gave me supposedly to explain your disappearance when I finally found you two weeks later on the third floor of the university building, in the corridor, standing in line outside the secretary's office waiting to pay your registration fee, the rays of your hair setting you apart, and I tried breaking through to you with sharp elbows and knees, like a bird chasing its mate through thick foliage— sharp twigs constantly wounding him—as when you grope through a disordered room for a mirror: "don't shove, mister, just wait your turn"; but I had to reach you—I couldn't do otherwise—reach your face, my mirror, after waiting for you in the same corridor so many afternoons, waiting for you to come out of some class, after so many wasted hours, and now, now "Angelos . . ." just that look of surprise in your eyes was worth having to split the unbreakable wall of

humanity which separated us, and then: "yes, let's go," you said, tightly clutching the registration booklet, "let's go down to the park"; but the corridor was long, groups of students everywhere, some near the window tearing a textbook to shreds to share it, others besieging the lame usher, others trailing an instructor who happened to pass like a comet through our dense cloud, others thrust up against the wall as in front of an execution squad while they waited to take an examination. "The corridor is about to give way under the weight of all this humanity," I said, "I'm so glad, I'm so glad I found you, Angelos," "You mean that I found you, Zoe," and you squeezed my hand as though in conspiracy, and I held it tight so we wouldn't lose each other in that voracious crowd; an army man with an arrogant look suddenly entered the secretary's office and the wrath of those waiting in line rose behind him, booklets fluttered in protest; some mustached students of former years hovered nervously in a corner waiting to seek readmission; the crowd drew back abruptly to make room for the professor, sir, who was on his way to the toilet; and oh, never, never had that corridor seemed more suffocating, more infinite, and when the staircase finally appeared out of the mist like a liberation, you opened your pocketbook and gave me the poem, which began, I remember: "I drink canned juice . . ."

But "I remember" is not a phrase to be remembered. What should be remembered is a staircase transformed into a deep-sea dive, a herd of people changed into fish that feed on others and themselves in rocky caves, a park becoming the floor of the sea, its benches shelves where oysters bed. "I remember" isn't a phrase to be remembered, and especially by me, who loved you through memory, through nostalgia for the light I could see before I was born, who wanted you always beside me as a confirmation in that corridor about to give way under the weight of humanity.

*Now, having escaped the fumes from the chemistry lab
in the basement, our backs turned to that crematorium of a
university building, we could see the dome of the tree in
front of us thickening with restless birds settling to spend
the night in its branches, and beyond, reflected from the
windows of houses across the street, the last light of day,
weak and melancholy, as though it had filtered through all
human sorrows.*

—Angelos, please forgive me, but I just couldn't see you.

—And you couldn't even call me?

—Angelos, you've got to understand me. I . . .

—So what have you been up to all this time, Zoe?

*—Nothing. I made two new dresses. One's beige, the
other dark brown, like the color of earth after a rain, with
a small white collar. I'll wear it next time I see you.*

—Next month, you mean.

*—No, tomorrow. I'll come back to register. Then the
lectures will start. We'll see each other every day.*

*—Was it your "someone else" who kept you away from
me?*

*—No, he's out of town. And he'll be gone for a long
time. It was just me. I'm afraid of you. Now give me a
cigarette.*

—These matches. God.

*—You know, I'd never smoked before. You're the one
who taught me. And I've been smoking secretly all this
time. It was a way of remembering you. Now you tell me—
I'm tired of talking about myself—tell me what you've been
doing.*

*—I've been washing my hands with jasmine, I've made
roses stoke a fire under the world, I look at fall as though
it were spring. Finally, I've been completely alone.*

*The intimate night covered us, and the birds in the
dome of the tree settled into silence. Opposite us, hidden in
the bushes, another young couple started an argument: "It's*

as I say, girl. That's all a lot of horseshit. You're just shame-
less." "All you know is how to sell a fast line. Monster. You
disgust me." "Just wait a minute, bitch. Who's the one who
runs around with any pair of pants that comes along?" "You
bastard. You bum. I swear I'll call the police." And then,
sharing a sense of how distant we were from their language,
from their very different world, we felt suddenly close, and
I bent down and kissed you, in that soft mid-November
evening, and you said to me:

—I always think of you walking with your head bent,
by the sea, which is somehow gray, your pipe hanging from
your mouth.

—And you taught me how to kiss, how to love a street,
a bus stop, how to die one afternoon.

The guard startled us with his flashlight: "We're closing up soon. It's almost nine.

—I'm late. Terribly late. I've got to run or there'll be
trouble at home again. I'd better—

—Wait. I'll let you go at the first lamp post. When will
I see you again?

—Tomorrow.

—Where?

—Here.

—What if it rains?

—I'll be inside.

—What time?

—Six.

You left with furtive steps, your pony tail twirling behind like smoke from a locomotive, your shadow growing
smaller, larger, until the dense crowd claimed you again.

At that time I still didn't know you, and unable to accept you whole as you were, I had divided you in two: your
body I'd called the earth, your head the moon; and the two,

I thought, were widely separated from each other, with the only bridge between them your long, slender, sensitive neck, like that of a Modigliani portrait, a bridge that made crossing from one world to the other at least possible but that didn't bring their opposed banks closer together, so that the chasm between them really remained unbridged, just as I myself had been born with the root of disunion in me, with both the voice and its echo, just as I found myself split in half when I met you, like a snake cut in two, its separate parts twitching on the indifferent ground, each struggling to join the other, to become one again, the tail curling in on itself, thrusting forward, struggling to find its head but, instead of getting closer, moving farther from its object until both parts of the snake expire separately; and it seemed the same fate was in store for me if I didn't find you, you who were an indivisible one, a woman in all your parts, perfect, shaped in the most attractive of forms, so that my dividing you into earth and moon was merely an attempt to get off easy, because we're always frightened of something sent to change us, and what we look for first of all is some way of maintaining a superficial order in the chaos we carry within us, some way of avoiding the weight of a final decision . . . but you were fated to close the bottomless chasm of my disunion, to bridge the two irreconcilable worlds between which I wavered, the two possibilities in me that jousted with each other endlessly, my two incompatible solutions, and that's why I say I still didn't know you at that time, even during those timid walks we used to take in the most remote parts of the city, when I still couldn't see beyond my own problem, the only difference being that what I once did alone, with my own body as company, I now did with you, allowing my contending selves to wrestle in your arena . . . and your pale head raised me to new, etheral levels, while your golden earth drew me down at a time when I

THE ANGEL

*didn't know the value of plowing, when I didn't know how
to control the plow, how to sow the seeds of joy, and yet
neither could I live only around your moon, because you
were there too, the whole of you, alive, undeniably real like
blood, while I remained so ungoverned, so unbalanced, very
much alone, as I told you often, and merely telling you would
make me feel lighter, since there was no one I could say it to
before, since I didn't really know what loneliness meant, having never known its opposite, and like the bird who tires of
flying in constantly changing winds, I could now find a
little rest on the branch of your neck, while gradually, without my suspecting it, you were teaching me the alphabet of
love, teaching me to distinguish the consonants from the
vowels, to utter, trembling, the first syllables, as I would
descend the difficult staircase step by step, sometimes falling but with you always there to raise me up again, your
patience with me immense, a mother's patience, I thought,
waiting so long for my hands to advance caterpillar-like to
your more mysterious worlds, to corners where others would
begin, corners which took me so much costly time to master:
the blouse, the brassière, the slip, the panties—all meta-
physical stages for someone who craves the physical . . . you
seemed endlessly various, so much of you to discover and
each discovery different from the last: a kaleidoscope turning, the shapes changing before the child's dazzled eyes,
only the magic of color remaining the same in all combina-
tions, while you would say to me: "you have the heart of an
adolescent and the body of a man, Angelos, what a strange
combination you are," and your voice was balm to my ears,
just as your hands were balm to my wounds, just as the
soft contour of your body underlined the hardness of mine,
a condition I hadn't known until it was projected in antith-
esis to you; you see, in the world I came from everything
was inverted, relationships the converse of ours; with you*

209

I would see myself black—as in the negative of a photograph developed in a darkroom—while you would see me white, and this made me happy, because I had faith in you and so became more credible to my own eyes—not to say more handsome; I needed your reassurance more than anything else, I never had my fill of hearing those words of yours, constantly echoing inside me (since I was so uncertain of my own self): "tonight the memory of your square hand, of your square body, tormented me very much . . ." words you had said about me, ABOUT ME, and this served as the cure for what I had said to you so many times: that we exist only in the imagination of others . . . after each one of our meetings in the park next to the warrior's statue, I would leave you invigorated, joyful, ready for an assault on the world, in fact, whatever the occasion, you always lit that spark in me, like that time you wrote the word "desire" in my palm, on the bus, and I didn't wash my hands for days afterwards so that I could look at it—I believed you because I needed your light, in your loose hair I discovered a thousand small secrets, and whatever we then did came of its own accord, without pressure, just as you too came to me so light-footed, bouncing, and though loneliness may have been in wait for us five yards from where we separated, we stubbornly refused to think of tomorrow, of mythical, non-existent tomorrow, since every moment was an explosion of beauty: together we came to know all there was to know, together we discovered everything, effortlessly, together in our first love, passing between the thousand Symplegades that threatened us, because in our tenderness we were stronger than rock, in our absolute ignorance of the world, we had more knowledge than the wise, in the darkness in which we lived, we were more aware of the light; otherwise, otherwise, how was the miracle of my metamorphosis possible, the miracle of my final escape through the prison wires: while the other prisoners called me "traitor," you lightened the load of my guilt for a crime I hadn't committed, you removed the signs of remorse, only for new signs to appear later, deeper signs, more unforgettable—but I won't tell you about those now: that period of first ignorance calls for hymns, even if the sundown was sometimes heartbreaking and our respective postures incompatible with the bench.

So a winter of investigation passed, followed by a spring of circles meeting, then a summer of separation, and the fall:
"Now I'm a complete woman, Angelos," you said.

From the rooftop of the world I call out to you: why, tell me why did you cut your hair? Why did you chip away your light? Why did you bring down your banner? What will the wind do now that it can't caress it? What will my hands do? Where, tell me where did you bury it? I see ringlets hanging from your head, blond ringlets like trickles of water curling away from a beheaded cataract. Nothing flows from your moon now. It remains, still beautiful, closed within its world. But there's no ladder for me to climb, no way for me to reach your dream.
—I got tired of having to comb it. I cut it off so I wouldn't have to bother any more. Don't look at me like that, as though you don't recognize me. My head feels so light . . .
I won't say anything about the summer that went by without my seeing you, about the letters I wrote you without being able to send them, about the walks I took outside your shuttered house, about trying to see people who knew you. I won't talk about the friend of mine who saw you in the

*street and came to me with his disappointment: "Now she
looks like everyone else," he told me. Even though his words
hurt me deeply, I'm strong enough to ignore them, because
I know that you haven't changed, I know that you don't look
like the others . . . But now, from the rooftop of the world,
I call out to you: why, why, why did you cut your hair that
October? I hold you responsible for the rains. I accuse you
of creating the clouds that formed. I blame you for causing
the trees to shed their leaves.*

*—It grows out quickly, Angelos. Soon it'll be as it
was before.*

*But don't you know, don't you know that I can't wait
until next spring? That I'm in a great hurry to go find the
solution? This uncertain state of affairs can't go on. Why,
tell me why did you so suddenly set a knife, a piece of metal,
a pair of scissors to your light? From the rooftop of the
world, I call out to you: you are guilty, you are guilty of
pruning your hair. My fingers may play in the stream of it
tomorrow, but I will no longer be able to bathe whole in its
free flow.*

*—I kept it all. I could roll it into a bun and pin it on
and it wouldn't look as though I'd even cut it.*

*But it's not the same. You yourself know very well that
it can't be the same. You can't solder light to light. You
know very well that light isn't made of metal, that the oxygen of this atmosphere can't solder it together. When light
breaks . . . That's that.*

*—Oh, God, you make me regret having done it so
bitterly. I made up my mind to do it one second, and the
next second I already regretted it. My only hope was that
you might like it this way.*

That was that.

.   .   .

A number of times thereafter I asked myself: why is it you and not someone else? Why you, with that face, that voice, that walk? How did I happen to find you? Why did you find me? What had either of us done to deserve meeting the other in this many-faced chaos and there to sow our sorrows in the seasons of the year? There was Philipou Street, Tsimiski Street, Nike Avenue, the side street off Aetorrache. There was the neighborhood around the Old Station, the Courthouse square, the municipality of Kala-maria, the quarters of Upper and Lower Toumba. Why did I get trapped by Ierissos Street and ask your street to carve out the course of my life?

I agree with you that Eleni swung her behind too much. And Thalia was looking for corny sentiment. Katinitsa straddled a motorcycle and disappeared around a corner, backfiring. Aura was too in love with what was not made of matter. My cousin smelled or urine-soaked virginity. And too much catechism withered Margarita. You were left, only you, with the taste of bitter almonds and banana on your lips.

II

—*Let's go.*
—*No.*
—*Let's go.*
—*No. I've got to get home.*
—*I won't let you by.*
—*Let me go, I tell you. And keep your hands to your-self. You look like a traffic policeman.*
—*Let's go.*
—*But don't you see you can't be that selfish?*
—*And don't you see you can't play with me like that?*

—I'm late and I want to get back. Why don't you let me by?

—Just because. Out of stubbornness. We're going to go.

—Where?

—To my room.

—By force . . .

—Yes.

—I can't, I tell you.

—You can't get by me.

You lowered your head and with a submissive voice:

—All right, let's go, you said. Might makes right, I guess.

You had now taken off your pumps and made yourself comfortable on the bed, adjusting the pillow behind your back, and I lay my head on your small belly; I was still wet from the water hoses they had turned on us, my ears still buzzed with echoes of the demonstration, I could still hear the windows of the British Consulate breaking, I could see the police chasing us with clubs, and then you and your girlfriend passing by on the sidewalk opposite me, so that I abandoned the fight and went after you, drew you into the alleyway, and finding through you a chance to release my pent-up fury, I brought you home by force . . . now, on the bed, we kept changing positions, looking for the most comfortable one, and you divided the bed in half with an imaginary line, saying that I mustn't cross the border, but we quickly abolished the border, and I found myself unbuttoning your red blouse with trembling fingers, freeing your breasts, which were on fire from the blouse's flame, and you said "put on a record so we can't be heard," and I got up, wound up the old gramophone, put on the same old record without changing the needle, glanced over at you waiting there, saw the bed's nest in the half-light, your half-stripped body a beautiful image, came back to you: "Do you love me?" "Very much; and you?" "Like my child, like my lover, like my husband," and you huddled up, your hands became sandy beaches calming the ocean waves, your breasts twin stars, your thighs spread their dicotyledonous flower, you opened to my troglodyte desire, "What enormous panties you're wearing!" "I stole them from my mother," and you laughed, I laughed, I asked if I was too heavy on you and you said "No, your heaviness is sweet," the needle scratched out its voiceless circles, and then, in the silence of that room, I heard your voice, all vapor, wrapped in expiring breath, utter: "Put it in straight, more to the left, that's good, leave it there."

When you left, it had turned dark outside; I don't know how much time had gone by, but I still lay on my bed, numbed by the sweetness I had tasted for the first time, relaxed, indifferent, empty. The relief I felt had nothing to do with happiness, because happiness is something one is afraid to lose, while this new-found feeling of vast emptiness was a miracle of inexplicable light. Never did a cigarette taste better between my lips. Never did I feel such healthy hunger. I kept finding your hairpins on the pillow: they weren't the same ones that you'd bought at the stand but mysterious phenomena that had fallen from space like meteorites. I smelled my fingers, which still held the odor of your chaos, and all the sweetness I had felt on entering that chaos came back to my senses. Until that moment the act of love had been for me an act of remorse, of agony, of guilt. After the appeasement of my cannibalistic urge I would be flooded with disgust, I would break mirrors. Relief such as this was without precedent; surely I was not in paradise but on a gentle beach where waves—instead of vomiting forth the carrion of fish and sea gulls—brought in their curling foam, the sea's harvest.

I couldn't quite believe it yet. Was it really me? Wasn't it actually someone else in my place? And if it was me, as I *would like to believe, then what had I been doing that whole year we were together? How could I have let so much time go by? Of course, until that fall you weren't a "complete woman." During the past summer, the "someone else" . . . At the thought of him a cloud moves in to threaten my serenity. I chase it away. It's better to admit that I was inexperienced, that from the time I emerged out of my mother's matrix I never went back in one again. Only today did I become a man. Today, when I dreamt of the sun rising out of its setting, when I got involved in the demonstration for Cyprus, when I got doused by the water hose, when I fought with you in the alleyway—today, when I heard the words: "it's painful ecstasy, it's wonderful, Angelos."*

I twist on my bed. I miss you. I feel your absence intensely, tangibly. I don't miss the image of you, the dream-icon I worshipped in the shrine of my heart; I miss your hands, your nails that scratched my back, I miss your legs, your fever, your breathing, I miss that deep and mysterious chaos of yours, sweeter than a date, with more syrup than baklava, more tender than a meadow of untrodden clover. And the room, full of objects that were bound in with our lovemaking, excites my senses. I must get out.

I now walk alone, tapping tree trunks as I pass, counting street lights, glancing fleetingly into the lighted shops; I walk in the fully advertised air of night and reflect that today, the day of my real birth, the two became one, the moon merged with the earth; your neck is no longer a bridge connecting two opposite worlds, it too is of the same essence as the earth, it belongs to your body, like your hair, the same blood flows through your veins, which hold you tightly enclosed in their net; you are the city and I the vardar wind that blows down your narrow and broad streets; you are the tree and I the breeze bending your branches; you are the earth and I the sky surrounding you; the line of your

*horizon can be seen clearly against the cloudless night; you
are the woman and I the man touching you. Seeing this
dividing line at our frontiers fills me with endless joy, like
that of a child on first discovering the world.*

*I stroll on and on through the city, which is slowly
emptying of its inhabitants. My steps give rhythm to my
thoughts. I now know that I'm standing on my own feet. I
don't need the beggar's crutches. I watch the moonrise
calmly. Your words circle inside me. Your voice flits about
like a bird in its cage. But I won't let it out. Your nibblings
in the prison of my ear become the source of new stimula-
tion, new delirium. Where are you? What are you doing?
What are you thinking?*

*I return to my room after deliberately wandering for
hours, and seeing the bed unmade as I left it, the record
with the needle in its grooves, your blond hairs in the comb
you used before leaving, your black question marks on the
wet sheet, I realize that the sour, rancid air of my room no
longer repels me, that for the first time I have a place where
I can live. You, Zoe, are there. You're waiting for me, diffused
presence. I sink into the sweet chaos I knew inside you,
velvet, green, soft like a full honeycomb, your sweetness
melts me, I can't resist it any longer, I can't, my joints become unhinged and the sea of sleep rushes in through a
thousand crevices.*

*At midnight, though, I get up. The word "chaos" won't
let me sleep. I want to understand that new void that I discovered, to explain it more fully to myself, to see it in
images. What will the sequel be, I ask myself as I bite into
the pencil, what will follow our first knowledge of death?*

*A raincoat of kisses. A wall to lean against. We have
no roof for our love but the damp night and the withered
tree of the inner courtyard. Our only witnesses: two wild cats.*

—*How long will your grandmother be in the house?*

Our love grew in remote corners, in dark, unfrequented side streets. As far as possible from main roads, as far as possible from people.

—Where are we? I'm completely lost.

To hide our love, we also discovered all the secret places, like fish who live at the bottom of the sea and never come out of their caves, surrounded by awesome rocks that tower above them—like those newly built apartment houses.

—It'll be better to walk.

The dampness of the night pierces through us more dangerously than the worst doubt. And as a result we've become numb. There are never enough kisses. However many the night harvests from our lips, she asks us for still more. Night is gluttonous for kisses—until the sun's kiss dispels her totally.

—I like to have your black bruises on my neck.

A light went out in that apartment house. Some fish is getting ready to emerge. Shall we go into this cave they're building? It's unoccupied. It'll do for us: two exiled fish in turbid waters.

—I'm afraid.

I took you by the hand; we jumped over a lime pit, stepped on a mound of sand which crunched its way into your shoes, went up the half-finished staircase like thieves, reached the second floor: boards, shovels, brushes for white-washing, bricks, cement sacks; we went on to the third: the staircase was bare and anomalous, below the void deepened, there wasn't a soul inside, not even a guard; we crossed on a plank and, leaving the dark hallway, entered a future apartment where they were putting in the door frames: tools abandoned by the workers who would continue their job in the morning, the rooms narrow, low-ceilinged, the light from outside falling in oblique slashes, no sound except that of

our footsteps leaving a hollow echo in the empty building.
—This is where we'd put the bedroom. There wouldn't
be anything in it but an enormous wide bed. We'd grow
tropical plants as curtains on the balcony, so we'd wake up
in the morning and think we were in another country. I
turned and looked at the room the way it was: naked, inhuman, unfinished, and cold. Darkness filled it. The window was like a gouged eye. The floor like a skinned torso.
—Let's get out of here.

And from there we continued walking, separating on
Egnatia Street only to come together again behind the PAOK
stadium, where the street lights ended, and following the
length of the field arm in arm, we reached ground dug up
for a foundation: bulldozers and cranes sleeping like metal
mammoths over the deep incisions in the earth; we walked
on, along streets still unlaid; here too a new building in-
scribed its skeleton on the night, everything remained unsettled: the stones, the soil, the buildings; and so, tripping
over tumors of earth removed in surgery, scratching our
legs on scrub which would be the last to surrender to the
machine's barbarity, we entered the small forest that served
as a haven for illegal couples.
—I like suspect places.

And I liked the moans of an erotic orgy, I liked the city
as it stretched under our feet, the prison . . .
—Don't kiss me there . . .

You were startled by two policemen who passed by
close behind the pine trees without seeing us, and from the
height of the forest, from its edge . . .
—I feel an enormous guilt, you told me, I feel remorse
over what I'm doing. I know that one day I won't be able to
see you any more, and then how will I live without you, you
who taught me how to smoke, how not to be ashamed, how
to know the joy of grass beside you.

. . .

It was winter, and the phone rang.

I had got used to its ringing, to my picking it up, to hearing your voice at the other end, since I was no longer he who searched for you desperately as for water, who waited for you interminable hours in the recess of a doorway, whose heart beat wildly as he took shelter from the rain, who passed outside your house on a street wrinkled from loneliness, who, shut in for whole afternoons, anxiously followed the elevator's motion, its stopping at the fifth floor, the shy ring of the doorbell, then your shadow behind the opaque glass panel of the front door—by now you had learned to come without pretext, without the thousand obstacles that you used to line up for me, now you came honestly, decisively, and we stretched the buttoned mattress on the floor there to surrender ourselves to the sating of our young senses, and your hair was getting longer and you had started to look like my first Zoe again . . . But today your voice in the receiver seemed strangely alarmed.

—Angelos, I've got to see you. Right away.

—Where are you calling from?

—From a pay phone.

—Can't you tell me what it's about?

—No. There are people all around . . . In the park, all right? Next to the statue, in five minutes.

I didn't even have time to explain to my friend why I had to get up and go, and I ran, vaulting down the stairs without waiting for the elevator; I arrived first at the designated place: it was nighttime and freezing cold, secrets hung from the tops of trees, the mist was so attenuated that it couldn't stretch further and yet it held together, the street was deserted, the park more densely so, the statue of the warrior was freezing also, unwreathed; and I kept pacing, rubbing my hands, watching my breath outlined in the air, finally lit a cigarette to get warm, and then I saw you emerge from a cluster of trees, a frigate loaded with high-priced femininity, free of cheap scents, swinging, rocking on your own waves, your hands in the pockets of your tan raincoat.

—Angelos, I'm afraid I'm going to have a child.

Your small voice hung like a stalactite in the night.

—I didn't want to tell you so you wouldn't start worrying too, but my period is five days overdue and no sign yet. I'm going crazy! What are we going to do, for God's sake? The shame . . . I mean it would be better to . . .

—Maybe that's the solution, Zoe.

The next day it snowed: a sudden snow that covered the streets, defeating the feet of men and all wheels. The city seemed to turn quiet in its shroud. Toward night, what didn't turn into slush froze, and the streets became dangerous.

I saw you again the following day and you were even more frightened, since another day had gone by and "it hadn't come." We sat at the taverna with the good bouzouki music, drinking one ouzo after another to build up our courage; the whore in the corner opposite us kept eying us, her look merciless, the owner kept watching us as though we were outsiders in his shop, the two of us lost in a chaos of calculations, beside the pregnant wine barrels, scribbling then erasing numbers on the back of a cigarette pack: numbers, dates, when, how many, and you got February wrong, it has twenty-eight days, not twenty-nine, "with the freezing weather even trains are delayed;" in the end we came out of the taverna having gained one day—no small feat.

Outside reigned a silence, as stark as an eye left naked by fallen eyelashes: white only, and its pupil the night. We slid down the icy street and I held you tight so you wouldn't fall; you were wearing your hood, which made your face look smaller than usual, a lamp covered by a lampshade. A child, what would we do with a child, even if we got married, what meaning would a child have: one more misunderstanding among so many others, girl or boy or something in between these that would be appropriate to the hermaphrodite world—a child not so comfortable in its non-existence, one more misfit, no, this could never be the solution we were looking for, a solution that would merely create a problem for another creature, no, no, come hold me by the hand, we don't want a family, we're living in a house of guilt and every new tenant only multiplies our guilt, until my father's house, a house of prayer which became a house of commerce, is finally torn down, we don't want . . . we don't want . . . come, let's dance a waltz, a tango, a charleston, we're what they made us, the end will come through us, our ancestors will have no progeny as they would want. We circled; I got dizzy from the ouzo and the whirling; I saw the streets bend and curl closed like hoops, the houses mirrored as in a pool, their foundations skyward; soon I saw you disappear with the hood over your head, diminish inside the larger hood of night.

The phone rang again on Sunday afternoon when the ice melted and the only snow left was on Kouri, where my friends would go skiing: luxury snow, luxury friends; I rejected them, standing guard over the phone as over a frontier post, and it was you on the line, your voice warm, gay:

—It came. It came. Today. Now you can be as happy as I am. Our troubles are over. Yes, I'll see you tomorrow. Bye now. And celebrate . . .

But what was it that had come, I wondered after I put down the receiver? A step below my joy of the moment, I didn't know what had come, I couldn't see it in images. Was it a flow of blood between your legs absorbed by cotton? No. Was it "the curse" that came late? No. What was it, then?

How could I express it, how could I see it so as to believe it? A flowing rivulet, offspring of ice, in the emerging down of grass. It came, yes, it came.

Spring had come.

But the news didn't reach us as we were expecting it would.

I was still caught up in the sweetness of your last spasm as you writhed free, and, with the jealousy of a woman who has finished first, you started drawing lines on my face with the indelible pencil you held, started uprooting my hair, marking my back with grooves, and it was spring, the first in my life when I didn't feel like killing myself; in the past, the abundance of life around me, the exaltation of the air, the coupling of birds, the vitality of people made me want to tie a stone around my neck and dive into the muddy bay; but this year we drank the blood of a slope together as we rolled through the tall grass, and the smell of your body after-wards, a meeting of sweat and love, was that of dry straw ripening in stacks on harvested fields—I was still left with the sweetness of your last spasm, the sweetness of the last time we embraced, since the last time was always the best, erasing all others from my skin's memory, when you sud-denly said:

—Angelos, we won't be able to see each other for a while. The "someone else" has come back on leave. You can't imagine what a stranger he seems to me! But . . . We'll have to be patient. Right? Promise me, please promise, that you'll think of me in the meantime.

You were and are the whole world for me. The room where we met formed the walls of our world. The streets where we walked, the veins of our world. The parks where we sat, the seas of our world. The city where we lived, the

223

theater of our world. The people we saw, the audience of our world . . .

—Promise me, sweet boy of mine, that you'll think of me.

We forget many things, as you know, but never the first dawn. The one that peels the night off the sky and wipes away the festering pimples of the stars, caressing its forehead, tired from its all-night vigil over the chaos. We forget, but never the first time . . .

From that day on, spring meant confinement. Interminable hours of watching the day's fireworks light up and die; I smoked, I waited, I started drinking. Our houses were so close together; we ourselves were so far apart. The world outside was foreign to me, hateful, like the Army. How could I dress up in phony armor? Except one night when I happened to see you in a movie theater without being able at that distance to distinguish who was sitting next to you, and the spacious theater suddenly narrowed to fit the measurements of our room.

—You came, you came, you managed to arrange it!

—I escaped the traps of the world, the prison of home, the eyes of people.

—How long can you stay?

—Not very long. I made up a story about having to go to the dressmaker's.

—You always come only to leave. You never come to stay.

—Don't start getting morose again.

—Just like in the beginning when each new meeting always remained dangling. If it bothered me then, it kills me now.

—When you smile like that, you kill me.

—So what have you been up to during the century since I last saw you?

—Our kitten died. We buried it in the courtyard. I cried a lot because I loved it.

—I feel even more alone now that I'm with you.

—You've stopped loving me . . .

—No, it isn't that. But when you come like this you're bad for me. You wake me out of my lethargy and then how am I supposed to fall asleep again on an earthly level?

—When I see you, I'm happy. I don't think about anything else. I've been here so long and you haven't kissed me yet.

—I started growing a mustache too, like your "someone else." In the end, you know, we come to look like the people we hate. Or we hate what we once loved. But we've got to— do you hear me?—we've got to find a solution.

—Every time you kiss me, I feel faint. Be careful, now —the bruises at the nape of my neck.

—When is he going away?

—He's been transferred. Now he'll be here for good. I should've told you. I didn't know how . . . It won't change anything between us two, Angelos. Only we'll have to be more careful. I'm not afraid. I don't love him. It's you I . . . you . . . Oh, give me your hands so we can burn the borders of the world.

—Now he'll be here for good?

—It doesn't matter, I tell you. We'll go on as always. I have my plans. Only you must shave off your mustache. A world without mustaches would surely be a brighter world.

—I don't know what's wrong with me. I'm shaking . . .

—With him, Angelos, I don't feel anything, believe me. You and I suit each other. Our bodies are cut to the same measurements. They're shaped for one another.

—Talk to me, talk to me, I've missed your voice.

225

—*You're sweet and heavy. At night, when I think of you, I can't sleep. How nice it is this way . . . Deeper, deeper . . . More, give me more . . . My God, what was that I felt!*

—*I'm afraid of the treacherous night.*

—*How your eyes shine! I see nothing but two flames in your eyes. That's the sweetest it's ever been . . .*

—*And your head on the pillow. The sunrise on my white mountain.*

—*Angelos, I never loved you so much. Give me a cigarette.*

—*I want you to inhale.*

—*I can't. It makes me choke . . .*

—*So many days for just one moment!*

—*I'm choking with happiness, I tell you.*

—*Are you leaving again?*

—*When I go outside, I'll want to kiss everyone I meet.*

—*You always come just to leave. You never come to stay.*

—*I have to. I'm late. I'll call you tomorrow.*

—*Always tomorrow, tomorrow. No, I don't want you to call me again.*

—*Then I'll see you. Thursday. At the university. On the third floor. I'm taking an oral in international affairs. In the afternoon. At six.*

—*And we'll come here afterwards?*

—*Yes.*

—*And we'll listen to a lot of records? And we'll destroy all the clocks?*

—*Yes, yes.*

—*I can't figure out our life.*

—*Neither can I.*

I found myself gazing through the narrow keyhole at the slick, cosmopolitan head of the professor, sir, after

*reaching the third floor of the university at exactly ten min-
utes to six and not finding you in the long, narrow corridor,
since you had already gone in with your five assigned com-
panions—today's examinations having assumed a faster
rhythm—so that I didn't catch up with you to give you a
little courage, to talk to you about Dumbarton Oaks, and
with my eye now glued to the keyhole I could see only the
bald head of your inquisitor gesturing sometimes negatively,
sometimes positively—I prayed this was in response to a
correct answer from you—and I could see his lips move
without sound, though I could imagine his voice, since I
knew it from his lecturing: a thin, nasal voice with a foreign
accent, a French "r" instead of our own; and that tongue of
his always in motion to keep the lips shining: "what do you
know, my dearrr sirrr, about the fifth article of the United
Nations charter?"—if there were at least some hope that he
might be moved by your beauty, but what could this surface
of civilized polish, of so-called nobility, of so-called manners,
what could it know of real beauty, this head that had glis-
tened so often at dinners and receptions, that had perspired
at so many frigid international conferences, that had taken
on something of the glow of every European capital but remained in the end a bulb that didn't light, a faceless face,
a lacquered portrait in some municipal library, lacking a
wound, something that would make it distinguished—a
naked, inhuman, cold mask, lips frozen in a smile, alum-
inum eyes. He then took out his scented handkerchief and,
unfolding the corners, wiped his forehead, shaking his globe
continuously. The group of five soon emerged. You were
with them.*

—He failed all of us.

—What did he ask you?

*—Something from the supplementary notes he pub-
lished. Which we hadn't bought. He asked me about the con-
ference of Dumbarton Oaks. I didn't know exactly what he*

was after. I had just started saying something when he stopped me. "Dumbarton Oaks, dear young lady, is totally beyond the range of your knowledge." He gave me an F.

We sat on our bench in the park, our faithful haven during stormy weather, and you had just begun to recover from International Injustice when I started talking to you in a voice that trembled at first but gradually became more confident:

—I think I've found it, Zoe. The solution that we've been looking for so long, that lay concealed behind each of our kisses, each of our embraces, that lay in wait for us behind every shrub, always a question mark after the period, the solution, I tell you, that we were looking for—I think I've found it. Don't be mystified. If you too believe in it deeply, you'll agree that it's the only one left. You know. I know. We know. Only one choice remains for us. And exactly because nothing influenced us, because nothing forced us to make such a decision, because we decided by ourselves and freely, because I love you and you love me beyond what is called love, because death by a bullet is preferable to an inevitable slow deterioration, because we don't know the material weight of men, their specific density, the weight of a mustache, the weight of a bald head, the weight of a charter, and God, may we never know it, because there is no absolute among men and we live among them whether we want to or not, because I could offer you a thousand be-causes, and in view of this, as they say, we must . . . I haven't been drinking. I'm in full control of myself. And I know that however unbearable it may be not to see you again . . . But, like a condemned man, I have surpassed the limits of pain . . . Only, help me. The knot in my throat is tightening . . . I don't know how to curl the rope around my neck . . .

—When? you asked without looking at me. When do you want to?

The huge night in front of us revealed not a single light.

—I didn't say anything about doing it tonight. Not to-night . . .

—Tomorrow, then?

—Yes, tomorrow, always tomorrow, always tomor-row . . .

—Tomorrow noon, then, everything will be over, you said, turning in on yourself like a newspaper ready to be discarded, like an animal whose only defense is to reduce its size.

—Everything was over from the first day we met, when you told me "this isn't going to happen again." Since then it's all been one long postponement, just as we are born with the sperm of death . . .

III

I TURN, *I return to the first period, to the first separation: the others that followed had no meaning; when I found you in that long, dilapidated corridor the next day at twelve noon exactly and suggested we go out for a breather, you said we were best lost this way in the crowd, two escapees returned to prison of their own accord and become judges of themselves, not because their crime was so great, but because they feared a life sentence more than the gallows; you were wearing your tan blouse that had a taste of earth to it, and I was holding my Athos pipe, just as on the first day, the first and last day, and we walked back and forth, even that long, narrow corridor becoming private, a place where you and I existed alone, just as the demonstration had disappeared the moment I saw you, just as the movie theater had become small as a room: together we could change everything, the whole world. "Angelos, the only thing*

I can't stand is the thought that we'll be in the same city"
—"I'll go away" —"where?" —"in a boat from Ouranou-
polis" —"where will you go?" —"I don't know, I don't know,
dont ask me, can't you see they're looking at us?" —"I want
you to write me wherever you may be, in whatever corner
of the world" —"let's get away from here" —"there'll be
fewer people on the second floor, let's go there"; the clock
on the second floor showed twenty to three: "the clocks have
gone crazy in this building; upstairs it said ten after twelve"
—"every floor has its own time, and we have our own too"
—"when will I see you again? I don't want us to separate
without first setting a date" —"in five years, let's say; all
right with you?" —"on New Year's eve" —"yes" —"so where
will we meet on New Year's Eve of 1960?" —"where indeed, where?" —"at the Blue Fox" —"no, that's not a firm
place; they may have torn it down by then and built an
apartment house" —"then on the edge of the harbor" —
"they may spoil that, too; besides, isn't it the no man's land
of the free port?" —"not in no man's land, I agree" —"where,
then?" —"in the Society of Macedonian Studies, up in the
foyer" —"yes, that will be there always" —"I'll write it down
on this cigarette box so we can remember it; let's go over
there near the window"; you gave me the indelible pencil
you always held in your hands, I started writing: "January
1, 1960, five o'clock in the afternoon, rendezvous in the
foyer," but the lame usher came over and chased us away:
"not in front of the dean's office, kids," he told us; we left,
now we had to get settled somewhere else; "shall we go to
the ladies' room and spruce up?" you said, and went in
first, saw there was no one else there, signaled me to come
in, and leaning against the door, I kissed you greedily, in-
satiably, interminably, until a rose grew on your lips; I cut
it off and held it, it gave forth a strange scent of bitter
almonds and banana; someone was pushing against the door

230

from outside; I pulled back, hid behind the door; luckily it was only the cleaning woman with her pail; we emerged from the ladies' room; in one hand I held your hand, in the other the rose; "where are we going now?" —"we're continuing the dive, reaching the first floor" —" 'I drink canned juice and dream of fruit,' do you remember?" —"remember isn't a word to remember, remember means that a stairway is changing . . ."; and here the hall was full of people: the freshmen, before thinning out through the sieve of time, crowded into groups outside the main lecture hall; waves of students passed over us, the clock on the wall had stopped at seven: "it's a good thing that the clocks are off, they make time more logical this way"; I didn't really believe what was about to happen. How would we separate? Where? In here, out in the park, at the bus stop, on the bench, near the statue? How would you look at me, how would I look at you, what would our last words be? The decision we had made struck me as incongruous for the first time: around us life was so real, while our bold act seemed so false; around us other couples were embracing, while we were breaking our embrace; their cries, their words, were our cries, our words; we weren't in any way different from the others; this dense wave of people made me see how irrational the solution we had chosen was; it required the strength that one has alone at night but that turns to dust in the light of day, evaporates in the road's traffic; yet we were bound together tightly by our decision; with hands clasped we walked to its execution, to our execution: "I must," I kept telling myself, "I must die." But how? Where? Time passed; we found a doorway dug in the wall, and there, in that wooden alcove shaped like a nest, in that corner, that cave, we took refuge from the sea of people surging around us, two exiled fish in turbid waters; we were looking at each other deeply, face to face, my hand in yours, the door

231

*like an ark, your breasts bursting through your blouse like
two doves, when the heavy shadow of your Lord fell upon
us and the doorway became a coffin.*

*—I came to see you, mister, he said. Yes, you. You don't
know me. So I'll take the liberty to introduce myself. I'm
Panayiota's fiancé.*

—Who's Panayiota?

*—The young lady whose hand you were holding so
tenderly a few seconds ago.*

*—You must be making a mistake. This young lady's
name isn't Panayiota. It's Zoe.*

*He laughed. A small, nervous smile remained under
the barrier of his mustache, which was the seal of his vir-
ility. His skin didn't seem to have ever passed through the
kiln of doubt. He picked at his fingers nervously as though
he were barely holding himself within the bounds of dignity.*

—What do you want.

—I'd like some kind of explanation on your part.

—Don't ask me for an explanation.

*—I regard as more than casual your interest in my
fiancé. Something which goes beyond the limits of friendship. You're taking advantage of her innocence and are trying to lead her astray.*

*—But we're not talking about the same person. You
have some Panayiota in mind. I refuse to give you any explanations regarding my Zoe.*

—I demand an explanation.

—I refuse.

—She herself can tell you her name.

*He pulled you near him, held you tightly against him,
and with you glued to his side like Eve before the fall, he
continued:*

*—Things are not as simple as you think. You may know
a great deal about the ancient civilizations of the Aztecs and*

the Maja, about the primitive morals of the Mau-Mau, but we live in a Christian society where we recognize the institution of property. Therefore, don't you start having designs on someone else's property. Third parties have given me ample information about your meetings. I recognize the possibility of a friendship among fellow students, but you, you . . . So I'm warning you for the first and last time. Leave my Yiota alone to continue her studies and break off all contact with her. Otherwise . . . What do you have to say?

—Nothing.

—I'm waiting.

—Angelos, Angelos, what will your last word be?

—Dumbarton Oaks.

—Now, what does that mean?

—Angelos, what's happened to you?

—Dumbarton Oaks.

—So no excuse, no apology, no assurance that I labor under a deplorable delusion? You admit your guilt?

—Dum . . .

—Angelos, you're burning . . . you're crying . . .

—Dumbarton Oaks . . .

—Come, Yiota, let's go, sweetheart. Men don't cry.

When I found myself alone in my ark, I still had the rose in my hand. Calmly, methodically, I started eating its petals one by one. I made bubbles of them with my tongue, then gulped them down—until I was left with just the stem.

I went outside, started walking, reciting to myself: "First there was I, then came you, afterwards he. For a while we were we, now you two are you, tomorrow you'll be they. I, you, he, we, you, they . . ."

A stranger to my own eyes, someone else to my own self, now a "someone else" to you, I see the Angel who lost the earthly battle . . .

233

. . .

I *walk along the street. I lean against a tree and the branch breaks. I step on the ground and the earth sinks. I dive into the sea and the water vanishes.*

I *walk along the street, at night, and the feel of my first death is warm against my cheek.*

I *walk, unable to shape a word, unable to relate events logically, unable to concentrate. The pain of separation drags me down; a dumb, dull, broad river, I roll down the streets through a night full of river mud, unable to clutch the jeweled banks, with their milk shops, cafés, and kitchens.*

I *walk along, passing rocks, falling, at times becoming a cataract, at times a calm pool of water in the current's whirl, at times a passionate churning that upends rafts, saps the foundations of bridges, floods sown fields, drowns chickens and dogs; I am the unworthy Axios, the narrow Evros, the bloated Strymon; on my unleashed waves travel crystals of ice, dead guerrilla women, uprooted trees, all of which I boil up in the anemic and polemic bay of the icy Thermaic gulf. Only the lighted neon signs penetrate the night of my river:*

TITANIA: "THE SWALLOWS RETURN"
PERMANENT PLEATING: SAVVA VOYIATZI
AGIP GAS

I *walk along, unable to understand the first death, the first separation, but believing in it absolutely, as we believe blindly in everything that's unfathomable, skimming over a chaos which has no relation to the chaos I knew inside you: this chaos is bitter, thorny, full of blood, abortions, asphyxiating gas:*

WATER GAS
SCOOTER HEINKEL—MOTORCYCLES
BEAUTY PARLOR: "VERA"

*And I can't carry so much night on my back, even if new
neon signs rip through it:*

FOTOGRAPHICA
RADIO—OPTA
PHILCO

*I walk along, and the streets seem like lungs emptied
of air, people like microbes you should touch only while
wearing gloves, gloves that make the fingers longer, just as
waiting for you makes seconds longer—and capital letters,
silent buildings, tortured colors, mold the image of my love
in the frame of the eternal sea:*

TANTEX
THE GREEK NORTH
NASCO
MELLA COLEST: the first cream hair tint

*And our voices become tunnels in our memory, become
lumps of emptiness which crush us against the vulgar decks
of the streets:*

PHOTOGRAPHY: Developing
Printing
Enlarging

*And I keep on walking along, walking along in the
river.*

235

GROCERY STORE: "THE SERRAIKON"
THE SHOP FOR WEDDINGS — BAPTISMS:
"ARISTON"
TERKENLY: *hot cheese pies*

Ripe fruit fell at the hour of separation, and I, irresponsible, took the way of birds.

Our beloved husband, father, brother, uncle, and grandfather

SOTIRIS PAPADIMITRIOU
Leather Merchant from Monastirion

who died yesterday, will be buried today in the Holy Church of the Ascension. We request that all . . .

Our beloved husband, father, brother, and grandfather

DIMITRIS TSOUKANIS
who died yesterday, will be buried . . .

Our beloved sister and aunt
SOFIA KOVALAKIDIS
76 years of age
who died . . .

Our beloved husband, father, son, and uncle
ANDREAS ADALIS
Cattle Merchant

Our little angel
GEORGE

Our beloved . . .
Our . . .
O . . .

236

. . .

Each morning I went by the house, I saw it further destroyed. The workers up on scaffoldings were finishing the demolition. After they tore down the roof and the upper walls, they started hacking away at the floors, lifting the beams, the metal railings, the remaining doors. They piled up all this material down by the entrance. And there they separated it: the wood with the wood, the metal with the metal. Each morning I went by, I looked indifferently at the house they were tearing down. Until one morning I saw— projecting from frames of toothless beams—the two squares, one blue, one reddish-colored: the walls of two torn-down rooms plastered against the neighboring house. They seemed so alone, so sad to have escaped destruction; the strong sun made their colors fade . . . Each morning I went by, and while the drills and the shovels worked incessantly and the workers moved constantly lower on the fractured walls, I couldn't look at those two square panels. The red and the blue, glued to the other house. They disturbed me . . . No, I don't feel any sadness over something that is deteriorating. When something is finishing, it doesn't hurt me. But the trace of your kisses on my cheeks, the bruises of your teeth on my neck, the color you left on my house . . . Each morning I went by, and while the trucks were carrying off the rubble and scrap iron, I read the sign:

DEMOLITION MATERIALS FOR SALE

And further down:

LIQUIDATION OF ALL MERCHANDISE

237

And further down:

FINAL DISSOLUTION

By order of the Court of the First Instance

No. 27365/11/55

Oh, what haven't I done since we separated—the old vision, the Great Idea—to re-establish the frontiers of our ancestors, of our uncle Alexander the Great, broadening the borders of our small country, widening the confines of our narrow room, until the allies betrayed us, our so-called friends, and we returned with bloodied wings; what haven't I done since I assimilated the refugees to find something to replace you, another country to take your place, another embrace . . . But there was always that terrible measure of comparison, and I was trying to find forgetfulness, which is impossible among men. If we were only bound by our expansion, this wouldn't prevent me from rejoicing. But that which bound us more was our destruction, and this I couldn't forget.

Meanwhile the seasons changed on the face of our city, which constantly enriched its front with apartment houses. Independent of us, summer polished the sea, burned the asphalt, thickened the air with milky dust. Fall took its place by denuding the trees, dampening the lights, shortening the fabric of day, and lowering the sky. Winter again sallied with the Vardar wind, hurled the veil of its fog, emptied the streets, and closed life early inside the houses, as during the Occupation. And spring came in awkward as a debutante, turned the surrounding hills green, covered the earth with flowers and the sky with kites.

"The light vanished and the young man lost his soul."

And then, silently, they buried me with onion tears.

. . . In any case, that first night on guard duty, while the snarled fishing net was being untangled and the spoiled bait unhooked, I may have gone from one floating gourd to the other without catching anything, having vainly explored a portion of my depths. In practice, I say, I may not have gained anything. But I was glad that the thread didn't break and that I was able to reach the end, the end which in its turn became another final beginning. The light wasn't far off now. The scattered blocks on my childhood floor came together tonight, formed a story, as though an invisible hand had turned up that side of them which completed my myth. And I felt a vast relief, as though an explanation had finally been found for the unknown, a motive for the inevitable.

And yet one side remained dark. Why all this fuss? Why should we make things so complicated when one of your kisses would have sufficed—one of your gestures— to get us disentangled so that we could start again from the beginning and again fail to find the solution? It was the eclipse of the moon, don't forget. And I could see that one part of it wasn't visible. But why did I discover more in that dark part of it, why did I prefer it that way to a full moon? This was a query unrelated to my deep relief, a question I asked myself forgetting where I was and that I had died— as I heard footsteps approaching. I assumed a defensive posture. "Halt. Who goes there?" I bellowed, my sword ready. "The patrol." "Let the leader advance singly . . . Halt! Eleven," I said in a whisper. "Thirty-two." "Advance . . . Halt! Advance on the password." "Saint Zoe." Just hearing your name on foreign lips made me feel they were stealing something from me. Then the leader came into the guardhouse and wrote "good" in the guard book. "Only you should shout out 'halt' a little louder," he remarked as he was leaving.

Not long after this the relief Underangel brought in a guard to replace me. He was from the barracks facing ours and I didn't know him well. I gave him the code numbers. The password amazed him, too. "What was that?" "Saint Zoe. Anyway, it's written down here," and I handed him the small piece of paper. I told him the patrol had just gone by, so he would be left alone for a while. I was moving off, sword on my shoulder, when I heard him muttering to himself: "Eleven . . . thirty-two . . . Saint Zoe . . . Saint . . ? You're telling me . . . She must have been some dish . . ."

ASIMIS' TRIAL before the High Court of the School of Reserve Heavenly Angels came at a moment crucial to the safety of that very school, as well as of Heaven in general. The wrought-up nerves of the regular angels who judged him found in this moment an opportunity to explode, although Asimis was completely unrelated to the cause of their panic.

A few days before the trial a strange noise was suddenly manifest near our star, like the ticking of a clock, and through the light we saw a cylindrical tube flash by us while we were outside on the black training fields, and each of us turned stone with fear. The noise it made was a metallic trilling like the voice of a night bird, and it wouldn't stop. It would return every now and then with mathematical precision; finally, our instructor, unable to explain this irrational phenomenon, shouted out: "We're being attacked by the Devil. Take cover!" And we all fell prone, our ears taut. The satellite would whistle by every three minutes, then disappear.

The news was very disturbing. The administration immediately ordered a stand-by alert. The night guard was doubled. And frequent trial alarms would jolt us out of our beds; loaded with all our equipment, we would take up our positions for the defense of our star against a surprise attack by the Devil.

Two days had gone by since the foreign noise stopped besieging us, yet the camp was still in an uproar. As the Regular Angels explained, this unknown body, sent from Hell and armed with so many instruments, must have fallen within the magnetic field of our star, and that was why it kept going round it until it must have either returned to its base with all the useful information it needed or disintegrated in our atmosphere, leaving its remains on one of our mountains. If the latter were the case, we would find the remnants someday.

The point was that the Devil didn't play games. And while we remained stationary, learning the old war tactics against him, he was progressing by leaps and bounds, intending to conquer Space with up-to-date technical means unknown to us. The regular officers were cracking, and the School God, who took up the matter with the General Staff of the Dead, was mystified because those higher up in Heaven, who couldn't be reached by such satellites, thought that He had failed in disarming the enemy and that Diabolical battalions were already hiding in the rough ground of our star. They even recommended that He start intensive instruction in guerrilla warfare. Our kind God tried in vain to explain his situation. They even threatened to replace Him if He didn't catch some prisoners in a counterattack. And then He, with the insensitivity of the Great, started taking it out on his subordinates. And they in turn on us. Discipline became more restrictive. Things seemed to be getting out of hand at the School . . .

After a number of postponements, the trial took place in the domed auditorium of the Administration Building. Behind a table shaped into a half-moon, on a high archepiscopal throne, sat the School Undergod—the School God Himself did not get involved in administrative matters— with two four-winged Cherubim on his left and two six-winged Seraphim on his right. Next to the Cherubim sat Holy Oversaint Pausikakos, and next to the Seraphim sat the School Intelligence Officer, a short, fat Holy Undersaint, who seemed to be acting as Secretary of the Court. They all seemed unnerved and sleepless as a result of the recent events. They fidgeted with their pencils, crossed and uncrossed their legs under the table.

In the heart of the huge empty room, Asimis stood at casual attention, facing the judges, with the rest of us—all witness—on his right.

Before the trial formally opened, the Undergod, serving as President of the Heavenly Court Martial, asked him if he was prepared to sign a confession of repentance, in which case the trial would not take place and Asimis would remain eternally in the ranks of angels. When Asimis refused, saying that he had no cause to repent his ideas, the Undergod leaned back in his throne and signaled the Holy Undersaint to begin reading—"within hearing of all angels assembled"—the indictment against the accused.

The Holy Undersaint rose and, in his squeaky voice, read of the formal charges: that Reserve Candidate Angel Asimis Asimakis had declared before third parties his lack of faith in the existence of Supergod; that he had attempted to proselytize for the cause of Super-Atheism; that he had fabricated his own theories about Space in conflict with established doctrine; that he kept an apocryphal and hieroglyphic diary whose few comprehensible paragraphs revealed his anarchic soul, etc.

During the deadly silence that followed the reading of the indictment, the Undergod called on the various witnesses to testify in hierarchical order. The first to step forward was our ferocious Holy Saint Onisimos. Dazzled by the galaxy of stars and sun medals displayed on the Undergod's chest, his voice turned weak and tremulous as he testified that Asimis had clearly shown antiangelic tendencies from the first day he reached the School; refusing to forget that he was dead, Asimis had daily committed infractions of discipline punishable under the Holy Regulations. He concluded that not only was Asimis' over-all behavior out of character with the high morals expected of an angel, but that his mere presence corrupted those around him. Our kind platoon leader followed, testifying that in his opinion Asimakis had been influenced by the earthly books he'd read, books on the black list of the Archbishopric. Then our Barracks Chief, Saint Baruch, emphasized that Asimis, with his devil-may-care attitude, spoiled the make-up and alignment of the bunks in the barracks. Finally, our squad leader, Saint Benedictus, testified that Asimis lacked a spirit of co-operation and always seemed a stranger in his group. The burden of defense seemed to be falling on us, his classmates.

The Undergod—the picture of impartiality—asked us if we had known Asimis during our earthly life. And when each of us in turn asserted that we'd first met him here, he told us to inform the court of our various attitudes toward the accused. No one of us, it's true, dared defend him openly, because Onisimos' agents had forewarned us that any favorable evidence offered by a witness under his command would merely create trouble for that witness in the long run. So the general impression formed by our opposing opinions was that Asimis served as a focal point of contradictions, a non-participant in the feverish competition at the school, a presence indifferent to everything, an inexplicable corpse.

Suddenly a Regular Underangel entered the courtroom like a *deus ex machina* and, saluting dynamically, reported that whole formations of satellites were besieging our star from the air, and that we could expect Satan to invade us any moment. The Underangel was planted by the authorities, as we found out later; his news served as a pretext for great commotion among the judges, who decided that, under the circumstances, there was no cause for prolonging a session devoted to a case of this kind. The Undergod leaned forward to nail the accused with a concluding question: "Just tell me one thing—and I want a yes or no answer

—do you or do you not hate Satan?" Asimis smiled to himself. "No," he said quietly. "I don't hate anybody."

His words seemed to fall like a silent grenade among the magistrates of Heaven.

The rumors, "the winged words," that the Devil was about to invade our star stopped almost immediately, as did all traces of the sound that had disturbed us like a strange knock in the mechanism of space. The general alert was relaxed and all of us—except Asimis, now exiled to a barren star for satanic rebels—returned to our daily routine.

Then one day the seniors left. There was a formal ceremony in the church courtyard, at which we were also present. After the liturgy, the School God bade the seniors farewell in His most emotional voice.

—New Angels, He said to them, your apprenticeship at the School has come to an end. Now each one of you has an obligation to honor his uniform, his wings, his very lofty mission. Moreover, you are now beings of a higher order, superior in knowledge and morality. Agents of the Divine Will between Heaven and Earth, your mission is to guide, to correct, to instruct, to console. Protectors of the pious, avengers of evil under the command of Supergod, whom you will serve, bearers of the saber and the sword, you have furthermore the power to kill. New Angels, we as a School will remember you always. We may have been too severe with you at times, but this was done for your own good, because we wanted to make you perfect. Heaven, now that Satan is undermining its supremacy, needs you more than at any other time in its history. He may surpass us technologically, but our own weapons will always remain the indestructible virtues of manliness, courage, purity, self-sacrifice. The School staff and I myself as your Father will always remember you. And you too will often feel nostalgic for life at the School once you've settled on the very remote frontiers of Heaven where you will be serving. Never forget what you have been taught here. Never forget that you are the indirect conveyors of the Beauty of the Eternal Brain. You are therefore created not eternal but perfect, and because of this, immortal in your perfection. "May the unapproachable light of angels dwell within your souls." From the bottom of my heart I wish you a good journey.

The God's words had already brought tears to many eyes. Then the Archangel took over to deliver the farewell address as head of the senior class.

—You stood by us well, Holy Fathers. You taught us the difficult way to true sainthood. You unburdened us of our human weight, of the sins of the flesh, of the tyranny of time. We are now ageless. You gave us wings and taught us to fly in the timeless, immemorial light. You taught us most of all the dignity of light. "Floods of tears and mourning, unrelenting memory of death," these are things of the past for us. Most of all, you have made us realize that Heaven is not exile but the beginning of a new life. That is why we shall never forget you. You had immense patience with us, God, Undergod, Cherubim, Seraphim, Holy Oversaints, Holy Saints, and Holy Undersaints. We have acquired the heavenly neutrality of gender. On the masculine side we are courageous, hard-heeled fighters, responsible for our actions. On the feminine side we are pure and virginal. You have instilled in us the seraphic attribute of "knowing" and the cherubic attribute of "loving." We are grateful to you. Now the bitter moment of parting has arrived: "how could a warm tear fail to flow from the heart?"

I want to thank you on behalf of the forty-first class, and to assure you that we will always honor the School's ideals because we are, because we have become, because you have made us, indestructible matter.

The end of his speech was acknowledged by the flapping of wings.

We watched them from the rear jealously. They were wearing dress uniform number 1; their wings glowed, their belts sparkled, their sabers clanged, their silver halos magnified the light. When would our day come too! How much more did we have to suffer! It was cruel of them to bring us to this ceremony; it had spurred our impatience, our eagerness to leave this confining camp and the terrible monotony of our life here.

The speeches, songs, and other festivities ended, and many of the cadet angels now came over to see us, to let us admire them—our former protectors, tyrants, torturers, counselors. Their faces were luminous with joy, and with their wings on, they actually did look quite different. I was musing about how Asimis would have laughed over their airs, their feeling of importance, their haloed stupidity, when Yannis found me.

—Congratulations, I said.

He too was shining head to foot. His legs had become thin and tapered like a swallow's tail.

—Thank you, he said. And may your turn come soon.

He took me aside to make sure no one would hear us.

—I'm going to our city tonight, he said.

I looked at him. Along with all the brilliance of his uniform, his expression showed an infinite melancholy.

—The only trouble is, he continued, to save my life I can't remember what street her house is on. You'd think I have amnesia or something.

—As soon as you see our city, you'll remember, I

reassured him. Everything will come back to your mind
automatically. You'll walk down the same street, your heart
fluttering as always.

—In any case, I'm taking a map along. So I won't get
lost.

—Where are they sending you? I asked.

—The 602nd Swordbearers' Regiment. On the frontier.

—Good luck, I shouted as I hurried off to join our company for exercises, my mind turning over what he had once
said: "I'll see her even if she doesn't see me. I'll talk to her
even if she doesn't hear me. I'll cool her with my wings and
let her think . . ." "Good luck," I shouted again as I took my
place in the line.

That day none of us could concentrate on our lessons.
At one point, someone shouted: "There they go!" and we all
looked up to sec the angels taking flight by twos and threes,
sailing through luminous space, becoming constantly
smaller until they were mere dots vanishing into the sun.

Our blasé instructor went right on: 'So, I repeat: a bat-
talion is divided into the following parts . . . A company
undertakes a delaying action against the enemy until the
others . . .

Our eyes were on him, but . . .

The school looked empty without the seniors. It seemed
bigger, more comfortable. In the P.X. there were now
enough chairs for all of us. At meals you could get seconds
and even thirds. There was plenty of olive oil. Our non-
commissioned officers were chosen according to the credits
that each had collected. Someone from our company became the Archangel, which made Onisimos very proud. Our
own Underangel was from the other platoon. Former
friends became barracks chiefs and group leaders and, as a

consequence, had trouble imposing themselves on us. Each of us changed his name to that of the saint he liked best. Now that pressure from the seniors was gone, we started bickering among ourselves. And we waited voraciously for the new candidates to arrive.

"I'll show them, those deadheads," someone would say. "I swear I won't bother them."—"They'll die, my friend, just as we did."—"I'll tell them not to be afraid of anything."— "You jerk, smile spiritually."—"You mug, I'm not joking. This is for real."—"Someone had better say the prayer."— "Our Lord Pantocrator, who allowed us to get through this day . . ."—"Who's laughing? You'll be on report tomorrow." —"Protect us with your holy angels, defend us with your might, guard us under your roof . . ."—"Cut the talking."— "Allow the coming night to be peaceful and sinless . . ." —"Planis, can it."—"My name isn't Planis, it's Saint So- fronios."—". . . of the Holy Virgin and all the saints. Amen." —"We want to sleep."—"Go on, you punk, shut your mouth."—"I for one am going to make those new bastards hop . . ."

And so the tradition of angels comes down through the ages from class to class.

Now that everything has taken on a surface calmness and I have nothing to say to the others, each day that goes by is one more step away from you. Yesterday it rained. A sudden thunder storm. The first on our star. But it wasn't the same as those I'd known; it didn't mean anything to me, since it didn't explain your being delayed . . .

No, there is no escape. Not even in Heaven. What if I do gradually lose my body? The prison is merely a different one, and there you remain forever, girl made of mist, girl with the tree's touch on your hair. The snow, your voice when you picked up the phone and told me . . . The ear has fallen off, but your voice remains. The eardrum is dead, but the last vibration is still alive in Heaven: long, infinite, persistent. It remains. It will go on remaining. All will be explained someday, though the explanation may be late in coming.

You ask to know what my position is in Heaven. I am still completely disoriented. I see the sun come up in one place and see it go down again in the same place. Then, where is the east? Where is the west? In the tranquillity we've found between the departure of the seniors and the delayed arrival of the new candidates, I'm beginning to suspect that Heaven isn't a solution but a flight. A flight from our insoluble problems. And this slow deterioration of ours is so painful far from those whose caress resurrected us!

There are times when I worry. I worry about the debts I left on earth. I worry about your hair. I ask myself that painful question: "what did you do?" and see all the streets we didn't walk, all the springs we didn't discover, all the words we didn't say. I become all worry over you. And there are other times when I say that isn't what's at fault; the fault is that we didn't keep the customs of our ancestors, that we didn't sacrifice a rooster when we layed the foundations, that we didn't bloody the cornerstone of the house we wanted to build . . . I worry about it all, vainly, superfluously, inanely. And there are times when I pierce through every cloud and discover you: an abandoned little thing huddled between the door and the wall.

"You left me, you abandoned me, it's your fault," I can hear you telling me at times. "You never saw me truly as a human being. You always liked to see me as an interval in your life, something to fill a void. You never caught hold of me by the heart. You caught hold of me by the breasts but never by the heart. I had told you from the very beginning:

250

'Angelos, I'll just be an episode in your life,' and you denied it. It's your fault. What else could I do? You knew how superficial my ties with the "someone else" were. And if I held on to him after I met you, it was just to test you. Of what value would it have been to give myself to you easily? I wanted to see your strength, I wanted you to grab me, to uproot me from the turbid waters in which I vegetated, from the depths which held me prisoner, to bring me into your world so that together we could make our own world. It's your fault. It's all your fault. Now my love is turning to hate. I want to destroy you, to cut you to shreds inside me. But it takes twice as long to tear down a world—killing the life within us at the same time—as it does to build it. And I'm alone, lost, confused in the night and silence of the city. My yesterdays are too nostalgic to think about. My todays are a sleepless vacuum. And tomorrow we're holding my white funeral and you're not here to send me even a few flowers. I know you escaped to an artificial heaven, that you went there to make your angelic name come true. But, deep down, I'm sure you haven't stopped carrying your very same self within you. I know this because I know you. You were always alone, and that's how you'll always be, because you never bent over the wounds of people, you never understood a person. You believed you were alone, because if you admitted the opposite, you would find yourself facing responsibilities you were afraid to face, as you were always afraid to look the truth straight in the eye. It's your fault. But whatever you may be, in spite of your ascension to the heavens, in spite of all that my despair makes me say to you, there really hasn't been a moment I've forgotten you, there hasn't been a second I've stopped loving you. And I go on waiting, hoping, for your Second Coming."

This is how I hear you talk in my moments of doubt, moments that have begun to multiply as our wings are further delayed. Only I don't believe in the Second Coming. I'd like to tell you this, to write it to you clearly: there are no seconds. There's only a First Coming and a First Going.

And again at other times I hear your voice, tender in the wilderness of our star, saying:

"Come. Please come. I want to tell you something. Let's go to the bridge over the train rails at the New Station. Behind us is the city, its sparse lights climbing the slopes of the hill. I want to tell you something, I want to talk to you. We're on the aerial bridge, Angelos, silently studying— each on his own—the complicated pattern of tracks glistening in the late twilight. No train goes by. Lines straight, curved, parallel, now separate, meet, disappear. Further down they come together again, embrace, disappear. We study them. Night moves on. Why did you wear your glasses? They won't help you see better, understand more. From the hanging bridge, facing the metal dead end which we see meshing under us, you and I have no other comfort except that of being close to each other, so close that if I stretch out my hand it will touch yours, if you bend your head you'll be against my shoulder. The lines, Angelos, will always be lines. We shall never understand their mysterious weaving. Now people are passing over the bridge. People returning from work with parcels, with bicycles. Women who have to support their children on their own, children already darkened by blacksmith work, men without homes. We too are like them. Only we're trying to find an explanation for everything. Sick hearts, both mine and yours. How monotonous it must be in the plains. What can two parallel lines running toward the world's horizon have to offer? It's nighttime. At least here . . . But look, look down there, next to the empty freight cars, that shadow holding a green lantern who controls the tracks by a switch, who regulates the course of the train about to arrive. Do you understand?

Everything is so simple sometimes—God, so simple! As we strain to unravel the secrets, someone always comes along like a shadow, holding a lantern, and a switch and sets us on our course. What's the use of staying here any longer? The Station is too romantic. It's getting chilly and I didn't bring my jacket. I'm cold."

And when I hear you talk to me like this, I soften. I realize how vain my worry is, how vain it is to find problems everywhere. And if you should be that distant star winking at me as though it's staying awake for my benefit, then I can sleep with ease under your eyelid.

But most of all I worry about your hands. It may be that your feet have sunk into the yellow toilet bowl, your breasts have filled with pasteurized milk, your eyes turned into broad beans for fasting, and your hair into grass which covers the whole of you; but I'm afraid that your hands may get coarse, that they may lose their first palor. Where are your hands and that shiver when you scratched my back? Because with your bruises, your words, your hands, I'm still searching, feeling, explaining the world. Oh, if only I could find your palm again someday and read your fortune in it, my fortune, the fortune of the quiet sun.

These were my thoughts until suddenly one morning, at muster, Holy Saint Onisimos told us:

—The wings have arrived. I saw them. They're new. According to the regulations, each one of you is entitled to one pair. After exercises you'll go to the supply depot and pick them up. Tomorrow I don't want to see anyone around without his wings. Do I make myself clear?

The company was all joy. The wings had arrived, our wings, finally. The day we could fly was now close. This unexpected news stirred up excited chatter all down the

253

line. It was the first time our Holy Saint had something pleasant to say at morning muster.

"The wings, oh joy, our first large wings."

—Cut it, the Holy Saint bellowed from the top step. Atten—shun!

I don't know why I was the last one to go into the supply depot. The line outside was long and I got tired of waiting, so I took off, checking back every now and then to see how things were going. The line seemed to diminish more slowly than the light of day, so when my turn came, the warehouse keeper was about to close shop. The place was palely lit by the last rays of the sun and an acetylene lamp.

—Where did you come from? the keeper asked when he saw me. Why have you been hiding all this time? The shop's closed. Come back tomorrow.

I told him if I didn't have my wings the following morning the Holy Saint would put me on report. I pleaded with him, I begged him.

—All right, all right, he said, and grudgingly moved to the back of the depot, which smelled of leather and paraffin. The air was dense with the odor of things stored there for years. The keeper was a paunchy regular Under-angel with the same face as the keeper of the cemetery. He said to me:

—One more month and I hand over this bedeviled depot. If you don't have troubles and want to find some, become a warehouse keeper. You'll always find things missing, they'll always be after you, you'll always think that . . . What's your height, anyway?

—One meter seventy, I said.

—Chest?

—I don't know.

—Stand there so I can measure you, he said, taking a tape measure out of his pocket. Now take a deep breath and hold it.

He mumbled "sixty-two" to himself. Then he measured my shoulder blades.

Size 6 should fit you, he said, and started looking through the pile of wings.

I studied them. It seemed they had just arrived from somewhere, still wrapped in straw next to the open cases. I bent over and picked up a pair. They were made of some material I didn't know—some kind of soft plastic, colored sort of bronze. I lifted them and they struck me as strangely light, so weightless they seemed already about to fly. They were labeled "Made in U.S.A.," and they had a long serial number.

—I don't have size 6, said the warehouse keeper, deep in a pile of wings. The trouble is, buddy, yesterday we had that other company, today yours, and you're the last of the last. But size 5 will do just as well.

—Is there much difference? I asked.

—Almost none at all. In fact, maybe the 6's would have been a little wide. The 5's will fit you like a glove.

Hurrying to get me out of there, he pulled them out of the pile, shook the dust off them, and walked toward the door.

—Here, he said, presenting me with a piece of paper. Initial this.

I signed.

—Number 63948, he said. And learn it by heart so you won't get them mixed up with somebody else's. Go on now, take them, and good luck!

I took them, said good night with prolific thanks, held them in my arms tenderly just as I used to hold my roller

255

skates as a child, and headed for the barracks. But my delight was so full that I felt the need to stop by the latrines first, carefully vaulting over the pools of urine that had formed outside.

I'd never seen the barracks in such an uproar. I'd never known such agony getting through the corridor. I shoved, dodged slashing blows, formed a shield out of my wings to reach my bed safely. They all wanted to put on their wings at once. They all wanted to see themselves in the cracked mirrors on the shower-room wall. And since no one could put his on by himself, everyone asked his neighbor for help. In theory we had been taught how to gird them in place, but the application proved to be another matter. There were straps we didn't know how to buckle or what their use was. "Get moving, buddy, you're taking all night!" —"Where does this hook go?"—"No, first pass it under your arm, then flip it around twice."—"Who's finished so he can help me?"—"Look at him! He's wearing them like donkey's ears!"—"Chief, mine are both right wings."—"All right, cut it. Who's got two left wings? Let's check them out."—"I'll go back to the warehouse keeper. He must have made a mistake."—"He's closed now. Go tomorrow."

Two or three had already returned from the mirrors, bearing wings, full of pride, when at the lower end of the barracks a bad fight started. It seems that someone inadvertently hit someone else with his new wings, causing a misunderstanding that had the two of them quarreling. A third party who came in to separate them shoved a fourth and the brawl spread to the whole barracks, since our new appendage on the back created quite improbable consequences. Wings struck where eyes couldn't see. Our arms, bound as they were by straps, couldn't reach where they had been known to reach. And so some beat the air, some knocked others down while trying to avoid being hit themselves. Pillows were hurled, trunks turned into barricades. Someone who tried to escape the massacre by jumping on his bed broke the overhead lamp with his wings. Darkness fell over the field of battle. Someone else, who tried to slip away underground, found his wings caught in the bed springs and shrieked like a mouse. Then a voice resounded: "Stop, for God's sake. The saint on duty's coming." And this seemed to have a magic influence throughout, because they all stood dead in their tracks. "Now," said the same voice, "while he's climbing up the stairs, each of you get back where you belong. Not all at once. One by one." They moved; emotions calmed down for a while, and no saint appeared.

The bugle announcing mealtime sounded soon thereafter, and with the same flurry, we started unbinding the straps around our shoulder blades. I had managed to tie only one wing in place and so made the line by the time we were called to attention. But many others didn't. The saint on duty noticed the gaps in the line and asked the Underangel what was up. "They haven't had time to untie their wings." he explained. "Well, run over and tell them to come as they are." And the Underangel went off on the double to execute the Holy Saint's order. They soon began arriving, some with one wing, some with both dragging on the ground, some without a halo, some with dangling straps; two candidates whose wings had got entangled came up like dogs with their rear ends joined, one pulling this way, the other that way, so that even the Holy Saint on duty finally had to laugh, which spared the whole group a reprimand.

In the morning, Onisimos stood on the top step to admire us. The company was in close order and we were all slightly hunched over. When the Underangel reported that some of us weren't absolutely satisfied with the fitting of our wings, the Holy Saint answered:

—Any changes are to be arranged among you. Find

out who wants to switch wings and negotiate the exchange on your own. I don't want any of you bothering the warehouse keeper.

When someone else asked if we could approach the other company for possible changes, our Holy Saint got annoyed:

—The fourth company has nothing to do with our family affairs. As I have said, make all arrangements among yourselves. Any questions?

In the beginning, my wings seemed to fit well, and while the switching was going on I didn't think of changing mine at all. They were of course a bit tight, but I thought this would necessarily be so until I got used to them. If they were wider—size 6, for instance—I was afraid they might be too loose, and I wanted them fully stretched, like the sail of a boat, at the time of my flight.

The trouble with my right shoulder developed on the third day. I didn't pay any attention to it. Only at night, when we took off our wings to go to sleep, would the point of contact on my back begin to itch. Besides, I wasn't the only one. Many of the others complained of suffering from imperfect fittings. One would have pains in his neck, another's shoulder would be sore, a third's armpits would be raw from the straps. It was always some point of contact that created the trouble. So I didn't say anything.

But before the end of the first week I had acquired a small wound in my right shoulder. The edge of the wing rubbed steadily against the shoulder blade. At night I would put some talcum powder on it, but soon I found I couldn't lie on my back in bed. Many of the others had declared themselves sick for one reason or another and were in the infirmary. I didn't want to be like them. I loved my wings, I

needed them, and I couldn't believe they would hurt me.
Deep inside me I refused to acknowledge that I was suffering. And yet the truth was that I walked along the uneven
ground of our star like an enormous crippled bird. When
the air remained still, I was all right. But the wind would
come up during exercises and fill my wing, turning it so
that the edge would scrape against the wound to revive the
pain brutally.

Meanwhile, the day of our baptism in Heaven was
getting near—a day on which all my hopes hung; the ex-
pectation of it made me endure all the tortures of posthumous life. It was for this day that I escaped your magnetic force, your law of gravity: in order to see the world
from another level and so understand the light, as I hoped,
independent of its relation to you. So how could I miss
that day? How could I not be there? And how, if I were
there, could I fly with a wounded body? I was finally obliged
to report to company headquarters with a request to be re-
leased from exercises.

There were many of us waiting outside the infirmary.
A hospital corpsman, totally bored, was taking down our
place of origin. He was obviously tired of caring for the
dead. Most of us were there with the same complaint: mal-
adjustment of wings. "This is a phenomenon," the sleepy
corpsman informed us, "that is observed in every class as
soon as the wings arrive."

The doctor was late in appearing. He was the same
one who had examined us the first day we reached the star.
Only today he seemed to me quite different. He hardly
looked at my wound. For him it was just one more symptom
among so many others. He hurriedly covered it with a lot
of talcum powder, but when he saw the blood surging to

redden the white surface, he looked more closely. "It's in an advanced stage," he said somberly. "It could have brought on gangrene. Why didn't you report in sooner, my boy?" I didn't know how to answer, what to say to him. Could I tell him that I accepted my body's revenge for its dissolution as punishment for my memory's betrayal of you? Could I tell him that the body you discovered didn't want to vanish and thus lose you? Could I tell him that though I may love these wings, my body didn't want to acknowledge its own death? What could I say? "To conceal a wound doesn't mean you're curing it," he added as he covered it with an ointment and gauze. It burned terribly and I had to bite my tongue not to cry out. "Vain self-sacrifice doesn't benefit angels," he continued as he bent over my shoulder. "Of course you deserve praise. But it almost pierced your shoulder blade," he concluded. He gave me two days' relief from duty and told the corpsman to tear the wing along the edge so that it wouldn't rub against my flesh any more and create a new inflammation.

—That's the way it goes, said the corpsman mysteriously when he took over. The doctor's right.

And he tore my wing along the edge. So there was now no fear of my mistaking my pair for somebody else's on those mornings when the saints on duty would go into the washroom and mix them up, forcing us to pick through an anonymous pile of wings with sleepy eyes. Now my wings had a distinctive scar. I felt them to be more my own.

I spent my two days free from duty in bed in the empty barracks. I thought of you intensely. Portioned memories of our wanderings in the park, by the sea, in the Upper City, kept turning over in my mind; I could see you moving through the current of humanity still holding all the exclusiveness of your dreams, circulating at times as a bodi-

less head and at times as a headless body. I could recall
your hair in its four seasons: when you had it tied up in a
bun, when you let it fall free, then your pony tail, and
finally when you cut it short. "Dreams circle in the cloud of
my hair like birds caught in the net of the sun. And no
matter how I fix it, try to hold it in place with hairpins, the
birds come back again and ruin it with their restless wings.
I cut it short to find some peace." But why, why . . . why
after so many moments of contact between us, so many
moments of touching, of contiguity, of intimacy, why do I
now miss more than anything that photograph we posed for
in the park, in which you and I were two separate persons,
you with your raincoat, I with my scarf, you with those
delicate legs that seemed to be emerging from snow, I with
my heavy boots seemingly sinking into snow, you with the
tree's touch on your hair, I with a shrub for a halo—why,
why do I suspect memory so much and long for that photograph as something tangible?

But, believe me, there's nothing worse than an empty
barracks, than forty waiting beds perfectly made up, than
forty silent, waiting trunks, than one person guarding absence, waiting for the barracks to fill with life, voices, commotion. I thought that I would be happy those two days,
that I could think of you without distractions, as I did the
first night on guard duty. But I found myself becoming restless in the solitude of the barracks, found myself praying
for the afternoon to come, for the others to return from
exercises so that the barracks would fill with dirt, mud, dis-
cord, life, life, life. Because now it's only among the others
that I can think of you, among the others who dictate my
own loneliness, who confine me more fully inside my own
boundaries; whereas their absence broadens your absence,
their void makes your void grow . . .

So, while in that strange state during those two days
—free from duty, a slave to memory—I said to myself since

things have come to this, since I have started losing the weight which you loved me to press upon you and which made you say "you're sweet and heavy," since I've started losing my tongue and since all else that used to make us human is becoming an obstacle here in Heaven, causing me to suffer, since I don't have your eyes to measure my growth and am like Narcissus without his mirror, since water comes from youth and ink is blood dyed black by despair, since the oil of my lampion is getting low and the shadows have become more numerous, since I am so idiotic as to want to keep the garments of a past glory ("you have strong hands, square arms") now that a winged gate is opening up before me, since "since" doesn't differ from chintz, and my mother's mince, and my grandmother's quince . . .

The wound in my shoulder started healing during those two days.

I stopped writing you. I don't know how to tell you exactly, how to explain it to you. I'm on the edge of an abyss. Of a primitive, undiscovered despair. No, it has nothing to do with those around me. But I, I myself, didn't find what I hoped to find in the light. It proved foreign to me. It betrayed me.

The crisis started the first moment I trusted my weight to the air. It was the long-awaited day of our baptism in Heaven. I didn't sleep all night anticipating dawn. In the morning, after muster, we started off for exercises, singing a morning hymn:

> *"We the reservists of Heaven*
> *March in unison*
> *With courage and conviction . . ."*

Our voices tore the skies. We were going for the summit. Up to now we knew the mountain only from the shadow it cast upon us in the afternoon and from our training exercises, when it always served as the refuge of a fictitious enemy. The foot of it made it look improbable: a monster turned to stone in the act of biting something. We stopped singing and moved into single file to climb the narrow path that led to the top. The day was full of laughter. The arms of Heaven had opened wide to receive us.

The summit wasn't peaked as it appeared to be from below but flat like a small plateau. We waited for the last of the file to arrive. Carved in the rocks we found the names of angels of other classes, code numbers, dates. The place seemed ideal for a first flight. The other mountains formed a protective wall all around, so that the plateau looked like a sheltered lake. The bugle sounded for the company to fall in. Holy Saint Onisimos wished us luck. Then one platoon after another rose in flight.

My turn came; I hesitated; someone behind me tried to push me, and the Undersaint reprimanded him; then I plunged. I moved my wings as they had taught us, and I floated off, but the light which had seemed so brilliant to me, the light whose limpidity is its glory, turned dull as soon as I touched it, like the shallow water along a sand beach. It didn't penetrate me in any way. I drove it out, I displaced it. The light would fold up in waves, and I could, if I'd had the means, weigh the folds and find out my weight. It was painfully clear that I had no relation to it whatsoever. "This light that besieges me is the light of strangers." I kept repeating to myself.

"And so he struggled, searched the air,
patrolled the skies, walked through abysses."

263

I was in danger of falling, of crashing against the bladed rocks of our star. I had gone up quite high to make sure the others wouldn't deflect the light. The sudden air pockets brought me vertigo and a numbness in my legs. All around me I could hear joyful voices, whistling. The others were enjoying themselves. But for me the timeless, unexplored, sleepless, euphoric, luxurious light was foreign.

As false consolation I said to myself this might be so because it's still the beginning; that, like all things too long awaited and finally arrived, it was bound to be a disappointment; that every relationship has its style and that maybe I hadn't yet found the right style for my relationship with the light. To avoid being shattered, I said that identity, that love, must develop a pattern, and that I was still too new to the light to have intercourse with it; that I should wait, warm it up first, warm myself up, before any ejaculation. And this might happen the second, the third, maybe the fourth time. I said all this to myself until . . .

The day before yesterday we flew a long distance. We went to another star, a neighbor, to attack in force. The presumption was that Satan had taken it over. We were supposed to make him withdraw from his defensive positions, to conquer all his strongholds . . . We flew for a number of hours in different formations, sometimes as a triangle with the base forward, sometimes in the form of a prism. We made our sortie, spread out, wildly shouting "Aiiirrr! Aiiirrr!" our sabers at the ready, and the only thing we managed to startle was a flock of starlings who flew off terrified by our howling. At the place where we later gathered for a "review of the maneuvers" we found numerous starling eggs in rock cavities hiding nests, but we didn't touch them, because they say that birds of that family are friendly to angels. Then we came back. There are no roads in Heaven, so I can't tell you exactly how many kilometers we covered. But again nothing happened during the trip back; again I couldn't participate in the light, again the light was foreign to me.

Now, as time goes by, this crisis threatens to destroy me. I want to leave, to go away, to move somewhere else. I don't care where. As long as I don't have to face this daily torture, this daily frustration . . . I who hoped to find in it the root of my luminous being, I who thought it would flow into my veins and make me phosphorescent, discovered that just as the sea is foreign to your eyes, so the whole of Heaven is ignorant of your hair.

That was it. That was it.

And yet no, no, NO. I want to shout yes, yes, YES. It's days now since I last wrote. Thank you. Thank you.

I saw Kostas. He was with the group of new arrivals who turned up the day before yesterday. I found him in the washroom, frightened, unable to understand where he was. He seemed to think he was still in Munich. It was the same old story in the shower room: "Your address . . ? Father's name . . ? What relation are you to So-and-so . . ?" Shouting, savagery, screeches. Only now we were the birds of prey and the new arrivals the fish.

He told me in the showers—while the water was alternately freezing and scalding us—that he brought me something of yours from earth. "What? What?" I asked. "I don't know," he said. "It's in an envelope. But it doesn't look like a letter." As he talked, the soap slipped from his fingers and it was impossible for him to find it again.

In the afternoon, as soon as we returned from flight maneuvers and after I got rid of my heavy suit of armor, I went to his barracks to find him. They had just shaved his head. He immediately jumped to attention. The others did the same. "So you're Kostas Kostidis?" I asked him with a smile that moved from irony to sadism. "Yes indeed," he whispered with closed lips, still at attention. "Follow me," I said with an air of authority, and we went outside, I in front, he behind.

I threw off my mask. "Oh, Angelos," he cried, "how could you change like this?"—"Sshh. Don't give yourself away. Besides, here they call me Saint Akepsimas." I warded off all those who came to bother us with the stereotyped phrase: "Saint, this fish is under my protection." I took him to the "Tarzan" spot. We sat in the pit.

—Where is it? I asked.

He took it out from under his shirt. I snatched it away before he had a chance to give it to me. I hid it under my shirt next to my heart. And I kept my hand there, as though to still the flutter.

—So she was alone, right? Alone?

—Yes, and she walked along with her head bowed.

—Where did you see her?

—On the street outside the university.

—What did she say to you?

—Nothing. When she found out I was about to depart, she came and brought it to me. She said she hoped I'd find you in the Kingdom of the Dead.

—What was she wearing?

—I can't remember, to tell you the truth.

—So she was alone, right?

—Yes, as I told you. What's wrong with you, anyway? You keep asking me the same thing.

He looked at me suspiciously with his blue eyes.

—And our city? I asked.

—The same as you left it.

—Have they opened the theater next to the Macedonian Society?

—No. They're still building it. But they finished the esplanade. It looks like a vast tombstone. As for the rest . . .
—What kind of weather do they have down there? I asked.
—Fall weather. Some rain.
—Fall? We have no seasons here.

I think I frightened him a little. My greed for news of the world was such that I succeeded only in shutting him up: he recoiled, gazing at me as though he didn't think I was all there. And how *could* I be with your envelope next to my heart?

Then I explained a few things about the School: that he shouldn't waste his energy writing useless letters ("it's just a trick of the administration," I told him), that in the beginning all efforts are directed toward bewildering the new arrivals, breaking their morale, making them panic; that he shouldn't be afraid of anything, and that I would go and pick him up at the barracks in the afternoons. The bugle sounded after a while, and we emerged from "Tarzan's" grave. —"On the double," I said, "even if your bones should ache unbearably the first few days."

At night, after lights out, I got up and went to the latrines alone. I locked the door, and then, with great care, as though removing the gauze from a festering wound, I unsealed the envelope. The scent of bitter almonds and banana hit my nostrils forcefully. And there I found, folded in the tulle wrapping of sugared almonds from a wedding, a lock of the blond hair you cut short that month of October.

From the rooftop of the world I call out: thank you, thank you. The next day I took the lock with me on our flight, tied it around my neck like an amulet. And then the miracle occurred: I no longer displaced the light that had wastefully flowed around me. As soon as I touched it, the light went through me unimpeded like a charge from a live wire. I wasn't alone in Heaven. You were now with me. Carrying your fragment of light on my chest, I was suddenly bound to the anarchic, timeless, sleepless light of the world:

"and I who was formerly in darkness have become luminous, beautiful in my new garment."

Words no longer suffice to express my wordless joy. The identity I couldn't accomplish by myself was realized through your grace. And I love everything, accept everything, in the light that holds you, light of my heart. I am—you've finally made me—eternal. And there is now ample room for you and me in this inner eternity of mine, where we can move imperishably, without ever meeting, without ever separating, because we're both of the same essence, we're no longer essentially opposite, we belong to the same tree, you are the branch and I the sap that feeds you, I am the branch and you the fruit it bears, you are the cloud and I the lightning that enters your womb, I am the cloud and you the rain that melts me, you are the lamp and I the wire that brings you light, I am the light, you are the light, we are now beyond conventional boundaries, beyond dividing lines, there where we daily learn that the light *exists*, that it doesn't live, doesn't die as we do, but *exists* independent of us, we live in its palm, the light studies us, we are rubbed out like lines and in our turn study other lines, because we always return to the light:

"you have made me lambent with the glory of eternity, and within me I am startled and burning."

Wedded in the year of the quiet sun, we ignore the kind of divorce that objects bring to the light, because here in

Heaven there are no houses, streets, parks, cars, the light doesn't break against them, and so we wake up in the morning wrapped in the same ray, we travel invulnerable to cold currents of air, at night we lie down behind the same cloud, leaving in our path a furrow of stars, and you no longer call me Angelos and I no longer call you Zoe, because we've learned that names only bring confusion, and we don't speak, we don't talk, because we've learned that words only create misunderstanding, we travel, diaphanous, with twenty fingers pointing toward the moon:

> *"you have bared my mind of earthly senses,*
> *robing me in senses unsubstanial, visionary."*

and how could one tell the others, how could one explain to them, that when once you touch the light, you become as through magic a conductor of it, that only when you start flying do you realize that you belong to the air, how could one tell them that behind all visible phenomena there is a third essence which isn't the essence of the fruit you eat but the essence of the light which ripened the fruit, an essence that can't be eaten because it *exists*, and whatever *exists* is unconsumable, how can you tell them that they—all of them—are the same as we are: indivisible particles in a river of sun,

> *"that you cleanse foul souls and illuminate the mind,*
> *that you raise my wordly substance to the Third Heaven,"*

only the roots of light that I planted in my chest live next to the veins, and the veins are worms because they feed on the heart, and the heart is the great sickness. So quite often the roots of the sun are stirred by the vibration of an artery, the blood searches for your source, like a snake seeking coolness,

*"your source which gives forth limpid and abundant water,
and those who drink of it with faith are granted everlasting
life,"*

but I can still find my lost transparency again, because you're
there, bound to me, I'm not alone in Heaven, we fly together,
now and always, in the indivisible, inchoate, ubiquitous
light.

The wings have begun to project roots in my back. The
unknown matter they're made of has become flesh, and the
straps have been assimilated. They're even sprouting some
tender down of a slightly bluish color to serve as our camou-
flage in the sky. The grafting has caught. So now we don't
take them off after exercises, and at night we sleep with
them on. We've grown accustomed to them. Nobody suffers
any more. Sometimes, though, when I happen to get up at
night and see the distorted bodies of the others, each one
wrapped in its own down quilt, their atrophied legs projecting from the covers, their fleshless arms absorbed by the
wings, the whole thing strikes me as a little strange. Some
of them get uncovered as they turn restlessly in their dreams,
and then a wing can be seen, standing upright and motionless in the barracks like the sail of a boat in the dead calm
of the sea. And when morning comes, in addition to all the
dust we have to sweep away so the barracks will look perfect
at inspection, we now have to pursue the down feathers
that fall off during our sleep to float around the room.

The day before yesterday I hurt myself on a rock, and
instead of blood, a yellowish-blue liquid poured out of me; it
thickened quickly and became dark like granite. I wasn't
in any pain, nor was I frightened. I accepted it as more
evidence, already superfluous, of my fundamental metamor-

phosis. Besides, how can you win anything if you don't first lose a great deal? And in the true scale of justice, a piece of light weighs more than a heart, and a few pounds of blood and a reservoir of water, which is the substance of our body. I don't know what it is that now runs through my veins; at least it doesn't hinder the light, at least it doesn't interfere with the smooth functioning of my four-leaved heart, at least it seems to have become uninflammable.

Only I'm now getting tired of writing you. My fingers can't hold the pencil firmly. They've become incredibly long, like a pelican's legs, and the fingernails have hardened into weapons. I can't bite them any more. It looks as though my whole arm is becoming the bone of my wing. The upper arm is disappearing. After a while it will become the wing's spine. And as I write you this, the whole of my gigantic right wing is in motion along with my hand, casting its shadow on the paper.

I'm almost through. I mean what more is there to say, even granting that I could write you? I wrote you because it was my only relief here in Heaven. While I was hard-pressed by the fear of change, while I had to face profound mysteries, I found a way out through words, I cast off cargo like a foundering ship, through words I created images, and I found I could understand the images better than the things they were representing.

Now we're waiting for the day when we'll leave our star and go off to serve on the frontiers of Heaven. In the afternoons I go and pick up Kostas at the asphyxiating barracks. We talk. But he's bored by me just as I was bored by Yannis. Anyway, he doesn't believe in returning, as Yannis did. The solution he's looking for is a different matter, "one way of looking at it," as Asimis would say.

Lately I'm often visited in my dreams by a somber-faced gentleman who looks very much like the "someone else." He has a mustache too, wears a striped tie, a double-breasted jacket, tapering pants; only his shoes are black, shiny, huge. They remind me of coffins for small children. He appears, doesn't say anything, doesn't ask for any explanations, just stares at his shoes as though acknowledging his own secret guilt. And this appeases me.

My fingers are trembling. The pencil keeps slipping. I don't know if you'll ever read what I've written, but I want to . . . I don't really know how to end. "What's your last word?" I hear you asking me, as at the moment we separated. Not Dumbarton Oaks this time, a name I taught you to stand for the unexplainable, not for a declaration we didn't know, a declaration we'd signed with our birth; "but what will your last word be, then?" you ask me insistently. Do you want to know? Do you want me to tell you, since you're on earth and I'm in Heaven, since we're separated by clouds that spread like a sea between us, do you still ask me, insist that I tell you? My hand trembles, my soul trembles: my last word will be my first word, as the first death is also the last, and all over again from the beginning, and all over again from the end: "I'm well and doing fine in Heaven. Don't worry about me. I'm well, I tell you. I'm well."

From the Star of Angels
Third Heaven
The day Herod massacred the Infants

THE PLANT

THE WELL

THE ANGEL

P.S.

Plants, fish, and birds are fundamentally one and the same. They may differ while alive, but when they stop living, they leave behind the same traces carved in the hard memory of stone. The butterfly is not the only flower that took on wings, nor the flying fish the only bird that took to water. We're fooled by their living on land, in the sea, and in the air. We think they differ because some rise motionless, some swim, and some fly. But plants, fish, and birds, when their bodies disappear, carve the same shape on the hard stone of memory.

A NOTE ON THE TYPE

THE TEXT of this book was set on the Linotype in a type face called *Primer,* designed by RUDOLPH RUZICKA, earlier reponsible for the design of Fairfield and Fairfield Medium, Linotype faces whose virtues have for some time now been accorded wide recognition. The complete range of sizes of Primer was first made available in 1954, although the pilot size of 12 point was ready as early as 1951. The design of the face makes general reference to Linotype Century (long a serviceable type, totally lacking in manner or frills of any kind) but brilliantly corrects the characterless quality of that face.

Composed, printed, and bound by
The Haddon Craftsmen, Inc., Scranton, Pa.
Typography and binding design by
WARREN CHAPPELL